KU-441-496

THE MEDUSA PROJECT
THE SET-UP

Also by Sophie McKenzie

GIRL, MISSING
BLOOD TIES
BLOOD RANSOM

SIX STEPS TO A GIRL
THREE'S A CROWD
THE ONE AND ONLY

THE MEDUSA PROJECT 1: *THE SET-UP*
THE MEDUSA PROJECT 2: *THE HOSTAGE*
THE MEDUSA PROJECT
WORLD BOOK DAY SPECIAL: *THE THIEF*
THE MEDUSA PROJECT 3: *THE RESCUE*

Coming soon:

THE MEDUSA PROJECT 4: *HUNTED*

SOPHIE McKENZIE

THE MEDUSA PROJECT
THE SET-UP

SIMON & SCHUSTER

ACKNOWLEDGEMENTS: Thanks to the following writers and readers for their story insights and writing advice, both general and specific: Dana Bate, Melanie Edge, Kate Elliott, Sharon Flockhart, Gaby Halberstam, Caroline Lawrence, Richard Lawrence, Joe McKenzie, Julie Mackenzie, Cliff McNish, Graham Marks, Robert Muchamore, Rose Saliba, Julia Scott, Daisy Startup, Olly Wicken and Moira Young. Particular thanks to Venetia Gosling and Lou and Lily Kuenzler for their invaluable feedback.

NOT FOR RESALE

First published in Great Britain in 2009 by Simon & Schuster UK Ltd
A CBS COMPANY

This edition published as a covermount exclusive
for *SUGAR* magazine in 2010

Copyright © 2009 Sophie McKenzie

This book is copyright under the Berne Convention.
No reproduction without permission.
All rights reserved.

The right of Sophie McKenzie to be identified as the author of this work has been asserted by her in accordance with sections 77 and 78 of the Copyright, Design and Patents Act, 1988.

Simon & Schuster UK Ltd
1st Floor, 222 Gray's Inn Road
London WC1X 8HB

This book is a work of fiction. Names, characters, places and incidents are either the product of the author's imagination or are used fictitiously. Any resemblance to actual people living or dead, events or locales, is entirely coincidental.

A CIP catalogue record of this book is available from the British Library.

Printed in the UK by CPI Cox & Wyman, Reading RG1 8EX.

www.simonandschuster.co.uk
www.sophiemckenzie.net
www.themedusaproject.co.uk

For Ciara and Cliona

'*So it is not science fiction, it is inevitable that within our children's lifetimes, molecular biologists will tweak the human genome. If we can re-create existing bacterial genomes, we will be able to create new improved human ones.*'

Terence Kealey, clinical biochemist, writing in *The Times*, Saturday 26th January 2008

1: Freak storm

I'm Nico and what I'm about to tell you is Secret and Dangerous and True. It's also several planetary systems beyond Weird. Here's how it started . . .

Picture this . . . Monday morning. A whole-school assembly in the big hall. Rows and rows of teenagers in lines of plastic chairs. I was sitting there, towards the back – dark hair, brown eyes – the guy all the girls wanted to get their hands on.

Only joking.

Anyway, there we all were, sunlight blistering in through high windows and the head teacher, Fergus Fox, droning on.

He's not just the head teacher. He's also my stepdad. I've lived with him in his boarding school since my mum died of cancer when I was five. We don't get on, for reasons which will soon become obvious.

But this isn't about him.

If it's about anyone, it's about her . . . Ketty.

She was sitting two rows in front and four seats to the left of me. You're probably surprised I can remember that little detail. Well, get used to it. When it comes to Ketty, I tend to remember everything.

That day she had her dark, curly hair in a ponytail, tied back with a piece of string. Very Ketty, that string. She doesn't go in for girly things like ribbon – she's practical. Doesn't wear loads of make-up or jewellery either and I've never seen her in a dress.

My eyes kept sliding over to where she was sitting. Which is when I saw Billy Martin put his arm round her shoulders. My mouth fell open. Everything else dropped away, even the sound of Fergus's droning voice. I waited for Ketty to push the arm away. But she didn't. Instead, she leaned in closer.

No *way*. But there it was. My best friend . . . with Billy Martin.

I looked away. Tried to calm myself. But my eyes kept going back to them.

I couldn't believe she'd go with Billy. What did he have that I didn't? Apart from a load of money, of course. But Ketty wouldn't be interested in that, would she?

I looked up at the stage and tried to concentrate on what Fergus was talking about. Some long, dull lecture about the appropriate way to wear your school uniform.

Billy's hand was on Ketty's arm now, his fingertips moving slightly up and down.

I tore my eyes away and felt the fury building in my chest.

It's your own fault, said the voice in my head. *You've been friends for months. You've had every chance to ask her out yourself.*

It was true. Worse, I didn't even know why I hadn't said anything to Ketty so far.

Actually, I did.

It was because I'd been sure Ketty would say no. I mean, we got on really well, but she was so completely into her running it was like there wasn't room for anything else important.

I didn't want to think about that so I tried to focus on Fergus again. But everything about him was annoying me now – his solemn face . . . his serious voice . . . I mean, he was talking about school uniform, for God's sake, not war or dying babies.

Billy squeezed Ketty's arm and smiled. I half thought of jumping up and pointing and shouting for the teachers to stop them. But even I'm not that crazy.

And then Ketty turned her head to look at him and right there, in front of everyone . . . in front of *me* . . . she smiled back at him.

A great, big, loved-up smile.

My stomach turned over. I could feel my face flooding red. I stared through the nearest window. It was open just a fraction. I imagined storming over to it and slamming it shut. Hard.

3

With a sudden swerve, the window swung wide open. I jumped. Before I could even register what was happening, the window slammed shut.

Several people sitting nearby looked round. I watched as the window opened and slammed shut again, then opened once more.

I glanced at the curtains beside it. As I did, they lifted away from the wall, like a gust of wind had rippled through them.

My eyes tore round the room. More curtains moved. Some floated up for a second and dropped again. Others flew high into the air. What was going on? Around me I could hear people gasping. Whimpers and anxious squeals from the younger kids filled the air.

'What's happening?'

'Why's everything moving?'

In the background Fergus's voice was a loud appeal. 'Be quiet. It's just a freak gust of wind. Stay in your seats.'

My eyes lit on the clock beside the stage – a big, open, white-faced clock with black hands and numbers. The clock hands moved – first slowly, then faster and faster, whizzing until they were a blur.

I blinked and the hands stopped.

Which is when it struck me. This was no freak wind.

It was *me*.

I was making everything move.

My heart hammered like a machine gun. I glanced away from the clock, to a vase that teetered on the table by the

4

stage . . . to the windows on the other side of the room. More curtains flew up. A chair tipped against the wall. The vase smashed.

Whatever I looked at was moving – violently, angrily. Like I was riding a wave of anger and every time I looked at something that wave crashed down.

How am I doing this?

For a second I felt like I was two people: one watching what was going on along with everyone else; the other somehow making it happen.

My eyes swept back to the clock. As I stared, it fell off the wall and crashed to the floor. *Jesus.* Screams now around me. A girl sobbing in the row behind.

'Help! Make it stop!'

My eyes flashed back to the window where the whole thing had started. It was still standing wide open. Mr Rogerson, the maths teacher, was walking towards it, hands outstretched.

Before he reached the window, I willed it to shut.

It did. Noisily.

I closed my eyes. My heart pounded. How was this *happening*?

From the stage, Fergus's voice sounded low and reassuring.

'Calm down, everyone. Like I said, it's just a freak wind. It's over.'

I took a deep breath and looked up, my pulse slowing. It *was* over at last. People in the hall were glancing round –

some nervously, others with wide, wondering eyes. The babble of voices rose.

'Did you see that chair tip up against the wall?'

'And the clock hands going mad?'

'Man, that vase just exploded!'

I looked over at Ketty. She was gazing round, her golden-brown eyes huge circles. At least Billy didn't have his arm round her any more. I stared down at my lap. Fergus was still talking over the hubbub.

'Just a freak storm . . .' he repeated like a mantra. 'Everyone be quiet . . . Show's over.'

Slowly the anxious voices died away.

'Stand and file out from the back, row by row,' Fergus went on. 'If you are close to the smashed clock or the broken vase, please be careful.'

I kept my eyes on the ground as we stood up. At least Fergus had assumed it was a freak storm. Not a freak stepson. My heart was still beating fast. What if I looked up and the whole thing started again? I shot a swift glance sideways, at my vacated chair. No movement. *Good.*

My stomach twisted with cramps as we walked out. None of this made sense.

Everyone around me was still talking about the 'storm'. And then a large hand clamped down on my shoulder. 'There you are.' Fergus spun me round and glared down at me. 'This way,' he said.

Reluctantly, I followed him away from the crowds. As we

reached his office Fergus looked round, as if to make sure we couldn't be overheard.

'What in God's name did you think you were doing?' he spat.

'What?' I said, startled. 'When?'

'Don't play games with me, Nico. I know it was you causing that mess in assembly.'

My mouth fell open. How could Fergus possibly know it was me? 'What?' I said, weakly.

Fergus frowned. 'How long has it been going on?'

My mouth closed, then opened again. My head felt like it might explode. 'I don't know what you're talking about,' I stammered.

Fergus crossed his arms. 'Okay, you don't want to talk to me. So listen.' He narrowed his eyes. 'The power you have is evil. I don't ever want you to use it again. Understand?'

I stared at him.

Fergus gripped my arm and gave me a little shake. 'Nico, are you listening to me? This power – moving things . . . telekinesis, whatever you want to call it . . . I'm telling you it's evil.'

'And *I'm* telling *you* I have no idea what you're on about,' I said, pulling my arm away. I turned to go.

'Come back here!' Fergus barked.

No. I stuck my finger up at him and dived back into the crowd. As I made my way up to my dorm, my heart started pumping hard again.

How did Fergus know that it had been me moving things with my mind? And why was he saying it was evil?

An ice-cold shiver circled my throat.

What on earth was happening to me?

8

2: Powers

Fergus didn't mention me giving him the finger later. Well, he didn't really have a chance. I arrived at the last minute for his history class and left as soon as the bell rang. As usual he picked on me all through the lesson, asking me the hardest questions, and giving me the least time to answer. Whenever I asked him why he gave me such a hard time in class, he'd say that because I was his stepson, it was important the other students didn't think he was showing me any favouritism. Like it might hurt their feelings.

What about *my* feelings? He never stopped to think how embarrassing his behaviour was for me.

It didn't used to be like that. When I was younger, we got on great. Maybe that was the trouble – Fergus still wished I was nine years old, or something. He certainly still treated me like I was.

After lessons finished, I went to the library and searched the internet. I wasn't sure what I was looking for exactly, then I clicked through to this psychic phenomenon site and there it was. Telekinesis – that word Fergus had used. Also known as psychokinesis: *the power to move objects without touching them*.

Apparently loads of people throughout history have claimed to be able to do this. In the olden days they'd be burned as witches. More recently they were likely to get their own TV show.

But no one had ever scientifically proven what they could do. And I couldn't find any records of people unable to control their abilities either, though similar stuff happened quite often in horror movies.

Not exactly a reassuring discovery.

It was almost 5 p.m. by then, and the light was fading. I went outside and spent about half an hour trying – and failing – to move a twig on the grass near one of the school benches.

I didn't get it. I'd hurled a clock off the wall when I hadn't been trying ... but now I couldn't move a twig? I slumped onto the bench, closed my eyes and tilted my head towards the dying sun.

'What's the matter?'

I jumped. Ketty was standing over me. She was dressed in her running gear – sweats and trainers. Her curly hair was still scraped back into a string-tied ponytail and her skin was glowing. She smiled, like she was really pleased to see me.

My heart skipped several beats.

'Sorry, I didn't mean to scare you.' She paused. 'You okay?'

'Course I am, babe.' I stood up, shoving my hands in my pockets so she wouldn't see they were shaking. 'Why shouldn't I be?'

Ketty's smile deepened. Her eyes really light up when she grins. And her nose wrinkles. It's beautiful.

'Whatever. I'll get on with my run, then.' She turned to go.

'Wait.'

She turned back, eyebrows raised. I ransacked my brain for something to say. Part of me wanted to tell her what had happened in assembly, but I was scared she'd think I was a complete freak.

After all, *I* thought I was a complete freak.

'Saw you with Billy earlier.' I smiled. 'You know he used to bully Curtis to do his homework?'

This was true, though a secret.

Ketty shrugged.

'So . . . you going out with him?' I held my breath.

Ketty shrugged again. 'Dunno,' she said. 'Maybe.'

Well that, at least, was hopeful. 'Hey, d'you wanna see a magic trick?' I said.

'Okay.'

I took the twig I'd been practising on and placed it on her hand. 'Watch,' I said. 'I can make this move without touching it.'

Praying I could make the thing at least twitch across her palm, I focused hard. Nothing happened.

A strand of Ketty's hair fell across her face as she watched.

11

I tried harder. Still nothing.

Ketty frowned. 'What's supposed to happen?' she said.

I could feel the panic rising into my throat. *Move.* The twig lay resolutely still. And then Ketty's mobile rang. I stared at it as she answered. It was new . . . and startlingly pink. Sleek, girly and expensive – it was the last phone I'd have expected Ketty to own.

'Hi,' she said to the caller. 'Yeah, I'm outside, I'll come and meet you now.' Ketty closed her phone and looked up at me. 'Gotta go.'

'Wait, let me try the twig thing again.' I laid it on my hand and stared down at it.

Ketty laughed. 'You're bizarre, Nico.'

'Not as bizarre as your new phone, babe,' I said, pointing to the mobile. 'I mean, *pink*?'

'I know.' Ketty made a face. 'It's . . . Billy gave it to me.'

'He got you a *phone*?'

How much money did he *have*?

'Yeah, it's got a great camera and brilliant sound quality.'

'Cool,' I said, trying not to sound bitter.

'That was Billy calling, actually,' Ketty said. 'Sorry, I've got to go.'

'Okay.' My face burned with humiliation as she turned and walked away. Could I have looked more of an idiot? Trying to move a stupid twig while her *actual* boyfriend had bought her an ultra-cool phone.

Furious with myself I chucked the twig on the ground. I felt like punching the bench behind me. As I stared at it, rage

12

pulsing in my chest, the bench fell backwards. It landed with a thud on the ground.

The rage in my chest vanished and I felt cold with fear. I stared at the bench. My mind had knocked it over. I was sure of it.

How was that possible?

I wandered over to a clump of trees. Beyond them the school's two playing fields stretched away. Most of my year were there. Ketty, of course, slim and scruffy in her running gear, with Billy and a few of his friends. Tom and Curtis were there too – heading for the sports hut, almost certainly to sneak a smoke in before the home room bell. Nearer me a bunch of girls were chatting, giggling over some magazine. All ordinary school stuff. I sighed.

'Nico?' Fergus's deep voice echoed across the grass.

I turned. He was striding towards me. I started walking away.

'Stop.'

It was pointless trying to resist. He'd give me a detention if I pushed him any further. Like I told you, even though he was my stepdad he always seemed to come down harder on me than any other pupil.

I stopped walking. Fergus marched up, panting slightly. 'I've been wanting to speak to you all day,' he said. 'But I've had the local paper on my back since lunchtime. Some bright spark called them about what happened in assembly.'

'The "freak storm"?'

13

'We both know it wasn't that.' Fergus paused. 'You know you were very rude to me earlier.'

'Yeah?' I stared down at his polished brown shoes. 'Well, you were accusing me of ripping up the assembly hall.'

'Which you *did*.' Fergus's voice rose. He checked himself. 'Look, I'm sorry . . . but are you seriously telling me it *wasn't* you?'

'Okay, no.' I sighed. 'But I didn't mean to . . . anyway, how did you *know*? There were three hundred people in the room.'

Fergus rubbed his head. 'I can't . . . look, I don't want to go into it. You don't need to know any of that . . .'

'Any of *what*?' Now what was he talking about? 'You're treating me like a little kid,' I muttered.

'I'm not.' Fergus's forehead creased into a frown. 'I just . . . I worry about you.'

I rolled my eyes. 'Which means you think I won't be able to handle whatever it is you think you know.'

'No. And I don't know anything except that the power you demonstrated is highly destructive. That's it. Come on, Nico. You saw what you did.'

He was lying, I was certain. He *must* know more. How else could he have worked out so quickly that what he was seeing was telekinesis – and that *I* was making it happen? Smashing clocks and vases with your mind wasn't exactly an everyday occurrence at Fox Academy.

'Now promise me we won't have a repeat of this morning's events.' Fergus attempted a wry smile.

14

I frowned. It didn't make sense. Surely any normal person would be curious about how or why I'd suddenly developed telekinetic powers?

'Don't you even want to know what actually happened?' I said.

Because I do. I want to know a whole lot more – and, anyway, I can't control what I'm doing, even if I wanted to.

Fergus shuddered. 'Absolutely not,' he said. 'Whatever you can do is evil. Your mother would have hated it. I *know* she would.'

I stared at him, my resentment building. How could Fergus know for sure what my mum would have thought?

'Are you listening? It's really important you don't *ever* try to use your telekinetic powers again. For your own good. Understand?'

I narrowed my eyes. How typical was this? Fergus treating me like a child who had to be *told* what was good for him. When was he going to see that I was old enough to work stuff like that out for myself?

'Promise me you'll stop, Nico. For the sake of your mother's memory.'

'Sure, Fergus.' I lied. He was just using my mum to get me to agree. He didn't care about her memory. 'Whatever you want.'

The next two days passed in the usual boring blur of school activities. There was a bit of minor excitement when the local paper's story on our 'freak electrical storm' came out. But everyone soon forgot about it.

I tried a few times to make stuff move again. But nothing happened. I was just starting to believe that maybe I'd imagined the whole thing, including Fergus's strange reaction, when I got a text that changed everything.

3: Meeting Jack

Like most schools, Fox Academy had strict rules about switching off your mobile in class. I usually kept my phone in my pocket, on vibrate, so if I got a call or a text I would know, but the teacher wouldn't.

It was double maths. Boring as hell. And I was almost asleep, when my phone vibrated. I fished it out of my pocket, checking first that our teacher, Mr Rogerson, wasn't looking. The text read:

That was no freak storm.
I know the truth. All of it, including what Fergus will never tell you.
If you want to find out who you really are, come to Nelson's Column, Trafalgar Square, 2 p.m., Saturday.
A friend.

I froze, staring at the words, then checked the sender. *Number withheld.* My first thought was that it was some

17

kind of wind-up. But who from? No one apart from Fergus knew that I had been responsible for what had happened in Monday's assembly. I glanced quickly round the class. Over to my left, Ketty was busily writing in her maths textbook. Next to her, chin propped in his hand, Billy was staring into space. Behind them Tom and Curtis were passing notes. On the other side of the room Lola and Lauren were surreptitiously peering into mirrors under their desks. Everyone else was working on their algebra. No one was paying me any attention.

I slid my mobile back into my pocket, heart thumping. If the text hadn't come from someone in my class then who *had* sent it? Who was '*a friend*'? The words drummed in my head.

Find out who you really are.

What on earth did that mean? I turned the whole thing over in my mind as Mr Rogerson droned on about some equation. How did the sender know my number? And how did they know that the storm wasn't real? I tried in vain to tell myself the text was just some weird bit of random nonsense, but I couldn't stop thinking about what it meant and who had texted it and *why* they'd sent it.

By the time the class ended I'd decided.

I *had* to find out.

I checked the suggested meeting place again. I knew where Trafalgar Square was, but getting to central London on Saturday wouldn't be easy. Fergus would never give me permission to go so far on my own.

Fox Academy is based north of the city, right at the end of the underground's Northern Line. If you want to go into town at the weekend, one of your parents has to sign a special permission slip. Fergus only let me go once, and that was on pain of a million detentions if I wasn't back by 5 p.m. I got back just before six. He hit the roof and I was grounded for three weeks.

Still, I'd sneaked out often enough since then.

I asked Tom if he'd cover for me if Fergus asked where I was on Saturday.

'No worries,' he said. 'What're you doing?'

I shrugged, doing my best to look casual. 'Just a date.'

Tom grinned. 'Fit?'

'Yeah.'

'Cool.'

Sorted.

The sun was shining in a bright blue sky and Trafalgar Square was heaving with tourists.

I'd got away from school without anyone seeing, then made it down to Charing Cross tube station in plenty of time. I was now standing by one of the lions at the base of the stone column in the centre of Trafalgar Square, waiting.

Almost fifteen minutes had passed and I was starting to think whoever had texted me wasn't coming, when I spotted a girl on the other side of the square.

Now, obviously, being male and not dead, I tend to notice pretty girls, but this one *really* stood out. For a start, there

19

was her hair. It was red and very long – almost to her waist. And then there was the way she walked – swaying slightly, like a model on a catwalk. She was dressed in boots and denim shorts and every head turned as she crossed the square.

I watched her too. After a few seconds I realised she was looking right back. In fact, she was walking towards me.

A few seconds later and she was standing in front of me – all long legs, creamy skin and slanting, pale green eyes.

'Are you Nico?' An American accent.

'Yes,' I said, trying to look as if unbelievably fit strangers approached me all the time. 'Er . . . how do you know my name?'

The girl smiled, revealing a set of perfectly white teeth. The smile didn't quite reach her eyes. 'I'm Dylan,' she said, rather coolly. 'Jack sent me.'

'Oh.' I stood there, feeling stupid. I wasn't prepared for this . . . some beautiful girl coming out of nowhere, talking in riddles. 'Who's Jack? '

'The guy who sent you the text about this meeting,' Dylan said, as if it was the most obvious thing in the world. 'He's my godfather . . . Jack Linden. Come on, he wants to meet you.'

She glided away. I followed, feeling completely bewildered. As we reached the edge of the square I stopped.

'Wait,' I said.

Dylan twisted her long hair in her hand. She raised her eyebrows. 'Yes?'

20

'How does this Jack Linden know me? How . . . where did he get my number?'

'He's kind of like a database expert . . . he can get hold of any telephone number he wants. He would have met you himself but he was worried you might have been followed.'

'Followed?' I stared at her. 'By who?'

'Fergus, of course.'

'Why would he follow me?' I remembered the text had specifically mentioned him. 'How do you know Fergus, anyway?' This was getting weirder and weirder.

'Jack'll explain everything.' And she glided off again.

Head spinning, I had no choice but to follow. Without speaking, Dylan led me up St Martin's Lane and along a very busy Long Acre. As we stopped at some traffic lights, I studied her face. She was undeniably beautiful – like a doll or a painting. But there was something cold and aloof about her I didn't like at all.

I suddenly missed Ketty.

We turned off the main road about halfway down. The bustle and noise of shoppers and traffic immediately calmed. Dylan took me along a series of short, increasingly deserted roads. We turned into a little cul-de-sac full of tiny brick townhouses. She stopped outside one with a red door and took out a key.

It struck me that this whole thing could be some kind of trap. Some elaborate plan to lure me away from home and rob me . . . or worse. My fingers tightened round the phone in my pocket and I braced myself, ready to run.

Dylan pushed open the door and indicated I should go inside.

'What about you?' I could hear the shake in my voice. I cleared my throat.

'I'm going home,' she said. 'I'm in London for a month, staying with relatives. I just came over to see Jack for the morning. He's inside.' She leaned into the hallway. 'Jack!' she yelled. 'Nico's here.'

She pointed to an open door at the end of the hallway. 'Wait in there.'

I opened my mouth to ask more questions, but before I could speak Dylan shut the door, leaving me alone in the hallway. My heart pounded. Rubbing my sweaty palms on my jeans, I crept along the dimly-lit hall. What the hell was I doing here? I reached the door at the end and pushed it open.

A kitchen. Wide . . . bare . . . full of pale wood, with a few designer appliances on the countertop and a huge stainless steel fridge in the corner.

So where was this Jack Linden?

I looked around anxiously. There were bars on the window, which looked out over a tiny, overgrown courtyard. I heard footsteps down the stairs and along the corridor. My stomach twisted over. I had to be *insane* coming in here like this.

And then the door burst open and Jack Linden swept into the room like a tornado.

'Nico?' He was breathless. Filling the kitchen with his presence. 'I can't believe it. You're *here*.'

22

He was tall, maybe in his late thirties or early forties, with dark wavy hair and wide eyes – a bright, startling blue. He laughed. 'After all this time,' he said. 'I'm finally meeting you.'

I nodded, unsure what to say. At least he seemed normal. I slowly let my breath out, beginning to calm down.

'Sorry, let me . . . I'm Jack. I'm . . . Christ, I don't know where to begin. '

'Um . . .' I hesitated. 'How about we start with how you know me?'

'Sure, er . . . let's sit.' Jack led me over to a couple of stools beside the wooden counter. We sat down and Jack adjusted the back of his jacket so the shoulder line sat neatly. I'd already clocked his suit. Dark grey, with silver buttons. Dead flashy and very designer.

'I . . . okay.' Jack blew out his breath. 'Years ago, before I got into, er . . . data retrieval, I worked for a scientist called William Fox. Fergus Fox's brother.'

My mouth fell open. 'My *stepfather*, Fergus Fox?'

Jack nodded.

'Fergus has a *brother*?' I said.

Why hadn't he ever mentioned that?

'*Had* a brother,' Jack corrected me. 'William's dead now. Like I say, I used to work for him, raising money to fund his scientific research. He was looking into gene sequencing. One Christmas William invited me and some other friends to a party and Fergus was there with your mum.'

'So you knew my mum, too?' My stomach churned. I

23

didn't often meet people who'd known my mum. She'd died when I was little from a rare cancer, and my own memories of her had almost faded. At least I wasn't sure any more what was a real memory and what was a story Fergus or someone else had told me about her.

'I didn't know her very well,' Jack admitted, 'but she made a big impression on me that night at this rather dull party. She was great fun ... really lively. We got chatting and she explained to me she was going to have a baby.'

I nodded. I'd heard my mum's story many times – how she arrived in London to study English, got pregnant by some man she hardly knew, and then met Fergus, a teacher at her college, who took her in when she had nothing and no one else to look after her.

'Anyway, to cut a long story short, William's research was going well. He had discovered a series of genetic codes which he was certain were connected to extrasensory abilities – a psychic gene, if you like. Eventually, he managed to create a synthesis of the codes ... he called it the Medusa gene. Anyone implanted with the gene would develop extraordinary abilities.'

'what sort of abilities?' I said.

'For example, the ability to move things without touching them ...' Jack grinned. 'Such as might appear to cause a freak storm.'

I suddenly realised what he was saying. I stared at him, shocked. 'You mean ... that gene's inside *me*?'

Jack nodded. 'William embedded the Medusa gene in a

virus, which is standard gene therapy practice. He then injected the virus into your umbilical cord while you were in your mother's womb. He predicted that the gene would take effect once combined with the hormones released at puberty. Does that make sense?'

'Well, no . . . except . . .' I gasped. 'That's what started this week . . . in assembly . . .'

'Ah, yes.' Jack raised his eyebrows. 'I read about that in your local paper and guessed it was really you. That's why I decided to get in touch. I assume the "storm" was Fergus's idea of a cover story?'

'Yes, but . . .' I stared at the mosaic tiles on the kitchen floor. It was all too much to take in.

'So Fergus knew . . . *knows* . . . about this Medusa gene?' I said.

'Yup.' Jack made a face. 'Look, Nico, I don't know what your relationship with your stepdad is like, but the truth is he and I never got on . . .'

'I don't really get on with him either,' I admitted.

Jack nodded slowly. 'So he doesn't know you're here with me and he didn't tell you anything about your . . . "gift"?'

'Er . . .' It probably wasn't a good idea to tell a total stranger no one knew where I was. Except . . . Jack seemed okay. Anyway, I needed to know more about this Medusa gene and Fergus certainly wasn't going to tell me.

'Fergus hasn't told me a thing. He never does – it's like he always thinks he knows best about *everything*. When he

25

realised what I'd done in assembly he got angry . . . told me never to use my telekinesis again.'

'What?' Jack's eyes blazed a fierce blue. 'That's outrageous. It's part of who you are.'

I frowned. *Was it?* With so little experience of my telekinesis – and no control over it – it was hard to feel like it was part of me. Still, maybe if Jack was right that would come in time.

'So how come I never met Fergus's brother . . . this William Fox?' I said, at last.

'I told you, he's dead . . . he died in an accident before you were born. Look, there'll be plenty of time to explain about all that. Would . . . I mean . . .' He hesitated. 'Would you mind showing me what you can do? It's just I've waited such a long time to see whether William's work paid off.'

I bit my lip. 'Er . . . I'd be happy to show you, but . . .'

'What is it?'

'Well . . . the truth is . . .' I stopped, feeling awkward.

Jack tilted his head to one side and gazed at me. 'You can't do it to order?' he said slowly. 'Sometimes it works, sometimes it doesn't?'

'Yes,' I said with relief. 'That's exactly it.'

Jack nodded thoughtfully. 'I'm sure I can help you with that . . . if you'd like me too, I mean.'

'God, yes.' The words blurted out too fast. I blushed.

Jack smiled. 'You know, maybe it would help to think about how mastering telekinesis might improve your life . . . What do you want? Power . . . girls . . . fame . . .?'

I stared at him, almost laughing. How could moving objects around bring me any of those things? Jack saw my expression and frowned.

I realised he was serious and looked down at the kitchen floor. What *did* I want?

The answer came back in a single word.

Ketty.

There was no way I could say that to Jack, though. Anyway, I knew it would take more than moving objects without touching them to impress Ketty. Still, a bit of money might help . . . at least then I could compete with stupid Billy Martin and his expensive mobile phone.

I looked up. 'I'd like to be rich,' I said.

A grin curled across Jack's face. 'No problem,' he said. 'I can certainly help with that! Now, let's get started.'

4: Making money

I tried again, but the tyre still wouldn't move.

Jack leaned against the garage wall, watching me thoughtfully. He'd brought me in here – the little garage next to the kitchen – after I told him how my telekinesis could easily get out of control.

'My car's parked outside,' Jack had said with a grin. 'And there's nothing else in here that matters.'

I looked round the garage. There wasn't much here at all. Just some shelves with stacks of old newspapers for recycling at one end, a few tools on a bench and the tyre I was trying to move propped up against the wall opposite.

'Have another go,' Jack said in an encouraging voice.

I focused on the tyre once more. *Move. Move, you stupid thing.*

Nothing. 'AAAGH!' I turned away in frustration and thumped the palm of my hand.

'Hey, Nico, easy tiger,' Jack said smoothly. 'I think . . . if you don't mind me saying . . . it looks like you're trying too hard.'

I nodded, my face burning. Why couldn't I just make it work?

'I know it's frustrating when you can't control it,' Jack said, shrewdly. 'But the telekinesis is already there, inside you, part of who you are. Just relax and it will happen.'

I nodded again, but inside I was all jangled up – how could I relax, feeling like this?

'Can we try something?' Jack said. 'I'd like you to focus on your breathing for a moment. Don't change the way you're breathing, just become aware of it. Okay?'

'Okay.' I concentrated on my breath. It was shallow and jagged to start with but, as I concentrated, it calmed a little. I closed my eyes and took a few deeper breaths. Ketty's face floated in front of my mind's eye.

'Nico?' Jack's voice made me jump.

My eyes snapped open. 'Sorry,' I said.

Jack smiled. 'No worries. It's easy to lose focus, but I'd like you to try again. This time look at the tyre but keep concentrating on your breath.'

I did as he told me. My mind wandered off several times, but Jack kept reminding me to watch my breathing and, after a few minutes, all my earlier frustration seeped away.

'Okay.' Jack rubbed his hands together. 'Now, breathe out, then, on the in-breath, say to yourself: *I will lift that tyre.*'

I did as he asked. It was funny. I couldn't imagine doing

29

this with anyone else without feeling ridiculous, yet Jack –
a complete stranger – made it feel like the most natural thing
in the world.

I focused on the tyre again. Breathed in . . .

I will lift that tyre.

'Good. Now, don't think about it, but on your out-breath,
make it happen.'

I breathed in again. *I can do this.* I breathed out. And the
tyre rose gently into the air.

I could hear Jack gasp beside me, but my eyes followed
the tyre up . . . up . . . to the ceiling.

'That's *amazing.*' Jack's voice was completely awestruck.

Yes. Adrenalin surged through me and in a split second
my focus vanished and the tyre plummeted to the ground.

No. Furious, I felt my mind connect with the gut instinct
to lash out. Seconds later the tyre was careering round the
garage, completely out of control. Again I had that weird
sensation that I was both watching it and making it move
simultaneously. As the tyre flew past the shelves my eyes lit
on the piles of old newspapers. The entire bundle flew up
into the air. Papers zoomed in all directions.

'Okay, Nico. Bring it back to your breath. Focus on your
breathing.' Jack's voice was tense beside me.

I tried to do what he said, but I was too frustrated with not
being able to control the tyre. My eyes followed it as it
bounced against walls and spun in the air.

'Come on, Nico, you can do this.'

With a huge effort, I brought my awareness back to my

breathing. I was almost panting . . . my breath coming out in fierce gasps.

'Okay, now slow that breathing down. Come on, calm down, Nico. You can do this.'

My eyes still on the tyre, I slowly calmed my breathing. As I did so, the tyre slowed down too. Gradually it came to rest above my head, hovering in mid-air.

'Now breathe out and lower it to the ground.'

I breathed in and then out . . . a long, slow breath. Without consciously telling the tyre to move, I held the direction to lower it in my head. The tyre wobbled for a second, then slowly, steadily, descended to the floor.

I watched it for a few seconds to make sure it had really stopped, then I closed my eyes. My head was aching but I felt exhilarated. Not in the wild, intense way I'd felt before, but with a new, deep-rooted, calm feeling.

A hand on my back. I looked up. Jack was smiling at me.

'Well done. You did it,' he said. 'Would you mind if I get my camera? Then I can film your telekinesis . . . study it when you've gone. That might help me work out how to help you better.'

'Sure.' I was so excited I think I'd have agreed to anything at that point – not that I could see any harm in Jack filming me.

He got the camera and I managed a couple more demonstrations with the tyre. I felt like I could go on practising for hours, but, after a while, Jack insisted we went back into the kitchen so I could rest – and have something to eat and drink.

We sat at the table and Jack ordered in some pizza, advising me as we ate that I should start a daily practice.

'Just ten minutes every day. Go outside, Nico. Find something small to work on and stay focused on your breathing. Once you've got on top of that, I honestly think you'll be able to move anything.'

I stared at him. Did he really think that?

I remembered Ketty and what I'd said to Jack earlier. 'So how can I use what I do to make money?'

Jack laughed. 'First things first,' he said. 'Practise every day for a week and we'll meet next weekend and, if you're ready, I promise I'll take you to a place where the Medusa gene will make you rich.'

5: Goals

I practised on my telekinesis as often as I could. Before and after school and even at break times, I'd go out to the trees by the playing fields and attempt to move whatever was out there – sticks, stones . . . even the bench again.

It was hard at first, especially without Jack there to remind me about my breathing. But the more I worked at it, the better I got. I found the idea that I had to *stop* trying so hard really weird – but I knew now how that felt, and after a few days I'd got into the habit of holding what I wanted to do much more lightly in my mind.

I kept my practice sessions completely secret. I'd always got on with everyone at school but I knew how anything – let alone something weird like telekinesis – could turn the most popular person into a big-time freakshow.

That meant I didn't hang out with my friends so much. Apart from Ketty, that is. I made sure I still saw as much of her as possible. We were still best friends, after all . . . even if she *was* going out with stupid Billy Martin. Every time I saw her, I made sure I listened out for something expensive that she might like. Not that Ketty was particularly interested in material things. She was more into running than owning stuff.

Still, there had to be something she really wanted. I didn't have any idea how Jack was going to help me use my telekinesis to make money, but I wanted to be ready to buy something good once he had. My plan was to hand it over, then, once Ketty could see I was just as able as Billy to give her stuff, ask her out myself.

It was Friday, the day before I was due to meet Jack again, and I was in a good mood. It was taking me a couple of minutes to get the right breathing going but, once I had, I could move whatever I wanted, for a few seconds at least.

Having just managed my first bit of telekinesis in the dorm – lifting my pillow off my bed – I headed outside. A group of us were meeting out the front of school to get the bus to nearby Hanmore Park and go to the movies. Ketty was already there, chatting with Lola and Lauren. I could see Billy hovering nearby. Ignoring him, I went over to the girls.

Ketty was in her normal going-out gear of jeans and trainers. But something was different. Lola and Lauren were ooohing and aaahing beside her, pointing at her hair . . . no, not her hair . . . I got closer . . . at her earrings. I did a double take. Ketty hardly *ever* wore jewellery and these were long, silvery earrings that glittered as they peeked through her dark, curly hair.

Lola caught me staring. 'Hey, Nico.' She giggled.

Ketty turned. 'Hey.' She made a self-conscious gesture towards her ears. 'They've got diamonds in them . . . what d'you think?' she said. 'I got them off Billy.'

Unbelievable. My heart slid into my shoes. What kind of teenage boy buys his girlfriend *diamond earrings*?

I forced a smile. 'Cool, babe . . . though it's kind of crazy giving you nice stuff like that. I mean, they'll fall out as soon as you start running.'

Ketty's face flushed. Lola sidled up to me.

'She's not going to wear them when she's running, Nico,' she simpered. 'Anyway, now she's got Billy, Ketty'll probably *stop* going running quite so much.'

Ketty and I exchanged glances. I knew from previous conversations that none of Ketty's girlfriends understood why she liked running so much. To them it was just something tiring and boring that made your body all sweaty and your hair look crap. For Ketty, though, running was everything. She said it made her feel good about herself in a way nothing else did.

I got that. But nobody else seemed to.

'If Ketty stops running, I'll eat those earrings, babe,' I said.

'Nico!' Lola giggled.

Ketty just smiled. A minute later, she drew me aside.

'Lola fancies you, you know,' she said.

I shrugged. I kind of knew that already. It didn't matter. Lots of girls behaved like Lola around me, all giggly and nervous. I wasn't interested in any of them.

35

'Hey, listen,' Ketty went on, breathlessly. 'I've just found out about this Youth Marathon. Well, it's really a half-marathon but that's still over thirteen miles. It's perfect for me.'

'That's great, babe,' I said, transfixed by the way her eyes were all lit up and shining.

'Not really.' Ketty's face fell. 'It's in Scotland and the closing date to enter is this coming Monday and it costs forty pounds to sign up. Then there's the fare to get there and finding somewhere to stay . . .'

I opened my mouth to say something sarcastic about Billy picking up the tab, but then it suddenly occurred to me *this* was my ideal opportunity. I could research the marathon and buy everything Ketty needed!

'How much d'you think the whole thing will cost?' I asked, as lightly as I could.

'A couple of hundred quid.' Ketty made a face. 'I asked my mum and dad. They said they didn't mind me going, but it was too expensive for what it was, and wouldn't I rather have a laptop . . .'

Better and better.

I made a sympathetic face back. Ketty had often complained to me how her parents hated her obsession with running. Not that she saw them very often. They lived and worked abroad and, since Ketty had joined Fox Academy at the beginning of the school year, I knew she'd only seen them once, at Christmas.

'What about your brother?' I asked.

Ketty talked about her older brother a lot. I'd never met him but, as far as I could tell, he was the only family member she was really close to.

'Yeah, I tried Lex too,' Ketty sighed, 'but he said he was skint until next week and I need the registration money by Monday.'

I nodded. Billy was watching me over Lauren's shoulder, a slightly aggressive expression on his square-jawed face. I caught his eye for a second and smiled.

Diamond earrings, my arse. I was going to buy Ketty something she *really* wanted.

It was a good evening after that. I mean, I had to endure the sight of Ketty and Billy with their arms round each other. But Ketty talked to me and her girlfriends just as much as she talked to him. I had no idea how to ask her how much she liked him, but I was confident it was less than he liked her.

The next morning I told Tom I had another date with my mystery London girl and asked him to cover for me again. He agreed, but only after teasing me about her.

'What does she look like, then?' he said.

I described Dylan, telling Tom quite truthfully that she was one of the fittest girls I'd ever met. I didn't add that I hadn't really fancied her. In fact, I exaggerated what we'd done quite a bit – just to wind him up. Tom swallowed the whole thing and made me promise to text him a picture of her. I forgot about it as soon as I reached the tube station where we were meeting, of course.

Ten minutes passed, and I was just starting to wonder if Jack had forgotten our arrangement, when a screech of brakes at the corner made me look up. My mouth fell open. Jack was pulling up, in just about the coolest car I'd ever seen – a sleek, black Aston Martin DB9.

'Nice wheels,' I said, trying to sound as if I rode in cars like this most weekends.

Jack grinned. 'Hop in. We've got a football match to get to.'

Football? To be honest I wouldn't have expected Jack to be a big fan of the game. He hardly looked like your average supporter. Today, as before, he was wearing a stylish suit with an open-neck shirt and designer sunglasses.

The Aston Martin zoomed away.

'Who's playing?' I asked. 'And, er . . . I thought . . . I mean, how is this going to make us any money?'

'You'll see.' Jack shot me a mysterious smile. I shrugged and sat back as he asked about my week and how I liked boarding at Fox Academy. I gave him a swift outline of how boring life at school was. Then I plucked up the courage to ask a question that had been on my mind since last weekend.

'Why are you doing all this?' I said. 'Helping me, I mean?'

'Several reasons.' Jack glanced sideways at me. 'I was part of the original project so I feel involved. But it's mostly because I want you to have a chance to fulfil your potential – and I know Fergus won't let that happen.'

'Why does Fergus hate what I can do so much? I mean, he actually called my abilities "evil" . . . said my mum would have hated them. He even tried to make me promise that I wouldn't use them any more.'

Jack was silent for a few moments, then he pulled the car over and parked. 'There's something I didn't tell you last weekend,' he said, his blue eyes bright and intense. 'Something that explains Fergus's reaction. But it's not going to be easy for you to hear.'

'What?' I said, feeling nervous.

'There was a problem with the Medusa gene. That is . . . d'you remember I told you it was embedded in a virus before it was injected into your umbilical cord?'

I nodded. 'You said that was normal in gene therapy.'

'It is, and William did all the necessary tests on the viruses he used, too – but the procedure is always risky.' Jack hesitated. 'Sometimes when you inject a gene code into what appears to be a harmless virus, the presence of the gene code makes the virus mutate . . .'

'Mutate into something harmful?' I frowned. 'But I'm fine.'

'I know.' Jack sighed. 'You were immune, but the viral DNA also seeped into the bloodstream of the carrier.'

'The carrier?' I stared at him, blankly.

'The person carrying the baby injected with the gene synthesis.' Jack shook his head. 'In other words, your mother.'

A cold wave washed over me. 'But . . . but my mum died of cancer,' I said.

Jack nodded. 'Yes. A cancer caused by the virus that the Medusa gene was embedded in.'

I froze. 'But that means the gene . . .' I could barely bring myself to think it, let alone say it. 'That means my gene, my powers . . . that means *I* killed her.' My voice was hoarse.

'No.' Jack shook his head again, more vigorously. 'No way. It was an accident. Or, if anyone's to blame it was William Fox. That's why Fergus felt so responsible for you . . . because of what his brother had done. And that's why he hates the gene inside you. But that's like hating the wind for becoming a hurricane.'

'But even so . . .' My voice was strained. 'Even so, if I didn't have the gene she wouldn't have died.'

'No.' Jack shook his head. 'That's not how your mum saw it, Nico. I met her twice – once before you were born, at that Christmas party; and once when you were a baby and William was dead. That second time, she *knew* that the Medusa gene . . . that it was going to kill her . . . and she saw the fact that she was going to die as a sacrifice she was making for you, so that *you* could be special. Your mum was *proud* of that sacrifice. And you should be proud too. You can't let Fergus stop that sacrifice from counting. You should make the most of what you can do . . . of who you are . . . for your mum's sake, if for nothing else.'

Jack smiled reassuringly, then revved up the engine. As we sped off, I tried to think it through. It was hard not to feel it was my fault Mum had died. And yet, Jack was right. I hadn't asked to be injected with a gene wrapped inside a virus. Just as William Fox hadn't known that the virus would kill Mum.

At least Jack had had the courage to tell me the truth, which was more than Fergus had done.

And if Mum had given her life for the Medusa gene the least I could do was make the most of its power.

Jack said nothing more as we zoomed round a series of streets, finally pulling up outside Arsenal's Emirates stadium. We went inside and Jack led the way to brilliant seats – they must have cost a fortune – in one of the directors' boxes.

Arsenal were playing a charity friendly against a Championship side I'd never heard of – Sweeton United. I tried to put what Jack had just told me to the back of my mind. At first I kept going over what he'd said but eventually the football sucked me in and I settled down to enjoy the match.

I forgot about my telekinesis – and Jack's plan for me to use it to make money – until the game was nearly halfway through. The home team, clear favourites, had already scored two goals.

Then Jack leaned over and whispered in my ear. 'You know, I've got a bet on at six to one that Sweeton will win three-two.'

I stared at him. Why would he have made such a specific – and unlikely – gamble?

Jack raised his eyebrows. 'Shame there's no one here who could help them score.'

41

My heart thudded as I realised what he was saying.

Did I dare do what he was suggesting?

I stared at the pitch. The ball was near Arsenal's goal, being successfully defended by one of Arsenal's best centre backs. Without really thinking about it, I directed the ball away from his feet, towards the Sweeton striker. It bounced off his shin and into the goal.

The Sweeton fans erupted in cheers. Jack punched me on the shoulder. 'Nice one!'

I stared at the pitch, too shocked to respond. Had I *really* done that? The striker looked as shocked as I felt. The score-board at the far end registered the goal. I *had* done it. I grinned.

'Two more like that, my son, and we'll be quids in.' Jack laughed, as the whistle blew for half-time.

The second half started well for Sweeton. Clearly buoyed up by their earlier goal, they scored ten minutes into the half without any help from me. Then Arsenal got the ball and all of a sudden I was leaning forward, intent on the play, making sure the ball swerved and swung away from the goal whenever it got too close. I was totally in the match, in the moment, only barely aware of Jack sitting beside me, watching me.

The score remained at two-all for a long time. I was so focused on the game that it was a shock when he leaned over and said, 'Only five minutes to go, Nico.'

That meant only five minutes for the winning goal to be scored. And the run of play for the past half an hour had definitely been with Arsenal. Panicking, I lurched forward in my seat, willing the ball to move down the pitch. Of course, as soon as I started trying so hard, the ball refused to move. I glanced at the clock. Only three minutes to go. Two minutes . . . Ketty's face flashed in front of my eyes, Billy's diamond earrings dangling from her ears.

I *had* to make this work. I couldn't let Billy buy her away from me. I had to show Ketty how much I cared about her . . .

6: Winning

I looked at the clock again. Only one minute of the match remained. A hush descended on the football stadium, as if the crowd had given up and accepted the two-all draw.

I had to help Sweeton score. But there was less than a minute to go and the ball wouldn't move for me any more. I could feel the panic swirling inside me. And then Jack put his hand on my shoulder.

'Breathe,' he whispered.

I breathed in, then out. My body released its tension. I focused once again on the game. The midfielders from both teams were fighting over the ball in the middle of the pitch. I waited for a Sweeton player to get a touch. Then I breathed in and lifted the ball. *Yes*. It soared all the way down the field. I breathed out. The ball bounced and swerved, just shy of the goal. Pushing away the anxious knot in my gut, I tried again.

This time the ball flew into the crowd. Crucial seconds passed while a new ball was produced. A corner. I glanced at the clock again.

Oh, crap. We were already in extra time.

'You can do this, Nico,' Jack whispered.

I breathed in as the Sweeton player stepped up to the corner flag. Breathed out as the ball rose into the air. My eyes held it as it curved. It was going to miss the goal. The crowd were chanting a countdown.

'Ten. Nine.'

I leaned with the ball, every fibre of my being flowing with it through the air.

'Eight. Seven. Six.'

Just a little push. The slightest touch. I nudged the ball with my mind, my hands mirroring the movement.

'Five. Four. Three.'

Wham! It thudded into the back of the net.

The Sweeton supporters roared. The final whistle blew.

I sat back, out of breath, exhausted.

The Sweeton player who'd taken the corner looked completely shocked that he'd scored. He was soon buried under his cheering team mates.

'Nico?'

I turned. Jack was open-mouthed, an expression of awe on his face. 'That was amazing,' he said. 'I honestly didn't think you'd be ready for that.'

My heart sank. 'So you were kidding about the bet, then?'

'Not at all.' Jack leaped up from his seat. 'I just meant I was prepared to lose the money. But you did it. Come on, let's go and collect our winnings.'

By the time we got back to Jack's mews house I was

starving, but triumphant. Jack swung the car into the garage where I'd practised with the tyre the previous week. He parked up, then produced a thick wedge of ten-pound notes from his wallet. I waited while he counted out forty pounds.

'My original bet,' he said, tucking the money into his pocket. He held out the rest of the cash to me. 'For you. That was *awesome*, Nico. *Amazing*. You're a complete bloody natural.'

I stared at the money, suddenly unsure. 'How much is there?' I stammered.

'Well, I bet forty quid at six to one, so you work it out.' Jack grinned and offered the cash to me again, but I shook my head. Now that the money was in front of me, it felt somehow wrong to take it.

'I don't know . . .' I rubbed my sweaty hands down my jeans.

'Don't know what?'

'Um . . .' I thought back to the football match. 'What I did was . . . sort of cheating, wasn't it?' I stammered.

Jack pursed his lips. 'Well, I suppose if you call giving the ultimate underdogs a fighting chance against a big shot team with more money than they know what to do with then, yes, it wasn't particularly fair. But life isn't. Come on.'

He offered the money again, but I shook my head. We stared at each other for a few moments. Jack frowned.

'It's . . . I mean . . .' I hesitated. 'I've got no problem really . . . I mean Sweeton scored one of their goals all by themselves . . . It's just . . .'

'Just what, Nico?' Jack said, his voice tight. 'Were you listening to what I said earlier? Your mother died for your gift. She would *want* you to use this amazing ability you have. She hated the fact that she was going to leave you all alone in the world. I know she would see what you did today as a small step towards helping you survive.'

I stared at him. 'Even if it meant cheating?'

Jack's eyes blazed. 'Using your talents to get ahead *isn't* cheating. It's just common sense . . . making the most of the cards you've been dealt in life.'

I held up my hands. 'Okay, okay, keep your hair on,' I said. 'This is all just really new for me.'

Jack smiled. 'I know. I'm sorry. I should give you more time to adjust.' He folded over the stash of bills in his hand. 'Look, you don't have to take it. I'll give it to charity.'

'Er . . .' I stared at the money, working out how much must be there now that Jack had taken out his original bet. 'That's got to be two hundred and forty pounds,' I said. That, surely, had to be enough money for Ketty to enter the marathon and find somewhere to stay in Scotland.

Jack chuckled. 'The boy can add up.'

I swallowed. My throat was dry. Jack held out the money again. 'Go on, take it,' he said. 'You can always give it away later.'

Well, giving it away was exactly what I was planning. I took the cash and shoved it into my pocket.

'Thanks,' I said.

Jack got out of the car. 'No, Nico, thank *you*.'

7: The deal

We went inside, to the kitchen, where Jack made me a large cheese sandwich. I was sitting at the table, wolfing it down, when Dylan walked in, carrying a shopping bag.

'Hey.' She smiled at me . . . a cool, slightly aloof smile.

Jack looked up. 'Hey, Dylan. What d'you buy today?' He turned to me. 'Dylan's only in London with her relatives for two weeks but I'm not sure there'll be anything left in the shops by the time she goes home.' He laughed. 'I've had to give her a key so she has somewhere to stash it all!'

Dylan rolled her eyes and took some sort of floaty green top out of the bag. She held it up in front of her. 'Like it?'

I grunted, feeling a bit embarrassed.

'Lovely,' Jack enthused. 'A great colour for your eyes.' Dylan shrugged, but you could tell she was pleased he liked the top. 'How did he do?' She pointed to me, though her question was clearly directed at Jack.

'Brilliantly,' Jack said. 'He has an amazing gift.'

I frowned. What was Jack doing? My telekinesis was private.

Dylan turned to me, twisting her long, red hair round her hand. 'So what's your thing?'

I stared at her. 'My *thing*?'

Jack cleared his throat. 'She means your psychic ability, Nico.'

My mouth fell open.

'It's okay,' Jack went on, quickly. 'Dylan knows all about the Medusa gene.'

Dylan glanced at him. 'You haven't told him?' she said.

Jack shook his head.

'Told me what?' I put down my cheese sandwich. 'What are you talking about?'

'Er . . . when William Fox created the Medusa gene,' Jack said, 'he didn't just implant the synthesis in you.'

I stared at him. 'You mean there are *others*?'

Jack nodded. 'Three others, all your age.'

'Where?' I turned to Dylan. 'Who?'

Dylan's face curved into a mysterious smile. She picked up a box of matches off the counter.

'Well, I tracked down a boy called Edward O'Brien a couple of months ago, but he wasn't interested in my help.' Jack shrugged. 'There's a girl out there somewhere, too. I'm still trying to find her, but it's not easy. I don't even know her name. You see, William destroyed all his scientific notes before he died. The identity of the four babies implanted with the Medusa gene was in those.'

'So how are you going to find her?'

'Fergus knows who she is. William told him before he died.'

'How can you be sure?'

'Well, Fergus knew about *you*, didn't he? And I know he'd spoken to Edward O'Brien, ages before I tracked him and his family down – frightened the wits out of the poor boy.' Jack shook his head.

'Oh.' My head was reeling again. It hadn't occurred to me for a second that there might be *other* people with the same ability as me. A knot of disappointment curled itself up in my chest. If I was honest, I'd kind of liked being the only one who could move objects without touching them.

'So did this boy – Edward whoever – have telekinetic powers too?' I said, flatly.

'No.' Jack shook his head. 'He didn't tell me much, but I'm sure of that. Anyway, William was adamant that the gene didn't work in isolation . . . that character traits, environmental factors, all sorts of random elements would determine how the Medusa gene developed. It's highly unlikely all four of you will have the same abilities.'

'So what other ways might the gene . . . come out in someone?' I asked.

Jack and Dylan exchanged glances.

'Most likely in some way that reflects other aspects of their personality,' Jack said. 'At least, that was William's theory. There aren't *that* many options . . . Mind-reading is one though . . . as is being able to predict the future.'

50

'Wow,' I said. 'That's amazing.'

Jack nodded. 'All four of you are likely to have a distinct and incredible psychic talent.'

'You only told me about two of the others,' I said. 'A boy called Edward O'Brien and a girl you don't know anything about. Who's the fourth?'

Jack glanced at Dylan. She was still holding the box of matches. She drew one out and struck it. She gazed deep into the flame, then held up her finger.

'Dylan's the fourth teenager with the Medusa gene,' Jack said, softly. 'Dylan?'

Dylan glanced at me out of the corner of her eyes. 'If I see danger coming, I can protect myself from getting hurt. Watch.'

I stared, as Dylan slowly moved her finger into the fire. She held it there for several seconds, her expression impassive, then slowly withdrew it. She held the finger up so I could see it clearly. It was unmarked.

I realised I'd been holding my breath and let it out.

'Never fails to bowl me over.' Jack grinned at me.

I nodded, feeling I was expected to say something.

'How did you do that?' I asked Dylan.

She shrugged. 'Jack showed me how to focus on my breath. I just do that, and it feels like my body gets this protective coat – like a second skin.'

'Does it only work when you know you're in danger?' I said, genuinely interested.

'At first it did, but now I can do it whenever I want.'

51

Dylan smiled coldly at me, her slanted green eyes narrowing like a cat's.

I nodded, wondering if she always sounded that arrogant.

Jack leaned forward. 'Nico, I wonder if you would consider doing a favour in return for me . . .er, helping you develop your own abilities.'

My hand unconsciously went to my pocket. I felt the thick edge of the folded ten-pound notes. 'What's that?' I said.

'You have better access to Fergus's papers and computer files than anyone else in the world,' Jack said, intently. 'As I explained, he undoubtedly knows who the fourth person with the Medusa gene is – but the girl herself is probably developing her abilities with no idea about what's going on. You *know* how terrifying it was for you when your telekinesis started. Imagine living with that for months . . . even years. I have to find the poor girl, even if it's just to pass on the information about the Medusa gene, like I did with Edward O'Brien.'

I nodded.

'Of course, if you don't want to go through your stepdad's things I'll understand,' Jack went on. 'But you are – without doubt – in the best position to do it.'

My hand fingered the bundle of notes in my pocket again. This money was my passport to Ketty. And Jack had helped me to get it. The least I could do now was help him help someone else. Anyway, Fergus didn't deserve my loyalty after keeping quiet about the Medusa gene all these years.

'Sure,' I said. 'No problem.'

8: Marathon lies

'For you.' I handed over the envelope.

Ketty opened it, a puzzled expression on her face. She drew out the Youth Marathon entry confirmation.

I bit my lip, waiting for her response. I'd gone online and booked her onto the marathon as soon as I'd got back from Jack's. It had been straightforward enough to fill out the entry form – I knew Ketty ran about three miles a day, which was above the entry requirement.

I'd printed it out and posted it with the necessary forty pounds cash and now, three days later, here was the confirmation that she was actually signed up for the race.

At last Ketty looked up. It was morning break and we were standing in the entrance hall. People were rushing past us in every direction, but all I could see were Ketty's golden-brown eyes.

'Wow, Nico.' She looked up at me, full of wonder. Then she wrinkled her nose. 'I don't understand . . .'

'There's nothing *to* understand.' I shrugged. 'You said

53

you wanted to enter the marathon and I've registered you.' I pushed four fifty-pound notes into her hand. 'This should cover all the other stuff you need – travel and food and staying in the designated youth hostel. You'll need your parents' permission to go, but you said before they were only objecting to the cost, so that shouldn't be a problem.'

Ketty's mouth fell open. 'But . . . but where did you get all this money?'

I shrugged. 'Been saving for ages,' I said.

Ketty raised her eyebrows. 'Don't lie to me, Nico. This is *loads* of money. We both know you don't have any savings *or* get this kind of allowance.'

Crap.

'Okay, okay.' I sighed. 'If you want the truth, I won it on a bet and I thought you could use it more than me.'

'You're kidding.' Ketty frowned.

'You're welcome,' I said, sarcastically.

Ketty's face softened. She reached up and kissed my cheek. I could feel myself reddening and coughed to cover my embarrassment.

'I'm sorry,' she said. 'It's amazing you've done this . . . like I said, I just don't understand . . .'

I rolled my eyes. 'I bet you don't give Billy such a hard time when *he* buys you something.'

As soon as the words were out of my mouth I knew I'd said something wrong.

'Billy's never bought me anything,' Ketty said.

I raised my eyebrows. 'Really? What about your new

54

phone and those fancy earrings you were wearing last Friday.'

'What are you talking about?' Ketty took a step away from me. 'The phone was a giveaway with some bank account Billy's parents set up for him. He'd just got a new upgrade, so he let me have the mobile from the offer.' She shook her head. 'And the earrings belong to his older sister. I was *borrowing* them because Billy offered . . . Just for the night. I didn't really want to, but he kept going on about them. You should know they're not my kind of thing at all.'

'Oh.' My throat felt tight. Ketty was looking at me like I had ten heads.

'Is that what this is about?' She frowned. 'Trying to look big by competing with Billy Martin?'

'No . . .'

There was a long pause. The school bell rang right above our heads. Ketty looked at her shoes. 'Anyway, me and Billy . . . we've just been linking. We're not going out or anything.'

'Yeah?' My heart leaped. I tried not to look too excited. 'Well, whatever – this money's got nothing to do with him.'

'So where did you get it?' Ketty paused, then her eyes widened. 'You didn't *steal* it, did you?'

'No.' I stared at her, astonished. 'No, of *course* I didn't.'

Ketty jutted out her chin. 'Where did it come from, then? And don't give me any rubbish about winning it on a bet. Proper gambling's illegal if you're under eighteen and no one at school has this much cash to lose.'

Panic swirled in my chest. My mind was blank. Part of me wanted to tell her the truth – but I was terrified she'd think I was a total freak.

'Okay,' I said. I could hear the desperation in my voice. 'I won it doing a trick . . . in a talent competition.'

Ketty screwed up her forehead. 'What sort of trick? Like that stupid twig-moving thing you tried to show me a couple of weeks ago?'

'No . . .' I cast around for something . . . anything that would sound convincing. *Stick as close to the truth as you can.* 'It was a trick, er . . . using balls.'

Ketty shook her head. 'Nico . . . I've known you for months . . . you can't do any tricks – with or without balls.'

The panic in my chest spread like fire. *Breathe. Breathe.*

'I can,' I said. 'I mean, it wasn't a *magic* trick or any-thing . . .'

Ketty put her hand on her hips. 'Tell me, specifically, what you did then.'

My mind spun. I lighted on the only trick-related activity I could think of involving balls. 'Juggling,' I said.

'Really? You can juggle?' Ketty frowned. 'Well enough to win a talent contest?'

'Yeah, I juggled with seven balls.' The claim blurted out of my mouth before I could stop it.

Ketty raised an eyebrow. 'Show me.'

Oh God. Oh God.

'I'll show you later,' I said, frantically trying to buy myself some time.

56

'Right.' Ketty looked away, her face a picture of disbelief. We stood in an awkward silence.

Shit. This was *so* not how I'd imagined this moment. Ketty was supposed to look up at me with big, grateful eyes and I was supposed to put my arms around her and . . .

'I don't think I should take your money,' Ketty said, stiffly. 'Seeing as you've now given me three versions of how you got it.' She held the two hundred pounds and the entry form out to me. 'Here.'

'I'm not lying to you about the juggling, I *promise*.' I remembered what Jack had said to me after the football match. 'If you can't use the money then give it to charity,' I said.

'I don't know.' Ketty hesitated. 'I *really* want to run in that marathon but . . . do you *promise* you didn't steal it?'

'Yes.' I rolled my eyes. 'I told you . . . I won a talent competition by juggling with seven balls. I'll show you . . . we'll go out on Saturday night. Yeah?'

Crap. Crap. Crap.

What had I said 'Saturday night' for? That was far too soon.

'Okay.' Ketty bit her lip. 'But I won't need all of it.' She handed me back fifty pounds. I had no choice but to take it. She pocketed the entry confirmation and the rest of the cash. 'Thank you.' She stared up at me.

Oh God, that wasn't how I wanted her to look at me. Her eyes were all wary and suspicious.

'Ketty?'

57

'I've got to get to Art.' Ketty tucked her hair behind her ears, all self-conscious. 'Er . . . thanks again . . . see you later . . .'

She turned and walked away. I sagged against the wall, watching her go and feeling like crying.

What had I done? I'd given Ketty all that money but, if anything, she seemed to like me *less* than she'd done before. Plus, even though she wasn't with Billy, I couldn't tell her how I felt myself. Not yet. First I had to prove to her that what I'd said about doing tricks was true. Proving my honesty and impressing her with my skills was obviously far more important than spending a load of money on her.

Which meant – and *how* had this happened? – learning to juggle with seven balls.

By Saturday night.

9: Saving Ed

The entrance hall was empty – all the teachers and pupils at their next class. Mr Rogerson, our maths teacher scuttled past, his arms full of textbooks.

'Shouldn't you be in a lesson, Nico?' He raised his eyebrows.

'On my way, sir.' I pushed myself up off the wall and headed along the corridor towards my history class. Fergus was already in there when I arrived though the class hadn't technically started. He raised an eyebrow at me, but didn't say anything.

It was the day after I'd given Ketty the money for the Youth Marathon. She'd barely spoken to me since and I was going quietly mad with frustration.

I'd quickly realised how insane my ambition to learn to juggle seven balls in four days had been. But at least I could use telekinesis to help. I'd been practising like mad ever since, unable to concentrate on anything else, though I'd still only managed to keep four balls in the air so far.

Fergus made some announcement about a new boy who had started at Fox Academy that day. All the usual stuff . . . please make him feel welcome . . . blah, blah, like head teachers do. I drifted off after a few seconds. It was the same during science and then maths. In fact, the only thing – apart from Ketty – that I noticed in the whole of my maths class was that Mr Rogerson's hair seemed to have slid slightly to one side.

'D'you think he's wearing a wig?' Tom whispered in my ear.

I grinned. 'I dare you to go up to him and pull it off.'

Tom grinned back. 'After you.' He glanced at the front of the classroom, where Mr Rogerson was busily writing an equation on the whiteboard. 'Hey, you said you'd show me a picture of your fit new girlfriend.'

I frowned for a second before I realised he must be talking about Dylan.

'Yeah, next time I see her,' I whispered.

'You're making her up.'

'I'm no—'

'Another whisper and you'll both be in detention.' Mr Rogerson's clipped tones temporarily ended our conversation, but Tom didn't let the subject of Dylan drop. In fact, he was still teasing me during lunch break. In the end I headed up to Fergus's flat to get away from him. I used to live here, but last year I told Fergus I'd rather be in the dorms with everyone else. I still had a bedroom, though, and keys.

I let myself in and sat on the sofa. There was a bowl of

apples on the table and I spent a few minutes attempting to juggle five of them using telekinesis. I could still only manage four.

Disgruntled, I put the apples back in the bowl and looked round. I hadn't been in here for weeks, but the flat was as tidy as ever. Fergus's timetable was clipped neatly to the fridge door, along with a picture of me and Mum from when I was about three.

I wandered over to take a closer look. Mum was smiling in the photo. What would she say if she knew about me and Ketty? I sighed. Chances were, that if she were alive, I probably wouldn't tell her. Most boys I knew didn't seem to talk to their mums about girl stuff.

The timetable showed that the whole of Fergus's lunch hour today was taken up with a staff meeting. Jack's instruction to look for information about the fourth teen with the Medusa gene suddenly popped into my head. Well, I might as well see what I could find while there was no danger of Fergus interrupting me. I could have another go at the juggling in a minute.

I scanned the bookshelves, then spent a few minutes investigating a cupboard that contained a load of private bank and tax info. Nothing remotely to do with the Medusa gene. I had a quick look round in Fergus's bedroom, but there was clearly nothing in here apart from clothes and a few old car magazines.

Maybe all the really important stuff was in his office. I headed out of the flat and past the boys' dormitories. I'd just

61

reached the back staircase that led down to the ground floor when I heard a muffled cry coming from the storeroom at the top of the stairs. I paused. The light was on inside the room – a glowing strip at the bottom of the door.

The cry came again – like an animal in pain. I threw open the storeroom door. The two people inside both jumped – Billy Martin and a boy I didn't know. Billy's face was vicious – screwed up with anger. The other boy looked terrified. Billy's hands dropped to his side and I realised that the other boy was holding his belly, like he'd just been punched.

'What's going on?' I said.

Billy swore. 'This loser just started in my Spanish class and he speaks and writes it perfectly.'

I looked at the other boy. He had thick, sand-coloured hair and blue eyes. He was tall, too. Taller than either me or Billy. But there was something gentle about him. Something just asking to be picked on.

'So you're beating him up because he's better than you at Spanish?' I narrowed my eyes. 'Or are you just annoyed 'cos Ketty dumped you?'

'She didn't dump me,' Billy snorted. 'I didn't *want* to go out with her – all she ever does is go running. And she's butters.'

'Don't call her that,' I spat, fury boiling up in my chest.

'Er . . . I think I'm going to go,' said the new boy.

'No.' Billy put out his arm to stop the boy walking past. The boy flinched. I gritted my teeth. The truth was I didn't particularly care about this new boy – but I was itching to punch Billy. What had Ketty seen in him?

I pointed at the new boy. 'So what's he done to you then, Billy?'

'I asked him really nicely to do my homework for me . . .' Billy clenched his fists. 'But the tosser said no.'

I glanced at the new boy. He must be the one Fergus had mentioned in history, earlier. He was standing perfectly still, his head bowed, like he was waiting for me and Billy to decide his fate.

I looked back at Billy. 'He shouldn't have to do your homework,' I said, my hands curling into fists. 'In fact, I'm telling you now, he's not doing it *ever*.'

'Or what?' Billy squared up to me.

I glanced round the storeroom, searching for a weapon. There was a mop in the far corner. Maybe I could make that fly towards me. I caught the new boy's eye. He frowned at me, as if he could see I was planning to grab a weapon – and didn't approve.

'Or *what*?' Billy said more loudly.

'Or *this*.' I shoved him in the chest. Billy stumbled back a step, then lunged forwards. I darted out of the way, grabbed his arm and twisted it behind his back.

'Leave him alone, or I swear I'll make you sorry.' I wrenched at Billy's arm.

'Ow! Stop . . . you're hurting me!'

'I'm not hearing you promise you'll leave him alone . . .' I twisted Billy's arm further up his back.

63

That's for saying Ketty's ugly.

'Okay, okay, I promise.'

I released Billy's arm. He rubbed it, then stormed out of the storeroom. Panting, I looked over at the new guy.

He was still staring at me. 'Thank you,' he said, his face breaking into an eager smile. 'Thank you . . . thank you . . .'

'I'm Nico,' I said, mostly to stop him from gushing on.

'Edward.' He held out his hand.

I shook it – just for a second. It felt a bit awkward . . . I wasn't used to boys my own age being this formal.

'So, did you start here today?'

'Yeah, my parents thought I'd be . . . better off at a boarding school.'

I grimaced in sympathy. From what I'd seen of Edward so far, he wouldn't be better off anywhere this side of a home school. What with his gentle, geeky air and his eager-to-please face, he might as well have *Beat Me Up* stamped across his forehead.

'You're Mr Fox's stepson, aren't you?' he said.

'How d'you know that?'

'He told me about you earlier.' Edward paused. For a second he looked alarmed, like maybe he'd said too much. Then he burbled on. 'Anyway, I know I said my name was Edward but most people actually call me Ed . . . My brother calls me ENOB. That's from my initials. My full name's Edward Neill O'Brien. Anyway . . .'

'Edward O'Brien?' Where had I heard that name before?

'Thanks for what you did, Nico.' Ed was now walking

64

hurriedly past me, chattering on at high speed. 'I owe you but I ought to get back to the dorm . . . check where my next class is.'

He scurried off. I followed more slowly, the memory of where I'd heard Ed's name before still niggling away at the back of my brain, just out of reach.

I tried, for a minute, to work out what it was. But then I reached the bottom of the stairs and saw Ketty in the distance – and all I could think about was my Saturday night problem again.

10: Quits

Friday. Another dull history class with Fergus. I was certain, now, that Ketty was avoiding me. We normally talked at the end of school, before she went running, but yesterday she'd rushed off to get changed without a word. That was Thursday – late-night shopping – so, to cheer myself up, I sneaked out of school and got the bus to Hanmore Park. It's the nearest town to school, with plenty of phone shops on the High Street. Tom and Curtis agreed to cover for me if Fergus asked where I was. In the end I was out of school for about an hour and a half altogether. Risky, but worth it. I bought myself a great new phone with the money Ketty hadn't wanted.

Since then I'd spent my entire time attempting to achieve my ludicrous juggling ambitions. I could now keep six objects in the air at any one time, though only for a few seconds. I'd stopped practising with balls – tennis balls were too big to manoeuvre and I couldn't find any smaller ones. Anyway, using different objects looked cool. The whole thing *was* cool actually. I loved watching the objects zoom around each other. However, I was only too aware that making stuff move on my own was one thing and doing it in front of other people, *especially* Ketty, was something else.

I'd spent most of the lesson so far with my new phone under my desk, looking online for tips on normal juggling that I could adapt to fit my own, telekinetic version.

Fergus asked Ketty a question. I looked up. She was a few seats over. Her hair was loose today, resting on her shoulders. I got the distinct impression she was using it like a veil . . . hiding from me. But maybe I was being paranoid.

Ketty answered Fergus's question, then looked round. She caught my eye and smiled.

My confidence surged. It was going to be okay. Ketty might have been a bit withdrawn the past few days, but we were still friends – I just needed to make her believe that I won that stupid juggling competition. I decided to catch her after class and make some definite plan about Saturday. I turned back to my mobile.

'Nico?' Fergus's exasperated voice cut through my exploration of juggling4dummies.com.

I glanced up. The whole class was looking at me.

'At last,' Fergus said. 'Am I interrupting something?'

'No, sir.' I slid my phone into my trouser pocket.

'Then perhaps you can tell me which highly important historical document we've been discussing?' There was a sardonic edge to Fergus's voice. He only used it on me – and maybe a small handful of genuine school troublemakers.

I glanced at the textbook on my desk, desperately hoping the open page would give me a clue. But all I could see was a map.

'Er . . .' I looked round the class, hoping for help or inspiration.

Ketty was mouthing something at me, but too fast for me to follow what she was saying. Billy was smirking in the back left corner. Lola and Lauren were sitting on either side of him, both looking anxious.

And then I caught sight of Ed. He was up at the front, his thick, sandy hair all tousled up – making him look even geekier than when I'd found him in the storeroom. But the eager-to-please smile was gone. Instead, he was frowning in my direction – his blue eyes intense.

'Stand up, Nico,' Fergus barked.

Crap. Crap. Crap.

I stood, my eyes still drawn to Ed's.

'Right, if you can't tell me what we've been discussing, I'd like you to empty out your pockets,' Fergus went on. 'Then maybe we'll discover what's so distracting that you appear to have failed to follow the past fifteen minutes' discussion.'

No. My thoughts careered ahead of me. If Fergus found my phone, not only would it be confiscated but he would want to know where I'd got the money to buy it. How was I going to explain that?

'Nico?' Fergus repeated. I shook my head. It wasn't fair. Fergus would *never* ask an ordinary student to turn out their pockets. As usual, he was picking on me.

Ed was still staring in my direction. All of a sudden, his gaze shifted and he made direct eye contact. I knew only a few seconds had passed but suddenly it felt like time had vanished. That everyone had disappeared apart from him. And then I heard his voice in my head.

Say this: Sorry, sir. We've been discussing the Magna Carta, sir.

I opened my mouth and said the words. As I spoke I knew that Ed was inside my mind, telling me what to say.

Like, I was present. And yet, not present.

It was, without doubt, one of the freakiest experiences of my life.

Fergus frowned.

'And the Magna Carta is?' He folded his arms, and stared at the floor, clearly expecting me to crumble.

I stood, my heart racing. Ed's voice sounded in my head again, but I was panicking so much I could barely follow what he was saying.

Calm down, Nico.

I blinked.

Just listen, Ed's voice went on. *The Magna Carta was an English charter, issued in 1215, which limited the powers of the king and which has been used as the basis for con- stitutions around the world. Many of our rights and freedoms come from that one document. That's what we were discussing. How an ancient piece of writing still affects our lives today.*

As he spoke, I repeated the words. I knew I wasn't saying them in the way I normally spoke, but there wasn't time to personalise them. It was my voice, but it was, undoubtedly, Ed speaking.

'Very well, Nico.' Fergus looked up at me, sounding puzzled. 'You may sit down.'

As Fergus looked up, Ed looked away. His presence inside by head vanished completely. I sat down, shaken. For a few seconds I was unable to take in what had happened. And then the bell rang for the end of class and everything fell into place.

Edward O'Brien was the name of the boy with the Medusa gene that Jack had told me about – the one who hadn't wanted Jack's help all those months ago. Jack had been convinced Fergus would know about the boy and he was obviously right.

Ed had psychic powers, just like me and Dylan – except, in his case, the Medusa gene had clearly given him the ability to read minds . . . and to communicate without speaking.

Everyone around me was moving towards the door. Ed was still at his desk, loading books into his bag. I leaped up. Ed glanced at me out of the corner of his eye. He sped up, hauling his bag onto his back, almost running out of the room.

Completely forgetting my decision to speak to Ketty after

class, I grabbed my textbook and pushed my way to the door.

Ed was already out. I looked both ways down the corridor. *There.* He was scurrying away, round the corner.

I ran after him, praying some teacher didn't appear out of nowhere and stop me for speeding down the corridors.

I caught up with him just outside the back door, in the so-called Tranquillity Garden. It's a small patch of grass with a bunch of flower beds. You're not supposed to talk or run around out there.

Needless to say, it's hardly ever used.

'Ed?' I said. 'Wait.'

He kept on walking.

'Stop.' I reached out and grabbed his arm.

'What?' He hung his head, as I let go of his arm.

'What did you do back there?'

'What d'you mean?' Ed assumed an extremely phoney look of puzzlement. 'Nothing.'

For God's sake.

'You got inside my head, man.' I frowned. 'Told me what to say.'

'You're imagining it.'

'You *did*,' I insisted. 'You can read people's minds. You've met Jack Linden. He *told* me about you. You've got the Medusa gene. Why won't you admit it?'

There was a pause. The wind rustled in the trees above our heads. Then Ed looked up, slowly. 'It's wrong, what I

71

can do,' he said. 'Getting inside people's heads is . . . it's evil.'

'No.' I stared at him. 'That's what Fergus wants you to think.'

'My parents think so too,' Ed insisted. 'Mr Fox told them about the Medusa gene a year ago. He offered me a place at school then . . . said I'd be safer here. But they didn't believe him. Then I started being able to communicate telepathically and—'

'Tele- what?'

'Telepathically.' Ed reddened. 'It means I can "hear" other people's thoughts and they can "hear" mine, if I want them to.'

A worrying possibility struck me. 'So . . . so how many of my thoughts could you "hear" just now?'

Ed shuffled from foot to foot. 'Not many,' he said awkwardly. 'I wasn't prying. You'd know if I was. I was just sensing the surface stuff, really – mostly all I felt was how freaked out you were about the idea of Mr Fox seeing whatever was in your pocket – which would have been obvious to anyone looking at you anyway.'

'God, Ed, you can read people's minds . . .' I grabbed his arm. 'Don't you see, it's *amazing*. Didn't Jack make you see that?'

Ed shook his head. 'We only spoke for a minute. It was horrible. I mean, he turned up out of the blue outside my old school, about a month ago, telling me I was going to develop some mad genetic ability . . . that I was one of four people implanted with this deadly virus-type thing. My parents were really cross he'd come to me directly rather than going through them.'

I frowned, suddenly remembering what the Medusa gene had done to my mum. 'You keep talking about your parents,' I said. 'Isn't your mum . . . didn't she . . .?'

'She died when I was four.' Ed looked away. 'Sandra's my stepmother, but I think of her as my mum. I mean, I don't remember my real mum much.' He looked at me. 'It must be the same for you?'

I shrugged, embarrassed. Then I realised what he'd said.

'How did you know I had the gene too?' I said. 'I never said.'

Ed sighed. 'I saw it in Mr Fox's mind the day I got here. He made me look him in the eyes and when I do that to someone, it's really difficult not to just go straight into their head. Mr Fox was trying so hard not to give away that you had the gene that I couldn't *help* but see it.' He paused. 'Look, I only helped you out today because you helped me with that boy yesterday. But we're quits, now. I thought you'd understand, seeing as you've got the gene too. Mr Fox and my parents are right. The Medusa gene is a curse – it *kills* people. I'm not going to use it any more, so please leave me alone.' And with that he scuttled away, back into the school building.

I stood in the silence of the Tranquillity Garden for a few moments. Ed was so wrong about the Medusa gene. I checked the time. I was already late for my next class. A few more minutes wouldn't make any difference.

I took out my new phone, called Jack and told him everything Ed had done and said.

Five minutes later I strolled back into school, a smile on my face – juggling seven pebbles perfectly in the air.

11: An expression of interest

Saturday afternoon, and almost everything was in place. Once I'd mastered the juggling on Friday I'd been tempted to show Ketty straight away, but I knew that doing it privately was one thing – and making it work in front of her was another, so I kept practising.

As soon as Jack had heard about Ed he said he wanted to meet up with us both on Saturday night. I'd explained that I was supposed to be seeing Ketty then, but Jack was undeterred.

'There's a pub called the Saracen's Head not that far from your school where we can all hook up,' he said. 'I'll make sure no one hassles you and your girlfriend for ID and your drinks won't cost a thing. You'll look good in front of her, while I speak to Edward.'

'Great, er . . . but she's not my girlfriend,' I explained. 'We're just friends.'

Jack laughed. 'Well, maybe Saturday night will change that.'

I was worried Ketty might have changed her mind about us going out, but she agreed to go to the Saracen's Head straight away. She still seemed a bit reserved with me, though – not easy-going and relaxed, like she used to be.

It was simple enough to get permission slips to be out at the movies until 10 p.m. on Saturday night. I had no intention of either going to the cinema or getting home that early, of course, but it's easy enough to fool adults. You just have to keep updating them with texts:

Bus broke down outside cinema, have to wait for another
Now bus stuck in heavy traffic cos of accident, should be back in 30
Still stuck . . . driver says at least an hour

That sort of thing.

Which left the one crucial detail that was threatening to spoil everything. How was I going to get Ed to come too? He didn't look like the kind of teenager who'd be comfortable in a bar, even a small, local one. The idea of him having fake ID was laughable.

I walked into our year group common room. Ketty wasn't there – she always runs on a Saturday, even when it's pouring with rain like it was today – but almost everybody else was. Billy, Lola and Lauren were sitting in one corner, laughing over some magazine. Tom and Curtis were playing table tennis.

Ed was perched on the sofa by the window, flicking through a history textbook. I shook my head. Somebody should really tell him how uncool it is to be seen studying on a Saturday afternoon. Movement outside the window caught my eye. Ketty was jogging past, her sweats and hair plastered to her body.

I looked back at Ed. He was watching her too. Which gave me an idea. I sauntered over and sat down next to him on the sofa.

'Hey, Ed,' I said. 'How's it going?'

'Fine, thanks.' He smiled.

I watched him warily. Was he going to try and read my mind again? But Ed's eyes were guarded and not quite focused on my own. I realised, with a jolt, that this was how he always looked at people – not quite making eye contact. What had he said about it before? That if he looked into someone's eyes, it was virtually impossible to avoid reading their thoughts . . .

Making a mental note to avoid looking directly at him myself, I cleared my throat. 'Got any plans for tonight?'

Ed shook his head. 'I thought I'd catch up on some reading. I mean, the syllabus here is different from my old school, so I'm behind in a couple of subjects.' He held up the history textbook.

I resisted the temptation to roll my eyes at this latest display of Ed's geekiness. 'I thought you might like to come out with me?'

Ed's expression grew wary. 'Where?' he said, cautiously.

'Just a bar in Hanmore Park – that's the nearest town to here. It's nothing special.' I made a face. 'We only get permission slips to stay out till ten, so you won't see much action down there, but it could be a laugh.'

Ed shrugged. 'I don't think so,' he said. 'My parents wouldn't like me going somewhere where they sell alcohol.' He frowned. 'How would we get in, anyway?'

'Oh, there won't be any alcohol,' I lied. 'The early part of the evening's just for under-eighteens. They'll kick us out by nine-thirty.'

I held my breath. Surely even Ed wouldn't fall for that? But he did.

'Oh, well that's okay then, but I'm still not sure I should. I mean, I do have all this reading to do.'

Unbelievable. I sighed.

'That's a shame,' I said. 'Ketty was really hoping you'd come along.'

'Ketty's going?' Ed's face brightened.

I grinned. 'So you've only been here two days but you know who Ketty is?'

Ed blushed. 'I've just . . . I've seen her running. She's . . . well, it's different. I mean, *she's* different, isn't she?'

More than you'll ever understand, mate.

'Yeah, Ketty's cool,' I said. 'She's a really good friend of mine . . . tells me everything.' I paused. *Here goes.* 'Actually, I think she likes you.'

'Really?' Ed's face flushed scarlet.

'Yeah,' I lied, praying he wasn't going to suddenly break

his own rules and attempt to read my mind. 'Ketty was going on about you earlier, before she went running. Said how good-looking she thought you were. *And* interesting.'

Ed's dark blue eyes lit up.

'Don't expect her to make it obvious, though,' I added hurriedly. I wondered if I'd gone too far. I was sure Ketty hadn't even noticed Ed existed. And she was certainly way too cool to go for someone so geeky. 'Ketty's much shyer than she looks,' I went on. 'She might seem like she's not interested but she's actually just really unsure of herself.'

'Okay.' Ed leaned forward, like he didn't want to miss a word I was saying. 'Thanks, Nico. I really appreciate you telling me all this.'

For a split second, he almost made eye contact with me, then his gaze dropped again.

A throb of guilt pulsed through me. I pushed it away. I was only doing this so that Jack would get another chance to speak to Ed . . . to make him see how special his mind-reading abilities were.

I was doing Ed a favour here.

'Right, well we're meeting out the front at seven-thirty.' I stood up, then punched him playfully on the shoulder. 'Good luck, man.'

12: The gamble

The Saracen's Head in Hanmore Park was already crowded when we arrived just after 8 p.m. I hadn't really enjoyed the twenty-minute bus journey over here . . . I was too preoccupied – mostly with my impending juggling but also, slightly, over how Ed was going to react when he realised he'd been tricked into a meeting with Jack.

I hoped Jack would show up soon. While he was talking to Ed, I planned to slip outside with Ketty and give her a juggling demo. Once I'd proved that I could do what I'd claimed, I was hopeful that she'd stop acting so withdrawn around me. Actually, I was hoping for a lot more than that. But now really wasn't the time to get ahead of myself.

At least Ketty hadn't seemed to mind Ed tagging along. And Ed himself was surprisingly at ease with us both. I'd called Jack beforehand.

'I'm not sure a pub's the best place for you to meet Ed,' I'd said. 'He's not exactly experienced in the night life department.'

Jack had laughed and told me not to worry about it – or our ID. 'Just give the password "white flag",' he'd said. 'That'll sort everything.'

And now we were standing beside the bar. It was ultramodern, all mirrored walls and pale blue lighting.

We were the youngest people in here by several years. I was cool with that and Ketty looked like she fitted in okay, but Ed – dressed up like a middle-aged yuppie in a crisp shirt and chinos – looked very uncomfortable.

I looked round. Most people weren't taking any notice of us, but a few of the older ones were giving us extremely dirty looks.

A man beside us bought a beer and Ed turned to me.

'I thought you said there wouldn't be alcohol,' he whispered. 'And where are all the teenagers?'

I grinned. 'I may have misled you on the exact parameters of the evening, Ed, but just because they serve beer here, doesn't mean you have to drink it.'

Ed opened his mouth to say something, then glanced at Ketty and clearly thought better of it.

I smiled to myself. He didn't want to look uncool in front of her. Some chance.

'I'll get the drinks,' I said. 'What d'you want?'

Ed glanced at Ketty again.

'Coke please,' she said.

'Me too,' Ed said, clearly relieved she hadn't asked for an alcoholic drink.

I rolled my eyes and turned to the bar. I had my fake ID

all ready to ask for a beer, but decided to try Jack's password instead. As soon as I said 'white flag', the barman nodded.

'Sure. No charge, mate.'

Wow. For a second, I was tempted to get myself a triple vodka or something on top of the beer. Then I remembered why I was here – and that, as soon as Jack took Ed away, I was going to have to show Ketty I could juggle with seven objects. Better to keep a clear head and stick to a small beer.

After a few minutes, while the three of us sipped our drinks and looked round, Jack sent me a text:

Back room. Left of gents. Come alone.

I made an excuse and left Ketty and Ed by the bar. There was a bouncer on the door next to the toilet. I said the 'white flag' password again. The bouncer opened the door and stood back to let me pass.

Feeling a little unsettled, I walked into a small cloakroom, where a woman in a silver dress was checking in coats and bags. I didn't have anything with me, so she just yawned and waved me through to the main room. It was buzzing, with slot machines against one wall, four card tables at one end and a roulette wheel in the middle. Staff wearing silver shirts (for the men) or silver dresses (for the women) wandered about with drink trays. Another man was calling out numbers by the roulette table, which was crowded with people watching the wheel spin.

Silver lights made the room sparkle. Both the walls and the floor seemed to be covered with dark red velvet. I'd only ever seen rooms like this in films.

Jack appeared beside me in another smart designer suit.

'Is this a casino?' I said.

He nodded. 'A small one.'

A couple walked past. The woman stared at me. I suddenly realised how out of place I must look – at least five years younger than everyone else in the room.

'What's the plan, then?' I said, wondering why Jack hadn't come out to speak to Ed in the main bar.

He laughed. 'That's what I love about you, Nico, you're up for anything.'

I glanced at him, suddenly worried. Did he expect me to play cards or something? I had no idea how to do anything more complicated than 'snap'.

'Don't worry,' Jack said, misunderstanding my anxiety. 'The owner's a business contact of mine. No one's going to challenge you.'

'Okay, but . . .'

'So Edward and this girl of yours are out by the bar,' Jack interrupted.

'She's not . . . er, yup, but . . .'

'And they're friends too? I mean, I know Edward's only just met her, but he likes her . . . they get on?'

'Yeah.' I thought of Ed's smile when I'd told him Ketty was interested. 'I think he likes her a lot, actually, but I don't see how that's relevant. I mean, I don't think Ed's going to

83

be able to handle this room,' I said. 'Even if he gets over the shock of seeing you, which I doubt.'

'He just needs a nudge.' Jack grinned.

He glanced across the room at a middle-aged woman in a smart black dress. She was watching us talk, an expression of deep interest on her face.

'What d'you mean?' I asked, feeling confused. 'I thought you just wanted to talk to him?'

'Mmm . . . slight change of plan,' Jack said. 'But don't worry, you'll still end up with loads of cash.'

'But . . .' I knew that I'd told Jack I wanted money. But that had only been in order to impress Ketty. Now that I'd realised flashing expensive stuff in her direction really wasn't going to work, I just wanted a chance to talk to her alone. 'You *are* going to take Ed off, aren't you?'

'All in good time.' Jack grinned. 'Now, I want you to go back outside with Edward and . . . what's your friend's name?'

'Ketty.'

'Okay, go outside with Edward and Ketty and wait. Act normal. Don't say you've seen me. And, whatever happens, just go along with it. Everything'll be okay. Remember I'm pulling the strings.'

Pulling what strings?

But Jack was already propelling me out of the casino and towards the bar area.

I made my way back to Ed and Ketty feeling more troubled than ever. What was Jack going on about? And when was he going to take Ed and leave me and Ketty alone?

Ketty and Ed were so deep in conversation that they didn't notice me coming until I was almost on top of them. Ketty looked really pretty, all smiling and fresh-faced in her jeans and red jumper. Beside her, Ed just looked geeky – his shirt even had ironed-in creases down the sleeves.

'Ed did orienteering at his last school,' Ketty said, as I walked up. 'It's like running with maps.'

'Right,' I said, Jack's words still racing through my head. What did he mean about 'pulling the strings'?

'What's the matter?' Ed said.

'Nothing. Er . . . d'you want more drinks?'

'I'll get them.' Ed fished out his wallet and turned to the barman.

I raised my eyebrows. Where was all Ed's confidence coming from?

Ed bought three Cokes and we chatted on for a bit. Ketty was clearly having a great time, explaining various school customs and procedures to Ed. He was all silent smiles and encouraging nods. I hung back, grim-faced, wondering what was about to happen. I didn't have to wait long.

After about ten minutes a youngish man in a suit and tie wandered over, his eyes on Ketty.

'Hello, miss,' he said with a frown. 'I need to ask you to step into the office for a minute.'

I froze. I wasn't expecting anyone to challenge us for being here. Hadn't Jack said that he knew the manager?

'White flag,' I said.

The man ignored me.

'I've got ID,' Ketty squeaked, picking up her bag. 'And we only drank Coca-cola.'

'That's not it, miss,' the man went on. He took the bag from her. 'I'm afraid we have reason to believe you are in possession of class A drugs.'

'*What?*' Ketty and I spoke together.

Ed's eyes widened into circles.

'That's ridiculous.' Ketty's lip trembled. 'Look in my bag if you don't believe me.'

The man thrust his hand into her bag. He slowly pulled out a small tube of pills.

Ketty gasped. 'They're not mine.' She looked at me.

'They're not hers,' I insisted. 'Someone put them there.' The idea that Ketty would take pills was ludicrous. Of all the people I knew Ketty was the *last* person who'd ever use drugs.

And then it struck me. This must be what Jack had warned me about – what he'd been referring to when he'd told me: *Just go along with it . . . I'm pulling the strings.*

The man remained impassive. 'Like I said, please, no fuss, miss. We'd just like a private word.'

I was too shocked to think straight as we crossed the crowded bar towards the casino room. Why had Jack arranged to have drugs planted on Ketty? It didn't make sense.

The man took us into the little cloakroom with all the coats and bags.

'I don't understand.' Ketty was shaking now. 'I've *never* taken drugs. Not even the tiniest bit.'

The door from the casino swung open, letting in a short-lived burst of light and chatter. The woman in the long black dress that I'd seen watching Jack earlier swept in.

She had short blonde hair cut in a sharp bob and smelled of a deep, musky perfume. Her dark, hard eyes took us in, then she turned to the man. 'Please take the girl outside, Scott.'

'Yes, ma'am.' The man opened the door and indicated that Ketty should leave.

'Where are you taking her?' Ed's face was pale under his freckles.

'What's going on?' Ketty looked over her shoulder at me, her eyes full of fear as she was led away.

I stared down at my feet, unable to meet her gaze. What was going on? Where was Jack? I forced myself to remember what he'd said: *Whatever happens, go along with it. Everything'll be okay.*

Ed looked like he was about to be sick. 'This isn't right,' he said. 'We weren't taking drugs. Oh, God, please don't tell my parents.'

I bit my lip.

'Don't worry, Ed, dear.' The woman smiled. 'Nothing's going to happen to you or Nico or Ketty, providing you do what I tell you now.'

Ed stared at her. 'How do you know our names?' he said.

'Oh, I know a lot more about you than that, Ed.' The

87

woman smiled again. 'In fact, there's something inside you both that was named after me.' She glanced at me. 'I'm Geri Paterson.'

'Sorry, but I don't think I have anything called Geri Paterson inside me,' I murmured.

A flicker of amusement crossed the woman's face. Like she was acknowledging the fact that we both knew the drugs thing with Ketty was a fraud but we weren't going to let on to Ed.

I decided I didn't like her.

'It's a pleasure to meet you.' Geri Paterson smiled.

Ed shook his head, clearly completely baffled. 'I don't understand,' he said. 'What d'you *want*? What have you done with Ketty?'

'First things first.' Geri smoothed down her sleek blonde bob. 'I think you'll both understand when you hear my code name.'

'Your what?' Ed frowned.

I just raised my eyebrows, determined not to let her see that I was almost as confused as Ed. 'So what's your code name, then?'

Geri's smile deepened.

'Medusa.'

13: The con

'Medusa?' I frowned. 'As in the Medusa gene?'

'Named after me, dear.' The faintest flicker of smugness crossed Geri's face. 'Not by its creator, William Fox, but by the people who paid for it.'

I stared at her. 'I thought Jack Linden raised the money.'

'Jack was the go-between.' Geri rolled her eyes. 'But the money came from us.'

'And who are you?' That was Ed. He still looked completely traumatised.

'Yeah,' I added. 'What's with the whole code name thing?'

'That doesn't matter.' Geri batted the question away with her elegantly manicured hand. 'We were hoping that Jack could bring you in without us having to force the issue but I understand, Edward, that you are in denial about the worth of your abilities.'

Ed stared at her, open-mouthed.

'What have you done with Ketty?' I said.

'Ketty is being held in the front office until you've both done what I'm about to ask of you. I wish it wasn't necessary to have planted those drugs on her, but I'm afraid *you*, Ed, made that the only option when you refused to co-operate with Nico and Jack.'

'What?' Ed said, his mouth still gaping.

"So, do you work for Jack Linden?' I clenched my fists.

'No.' Geri sniffed. 'Jack Linden works for me. His mission was simply to find you. I was the one who insisted he brought you and Edward here.'

'Jack Linden's here too?' Ed sounded close to tears.

'What do you want us to do?' I asked.

'Put simply, dear,' Geri said, 'we want a demonstration of your abilities in action. At this stage, all I'm looking for is proof that Medusa works – that the gene synthesis made a quantifiable difference to your development. Jack tells me he's seen you in action, Nico, and that you've experienced Edward's abilities, but . . .' she paused . . . 'I hope you understand I prefer the evidence of my own eyes.'

'But why *here*?' I gritted my teeth.

Geri looked surprised. 'That was for your benefit, Nico. Jack insisted you should be rewarded for your efforts and I felt that having you beat the house by gambling would incentivise you *and* be a satisfying outcome for us.' She laughed – a surprisingly light, tinkly laugh.

'You want us to *gamble*?' Ed said, aghast. 'At a card game?'

'Not exactly.' Geri turned from him to take us both in. Her

manner became more brisk. 'When we go into the casino room next door I want the two of you to accompany me to the roulette wheel. Once there, I will bet on various numbers. After a while, I will look at Edward and "think" the number I need the roulette ball to land on. Edward will hopefully "hear" my thought and then communicate the number he "hears" to Nico – demonstrating he can both receive and give information. We'll be watching to make sure Edward doesn't cheat by signalling the number another way. Having confirmed the number with me, Nico will then attempt to manipulate the ball to land in the right slot on the roulette wheel. You will both have to work fast and under pressure, but that's all part of the demonstration. We want to see how you perform under stress.'

'And what if we don't do what you say?' I said.

Geri tutted impatiently. 'Then poor Ketty will probably have to deal with a night in the cells, a caution from the police and the wrath of her parents.'

'That's not fair.' My heart was thumping with the injustice of it. 'None of this is Ketty's fault.'

Geri raised an eyebrow. 'Nico, I thought you were on board with all this? Jack said you were highly co-operative – that you were even looking for a way to make money from your abilities.'

Beside me, Ed gasped. I could feel his accusing gaze. But Ed was the least of my worries right now.

'I don't want anything if Ketty has to suffer for it,' I said. *God*, how could Jack have got this all so wrong?

'Ketty won't suffer,' Geri snapped. 'Provided you do what you're told.' She turned to the door. 'Come on.'

Seething, I followed her. How *dare* she put Ketty in this situation? How dare Jack?

'Wait.' Ed's voice was shaky but determined, his face bright red. 'What if we go to the police and tell them what you've told us and how you've set Ketty up? We know your name, we could get you arrested.'

Geri appeared unfazed. 'You could try, Edward dear, but my operation is completely above the law.' She paused, her eyes narrowing. 'I suggest you don't test me. You may not enjoy the consequences.'

Her threat hung in the air as she pushed open the door to the casino. Ed and I followed her through. Jack was standing beside the roulette wheel. He winked at me as we walked over. I looked away, feeling mutinous.

What did Geri mean . . . how could an operation be above the law? That meant being able to control the police. What kind of organisation was able to do that?

Geri took her place at the roulette table. At its head was a wooden bowl – the roulette wheel – that contained a circle of numbers in random order, each in a coloured slot – alternately black or red. A silver-shirted man stood beside the wheel, presumably ready to spin it. Beyond the wheel, a green baize-covered table stretched away – its surface covered in numbered squares corresponding to the ones inside the wheel.

Jack took Ed's arm and led him round to the other side of the table. Ed looked numb with fear.

'Place your bets,' the silver-shirted man called.

Geri pushed a pile of round, plastic betting chips onto the number two on the table. A couple of other people, also at the table, placed their chips on other squares.

'No more bets,' Silver-shirt called. He spun the wheel. The numbers flashed by in a blur. Then he chucked a tiny ball into the wooden bowl. It rattled round the rim, then bounced in and out of a few of the numbered slots. Both wheel and ball moved fast at first but, as the wheel slowed to a halt, the ball settled into the number six slot and stayed there.

Geri sighed as Silver-shirt raked in her chips.

The game continued for several minutes. Geri bet and lost on numbers twenty, then six, then two again.

Ed and I received a number of disapproving glances from the other players. We were obviously underage. Still, Silver-shirt was completely ignoring us and nobody else actually *said* anything.

'Place your bets,' Silver-shirt called again.

This time Geri looked up at Ed.

I watched his face. His eyes were boring into hers – with that same intense look that I'd seen when he'd helped me during that history lesson. He was obviously reading her mind – finding out whatever number it was that she wanted the roulette ball to land on. The other two players around the wheel didn't seem to notice.

Ed looked away and Geri glanced back down at the green baize table. She ran her pink, polished fingernail along the cloth, then looked sideways at me.

This was it. Now Ed's job was to communicate the number Geri had chosen to me.

I focused on his face. He was staring grimly at the roulette wheel. Geri coughed.

I willed him to look up.

Geri coughed again.

At last Ed raised his dark blue eyes and met mine. I steadied myself, waiting for the rushing sensation I'd experienced before.

There. A split second later, Ed's voice was in my head, forcing me to listen.

The number she wants is seventeen. And by the way I hate you.

He tore his eyes away and I felt a rushing sense of release as my mind was freed from his hold.

I looked down at the table. Geri was tapping her nails against the pile of plastic chips in front of her. It suddenly struck me that I was only going to get one chance at this – and that I had to make it look smooth. My heart pounded in my chest.

For Ketty.

14: All the moves

I took a deep breath and let the outbreath flow through me, down to my feet.

'Final bets please.' Silver-shirt looked disinterestedly round the table. He clearly had no idea that Ed and I had just communicated telepathically.

I could feel Geri's eyes on me. The hairs on the back of my neck stood on end.

'What number d'you think I should bet on, Nico dear?' she said.

I swallowed. 'Seventeen,' I said.

Geri smiled. Without speaking, she placed a slim tower of plastic chips on the black square numbered seventeen.

Focus.

'No more bets,' Silver-shirt cried.

A bead of sweat trickled down my back as he spun the roulette wheel. An expectant hush descended on the table. All eyes focused on the wheel. Silver-shirt threw the little ball into the bowl. It rattled round the wooden rim. Once round. Twice.

I tried to work out where seventeen was on the wheel, but the numbers were spinning by too fast. My mind raced, following the wheel round. Where was seventeen? *There.* It whizzed past and I lost it. But the wheel was slowing now, the numbers easier to see. I found seventeen again. My mouth was dry as the ball clattered in and out of a slot on the other side of the wheel.

It jumped to another, and another. Little bumps now. I concentrated on lifting it . . . flicked it over the next couple of slots. Then another two.

Seventeen was still several slots away.

I kept my breath steady. I mustn't overshoot the slot.

Flick. Bump. Into fifteen . . . into four . . . *Flick again.*

The ball landed in slot twenty-five. *Crap.* I breathed out, completely in the moment. The ball slowed. It was going to stop there unless I moved it again. Just one more tiny flick.

Yes. The ball rattled next door into slot seventeen.

A throb of exhilaration pulsed through me. I looked round, making sure no one was staring suspiciously at me, then glanced up at Ed. He caught my eye, just for a split second, his face registering pure relief.

Then he looked away.

One of the other players at the table groaned. Geri smiled at me and laughed her light, tinkly little laugh again. Silver-shirt took a pile of chips, added them to the slim tower already on square seventeen and pushed them towards Geri.

'Excellent,' she murmured to herself.

I made my way round the table to where Jack and Ed

were standing. Ed looked furious. Before I reached them, he turned and stomped out of the casino, closely followed by the man who'd taken Ketty earlier.

I grabbed Jack's arm. 'We did what she wanted. Make them let Ketty go.'

'Calm down, Nico.' Jack rolled his eyes, shaking my arm off. 'Well done, that was impressive.'

I shook my head. Didn't he realise the enormity of what he'd done?

'You shouldn't have threatened Ketty,' I said.

Jack looked at me, puzzled. 'Nico, man, Ketty's fine. I *told* you, I was pulling the strings all along. She's waiting in the front office now. Nobody's said a word to her yet. You can go in there and explain you've sorted out the misunderstanding over the drugs. Not only will you have money to spend on her, she'll think you're a *hero*.' He chuckled, clearly delighted with himself.

I frowned. Couldn't he see it wasn't that simple? 'But Ed will tell her what really happened.'

Jack shook his head. 'Edward's been warned to say nothing to anybody. Not Ketty, not his parents, not Fergus Fox.' Jack grinned. 'I've got him out of your way too . . . he wanted to see Ketty, but I've had him sent back to school in a taxi. You've got her to yourself.'

I thought this through. Maybe it wasn't too late to save the evening, after all. Jack was right. If Ketty didn't know what had really happened, I could still come across as a hero. Plus we could get some food, chill a bit and I could show her the juggling I'd promised. She'd laugh and be impressed and, after that, anything was possible.

'Okay, I guess that will work.' I hesitated. Now that my worry over Ketty had been ratcheted down a notch, it occurred to me that Jack owed me a couple of explanations. 'Why didn't you just talk to Ed like you said you were going to? And why didn't you tell me you were coming here with someone else?'

'Geri just turned up and took over,' Jack said. 'She's not someone you can refuse. And the only reason I didn't tell you about her before was that I didn't want to overwhelm you with too much information.' Jack sighed. 'I promise you, Nico, everything I said about helping you develop your abilities was true. All Geri Paterson and I want to do is to help you and the others. That's why it's so important to us to find all the people with the Medusa gene.'

I shook my head. I needed more information than that.

'What's this organisation you and Geri are part of? Who does she – who do you – work *for* exactly?'

Jack shook his head. 'I can't tell you that yet but it's an extremely powerful organisation. The point is, Nico, we have your best interests at heart.'

I thought about the fear in Ed's face earlier and my stomach cramped with anxiety. Even if everything turned out okay from this evening, I was beginning to see that Ed and I and the Medusa gene were just a tiny part of some mysterious – and far bigger – operation.

An operation that was dangerous, powerful and – for

reasons I didn't fully understand – extremely interested in the way the Medusa gene had affected us.

At that moment Geri appeared, an excited smile twisting across her thin lips. 'Excellent work, Nico,' she said, then turned to Jack. 'Has Edward left already?'

'Yeah, he refused to take any money.' Jack sighed. 'But, don't worry, I made sure he'll keep quiet about Viper.'

Geri nodded.

'Viper?' I said. 'Isn't that a snake?'

Jack and Geri glanced at each other. Geri nodded, as if giving Jack permission to speak.

'Each recipient of the Medusa gene was given a code name when he or she was implanted,' Jack explained. 'The unidentified recipient was called Viper.'

'*Each* recipient?' I said. 'Does that mean I have a code name too?'

Jack looked at Geri again, his eyebrows raised.

'Yes.' Geri smiled at me. 'Your code name is Cobra. Very fitting – the King Cobra is a powerful snake.' She handed me two fifty-pound notes.

I didn't get the whole 'snakes' thing but I had to admit I liked the idea of being seen as powerful. And I *had* moved that roulette ball perfectly. I pocketed the money. Maybe I could handle Geri and her organisation after all.

Anyway, all that mattered now was seeing Ketty.

'Come on,' Jack said. 'Let's get you out of here.' He led me out to the bar and across the room to a door I hadn't noticed before marked *Office*. 'Ketty's in there. I'm going to make myself scarce, but you've got plenty of money. Get a cab back to school later, okay?'

I nodded, all my thoughts focused on what I was going to say to Ketty. I knew having money wasn't going to cut it with her any more. I had to make her feel I'd saved her. I pushed open the door. She was sitting, hunched over, in a chair by the desk. As I walked in, she jumped up.

It was obvious from her tear-stained face that she'd been crying.

'Nico.' She flew across the room and hurled herself into my arms. 'They just put me in this room and left me here. I've been so worried. Are you okay?'

'Hey, I'm fine.' I hugged her back, struggling not to blush at being so close to her.

'What about Ed?'

'He's fine too . . . but, er, he wanted to go back to school. Look, I straightened it all out with that manager. I made them see those weren't your pills.' I thought fast, pushing away the guilt I felt at lying to her. 'Apparently someone in the bar dropped them in your bag so they wouldn't get caught themselves.'

'Oh, Nico, that's brilliant.' Ketty hugged me again. 'So can we go?'

'Sure.' I picked up her jacket from the chair she'd been sitting in and we went outside. 'I'm starving.'

Ketty beamed up at me. 'Me too.'

Ketty wanted one of those healthy kebabs, so we walked down to the kebab shop on Hanmore Park High Street. She ordered shish chicken and salad in a pitta. I asked for chips.

I could have spent ten times as much taking her to a fancy restaurant, but I didn't want to draw attention to having cash. If I'd learned anything from the past week or so, it was that flashing money around didn't impress Ketty at all.

In the end, I paid for our food without even breaking into my fifty-pound notes from the casino.

And it was great being with Ketty. She was more relaxed with me than she had been for days. Guilt prodded at the edges of my mind. I knew it wasn't right for me to claim the credit for sorting out the drugs situation – but it was hard when the result of Ketty's gratitude and relief was us chatting and laughing just like we used to.

As we left the kebab shop, munching on our takeaways, Ketty glanced sideways up at me.

'So tell me about this juggling you did to win the money for my marathon,' she said.

My throat tightened.

'Okay . . . it was a random street competition,' I said, carefully. I'd already planned out something that would be impossible to prove or disprove. 'They were just asking for passers-by to take part in, like, this talent show and whoever won got the takings for the day.'

Ketty wrinkled up her nose. 'And you really juggled seven balls?'

'Watch. I can do it with anything.' I picked seven fries from my bag and gave her the rest to hold. I placed the chips, slowly and theatrically, in my outstretched palm. Ketty giggled.

My heart raced. *This was it.*

I glanced round to make sure no one was watching, then breathed in and out slowly. When all my attention was in my breath, one by one I made the chips rise into the air and move round each other. My hands skimmed each chip as it fell, making it look like they were in control of the action. Though, in fact, my hands were really just shadowing the chips' movements.

'That's amazing. How are you *doing* it?' Ketty gasped.

As soon as she spoke, I could feel my focus on the chips slipping. Panicking, I tried to bring them gently down, into my hand, but they refused to obey me and flew off in different directions. One bounced off my own chip bag, still in Ketty's hands. As I glanced at it, the chips inside seemed to explode out of their wrapper. *No.* They burst like fireworks into the air and cascaded down, around us.

In seconds they were all on the pavement.

Ketty's mouth fell open.

I dropped to my knees, desperately trying to pick up the chips. I don't know what I was thinking. Maybe that if I got rid of the evidence, Ketty would somehow forget what she'd just seen.

'Nico.'

I ignored her, still scrabbling around on the pavement. It was hard and cold under my knees.

102

'Nico, what just happened?' Ketty's voice above my head managed to sound both scared and accusing.

I scraped up a chip that had fallen beside a drain grating and chucked it into the drain. What *had* just happened? Why did Ketty's presence make it so hard for me to control my telekinesis?

'Nico, will you please stand up.'

Reluctantly, I got to my feet.

'Nico, look at me.'

I looked at her.

Ketty's expression was one of complete confusion. 'Those chips just . . . how . . .?' she said. 'That wasn't part of the trick, was it?'

I opened my mouth to say that it was . . . to try and lie on my feet with some random nonsense about the angle of impact of the first chip leading to the spilling of the rest. But, as I gazed into Ketty's wide, bewildered eyes I knew that I couldn't tell her any more lies.

I'd tried to impress her with money and by showing off my telekinetic skills. Neither of these tactics had worked – which only left me with one option . . .

'Okay.' I took a deep breath. 'This is going to sound weird but I swear it's the truth.'

And I told her about the Medusa gene.

15: Argument

'And this same gene, or genetic mutation, was put into three other people too.' I finished my explanation. 'We've got snake code names. I'm Cobra.'

Ketty and I were still out on the street. It was a warm night but we'd been standing still for a long time. Ketty shivered. She had the same, serious expression on her face she'd had for the past twenty minutes. Her kebab sat on a nearby wall, cold and forgotten.

'Come on, babe, let's get inside somewhere.'

Ketty shook her head. 'I'm fine.'

She sounded a bit dazed, but then I guess it's not every day that you find out your best friend has telekinetic abilities.

So far I'd only explained how the basic skill worked, and a bit about the origins of the Medusa gene. I'd tried to show Ketty what I could do, but standing close to her, it was impossible for me to control my breathing and focus for more than a few seconds. Still, I'd done enough to convince her that I wasn't lying.

'So when else did you use these . . . powers?' Ketty stared at me shrewdly. 'There was no magic tricks street competition, was there?'

'No,' I admitted. I told her how Jack had contacted me and helped me develop my telekinesis. I didn't mention the football match and how we'd made money by betting on a result I'd engineered. 'Jack told us to meet here, tonight, too . . .' I stopped, not wanting to get drawn into an explanation of how Ed and I had used our abilities to gamble successfully at roulette.

'Us?' Ketty frowned. 'Who's *us*?'

Crap. Now I'd have to tell her about Ed. With a sigh I explained that Ed was one of the three others with the Medusa gene. 'He's come to our school because Fergus knows about the gene and thought he'd be able to hide it better here.'

'Mr Fox knows?' Ketty frowned. 'And he wants you to hide what you and Ed can do?'

'Yeah. Fergus seems to think the Medusa gene is an evil curse which should never be used. And so does Ed, so please don't tell either of them I told you about it.'

'I can't take all this in.' Ketty shivered again. Light, misty rain glistened in the light of the street lamp behind her.

'Come on,' I insisted. 'It's pissing down. Please can we get off the street?'

'I want to go back to school,' Ketty said.

'Sure,' I said. 'I've got money for a cab.'

Ketty said nothing. We set off up the hill towards the centre of the town. There was a dull weight in my chest as I

105

walked beside her. I wanted to say something to make everything okay, but had no idea what . . . maybe it was best just to let everything sink in for a bit.

The rain grew heavier as we trudged. And then Ketty stopped.

'What did you mean, earlier, about Jack telling you to go to that pub tonight? I thought tonight was just about showing me you could juggle.'

'Not exactly.' I explained how Jack had told me to bring Ed to the bar.

'So you tricked Ed into coming?'

'Er . . .'

'So the whole point of the evening wasn't for you to con me into thinking you could juggle?'

I winced. 'No . . . yes, well, sort of. Jack meeting Ed was just this extra thing. But then Geri showed up and we had to do what she asked. They said you'd be done for possessing drugs if we didn't.'

'Wait, so you *knew* that the drugs thing was a set-up . . . right from the start?'

I stared at her. 'No,' I said. 'At least, Jack warned me to go along with whatever was about to happen, so I thought it *might* be part of his plan, but I wasn't a hundred per cent sure until . . .'

'So you *did* know.' Ketty shook her head. 'I don't believe it, Nico. You're supposed to be my best friend and yet you let me think I was going to be sent to jail for owning drugs which you *knew* had been planted in my bag.'

106

'No . . . it wasn't like that, I . . .'

'*And* you've been lying to me for weeks.' Ketty's voice rose, furious now. 'All that crap about a talent competition . . . why didn't you just *tell* me about the Medusa gene then? Or when it started, in that assembly?'

'I . . . I . . .' My mind was in free fall. Panic-stricken I tried to remember how I'd felt . . . why I'd kept quiet. 'I *did* try to show you . . . with that twig back at school. Remember? But it didn't work and I thought you'd think I was a freak if I told you without being able to prove . . .'

'I thought we were *friends*,' Ketty was shouting now. 'But all you've done is lie to me and take me into a really bad situation where I was terrified and . . . and in the meantime, all *you're* doing is conning people out of money.'

She stomped off up the street, away from me.

Desperate, I ran after her. 'Ketty, wait! I'll get us a cab. Come back.'

'You think you're so special, but you're just making money by cheating people,' she shouted. 'You're pathetic.'

We were right at the top of the hill now, at the main crossroads of town. Loads of people were milling about. Several of them stopped what they were doing to stare at Ketty yelling.

'Please, Ketty.'

A bus going back to school pulled up at the bus stop a few metres down the road. Ketty broke into a sprint. 'Leave me alone,' she yelled.

Seconds later she'd jumped onto the bus and it had zoomed away.

I stood, looking after the bus. My hair was plastered to my head and my clothes stuck to my body. Rain pounded all around me. A drop trickled down the back of my neck. But I was barely aware of anything other than the cold, hard stone which had lodged in the pit of my belly.

Everything I'd done had been for Ketty.

And it had all been for nothing.

16: Scotland

I arrived back at school soaked through, having walked all the way instead of waiting for another bus or catching the cab I could easily have afforded. A furious Fergus met me at the front door.

'I've been trying to call you for half an hour,' he snapped. 'Ed's just explained you've been with Jack Linden . . . using your telekinesis. How could you, Nico . . .? After everything you promised.'

I hung my head and stood, dripping, on the school front step. I was so full of what Ketty had said to me, so numb with misery, that Fergus's anger didn't really touch me.

This clearly infuriated him further. 'Get upstairs and get dry,' he said through gritted teeth. 'Ed told me you've been in a bar which I suppose means I won't get any sense out of you until tomorrow morning, but we'll be talking first thing, young man.'

A pulse of irritation flickered through me at the thought of goody-goody Ed grassing on me. I was about to explain that, apart from a few sips of beer, I'd drunk nothing stronger than Coca-cola all evening, when it occurred to me I'd much rather defer Fergus's 'talk' until morning, if I possibly could.

Fergus insisted that I handed over my winnings. I gave him the two fifty-pound notes without protesting, then made my way, soggily, up to bed. The dorm was empty. It was still only nine-thirty on a Saturday night, after all. I took my clothes off and crawled under the covers. I closed my eyes, but could still see Ketty's angry face. I screwed my eyes tighter shut, feeling tears prick against the lids. A huge sob welled up from my guts but I forced it back, just as my mobile rang from my trouser pocket.

Was that her?

I leaned out of bed and fished out the phone. *Jack calling.* I hesitated before answering. Frankly, I didn't care if I ever spoke to Jack again. If it wasn't for him, I wouldn't have lost Ketty.

I answered on the sixth ring.

'Nico, my man.' Jack sounded cheerful and breezy. 'I won't keep you, as I'm sure you'd rather be with Ketty than—'

'I'm not with Ketty,' I interrupted, my anger rising again. 'Thanks to you, she hates me.'

'What?' Jack sucked in his breath.

I explained, briefly, what had happened after we left the bar. 'You were wrong about her seeing me as some sort of hero,' I went on, bitterly. 'And you were wrong about Ed keeping quiet, as well – he came straight back to school and told Fergus everything.'

'*What?*' Jack snarled. 'And what's that *idiot* going to do?'

'I don't know,' I stammered, shocked by the sudden fury in his voice. It might be okay for *me* to say Fergus was an idiot, but it didn't feel right when Jack did it. I took a deep breath. 'Anyway, I guess I'll find out tomorrow. Fergus says he wants to talk to me in the morning. And I don't think he's planning on raising my allowance.'

There was a long silence on the other end of the phone.

'Jesus Christ,' Jack said through gritted teeth. 'I had no idea either Edward or Ketty would react like they have.'

'Yeah, well . . .' I tailed off.

More silence.

'Jack?'

'I'm just thinking,' he said, sounding a little calmer than before, '. . . about you talking to Fergus.'

'What about it?' I sighed inwardly. No doubt Jack was going to suggest I concealed as much as possible about Geri Paterson and the demonstration she'd just forced me and Ed to give.

'I think you should tell Fergus everything,' Jack went on.

I sat up, surprised. 'Really?'

'Yes. I feel very guilty that, thanks to me, there's a wedge being driven between the two of you.'

I frowned. Jack didn't *sound* like he felt guilty.

'Well, we weren't exactly close before,' I said.

'Still, I was wrong to encourage you to keep secrets from

111

your stepdad.' Jack paused. 'There's only one thing I'd appreciate you *not* mentioning . . .'

'What's that?'

'The fact that we're looking for the fourth person with the Medusa gene.'

'You mean Viper?' I said, remembering the code name Geri had told Ed and me about earlier.

'Yes. Whatever you think of me you have to understand that my only objective is to help you and the others come to terms with your gift. That's what Geri wants too – she might be an overbearing, control freak with too much power at her disposal, but she's not a bad person. She wants to *help*. And if Fergus knows we're looking for Viper, he might take steps to make sure we never reach her.'

'Tell me who you and Geri work for,' I said.

'I can't right now, not over the phone,' Jack insisted. 'It's too complicated. But I promise I'll tell you soon.'

I thought about what Jack was asking. He had a point – whatever else he'd done, he had certainly helped me use my telekinesis. I had no reason to doubt that, whoever Jack was working for, all he wanted was to understand the effects of the Medusa gene experiment and to help me and the others develop our abilities. After all, if he'd wanted to hurt me he could have done so very easily already. And the same was true of Geri.

'So, will you keep your eyes open for any information?' Jack hesitated. 'I mean, I know you must feel that you've been really manipulated, especially with Geri weighing in like she did this evening . . .'

'Yeah,' I grunted.

'Well, all I can say is that I would have handled things differently if she hadn't been there.' Jack cleared his throat. 'As for Ketty, I'm not big on giving advice but, bloke to bloke, here's what I know about girls. Only a few are the real deal. If Ketty didn't really matter, then don't waste time on hurt pride. With your looks I can't imagine you'll have any problem landing someone else. But if she *is* special, then fight for her. Give her a chance to cool down, then find her. Explain how you feel. If it's meant to be, she'll listen.'

The call ended and I fell asleep soon after, in a slightly more hopeful state of mind.

The next morning I decided Jack was right. It was Sunday, a day Ketty always went for a long run. I'd give it until the afternoon, then try and talk to her again.

Fergus hauled me up to the flat first thing and laid into me, big time. He was furious that I was using my telekinetic abilities when I'd promised I wouldn't . . . that I'd lied to him . . . that I'd cheated in the casino last night . . . that I'd even been in a bar and casino in the first place . . . that I'd dragged Ed and Ketty into danger . . . and that I'd let Jack Linden into my life.

'Why didn't you come to me?' he kept saying. 'Why didn't you tell me Jack had contacted you?'

I'd done as Jack had suggested and confessed everything

to Fergus. Well, almost everything. I didn't tell him about winning the money on football and – as requested – I didn't tell him Jack and Geri knew there was a fourth teenager with the Medusa gene.

Fergus paled when I mentioned Geri's name.

'God, I hoped Ed had got that bit wrong,' he muttered. 'You must stay away from that woman, Nico. I mean, Jack Linden's bad enough. Untrustworthy sod. He was a really bad influence on William, encouraging him to push the boundaries of his research all the time – research which William should *never* have got involved with. But Geri Paterson's in a different league.'

'How do you know?' I asked, curious.

'I met her once, briefly. But my brother told me about her before he died, after he realised the Medusa gene was lethal. She provided all the funds for his research. Jack was just the go-between.'

'But where did *she* get the money from?' I frowned.

'I don't know. But William told me the funds were pretty much unlimited *and* that she had a huge hold over the police. Anyway, we're not here to talk about Geri Paterson.'

He changed the subject back to my shortcomings. I sat back in my chair and let the rest of his lecture wash over me. I was planning what I was going to say later to Ketty. Maybe if I finally told her how I felt about her, she'd understand that everything I'd done – all the lies I'd told and the money I'd managed to win – none of that was to make me look big. It had all been for her.

'And so . . .' Fergus sighed, 'I feel I have no choice but to ground you from today through to the end of the Easter holidays.'

I snapped back to attention. 'What?' The three-week holidays were due to begin at the end of the week. That meant almost a month of staying inside the school grounds. 'You can't.'

'It's the only way for me to make sure you understand how serious what you've done is . . . and to keep you safe. There must be no more communication with Jack Linden and Geri Paterson. And, obviously, no more telekinesis.'

'That's not fair,' I said.

Fergus leaned forwards. I noticed, for the first time, that there were deep lines etched across his forehead. 'I wish you understood just how much you mean to me, Nico.' His voice was strained.

I looked down at the scuffed and scratched wooden floor. Fergus *never* talked about feelings like this. What was going on?

'I loved your mother very much,' Fergus stammered on. 'And . . . and I love you.'

I focused on a patch of floor where the whorl of wood combined with a particularly deep scratch. My face burned. It wasn't that I didn't love Fergus back. I did. It was just that talking about it felt awkward and embarrassing.

'I realise we live in . . . in strange circumstances, what with this being a school and me being your head teacher. And I also know that I'm not the most demonstrative person in the world,' Fergus said stiffly. 'But I've tried to be a good stepfather. Up until a couple of years ago I think we had a good relationship. And then . . . I don't know what's happened since, Nico . . .' Fergus tailed off.

You don't want to let me grow up.

You try to control my life.

You don't listen.

I was staring so hard at my patch of floor it had started to look like a face with only one ear.

'Nico?'

''S all fine,' I mumbled.

Fergus sat back. 'But it's *not* all fine, is it? Come on, talk to me, Nico. I'm listening.'

I looked up at last. Maybe if I tried to explain to him . . . maybe he'd see I hadn't done anything deliberately to hurt him. I just wanted . . . needed . . . to be treated with respect.

'I just . . . I just wish you would stop treating me like a baby.'

'How do I . . .?'

'Well, take the Medusa gene . . . you *knew* that it was inside me . . . that the virus William Fox used to implant it actually killed Mum. And yet you let me think she died of some random cancer.'

'But she did,' Fergus said. 'A cancer that my brother created. I know William didn't *mean* to create it, but he took risks, egged on by Jack and paid for by Geri.'

'But you didn't even tell me he existed,' I said.

'Don't you understand, Nico?' Fergus sighed. 'My

116

brother and I were reconciled before his death, but we hadn't been close for months . . . years, even. Not since he got obsessed with the Medusa gene. And after he'd come to me and told me what he'd done – and the effect it was going to have on your mum – I got rid of all reminders of him . . . because every time I saw his face, I saw her death too. I decided you were better off not knowing anything about him or his work. And, I'm sorry, but I still think you're better off not knowing—'

'That's what I'm talking about. Right there. *You* deciding what's best for me.'

'Of course that's what I do.' Fergus's voice rose. 'That's my job as your stepfather.'

I sighed. What was the point of trying to talk to him? He was never going to understand.

We sat in silence for a few more moments, then Fergus muttered something about cooking me some breakfast and I muttered something back about getting my breakfast as usual at the canteen and I stumbled out of the flat.

As planned, I waited until the afternoon, then went to look for Ketty. She was nowhere to be found. Lola thought she was still out running, though Lauren said she'd seen her strolling in the grounds with Ed. I checked several times later and they were both still missing.

I could only assume they were outside somewhere, discussing what a horrible person I was.

I felt really ill that evening. Flu, probably brought on by getting soaked the night before – or so Fergus insisted. He

117

found me in the common room, still hoping to see Ketty that night, and hauled me up to the flat. I spent the next three days in bed, feeling extremely sorry for myself. I called Ketty over and over on my mobile and left at least three apologetic messages, but she didn't answer and when I crawled downstairs, which I did at several break times, I was unable to find her before some teacher intercepted me and, grumbling that I was spreading my germs, sent me back upstairs to bed.

Lola, Lauren and Tom came to visit briefly on my second evening. None of them mentioned Ketty – though Tom did tease me about Dylan again.

'Still no picture of that mystery girlfriend, Nico?'

'Yeah, yeah,' I said, barely listening. 'I'll sort it next time I see her.'

I felt a lot better when I woke up on Thursday. That evening I wandered down to the common room, then along to the girls' dorm, looking for Ketty. One of her room-mates said she was out running. I rolled my eyes. Didn't the girl ever stop?

Ketty was clearly avoiding me. Which meant that the only place I was going to be able to see her was in class. I decided that I had to go back to lessons tomorrow, Friday. It would be the last day of term and I was worried that if I didn't see Ketty then, I might miss her altogether. She hadn't said anything about visiting her parents in Singapore for Easter, but there was every chance that she would. Fergus agreed I was well enough. He also told me he was going away from early tomorrow for a couple of days . . . that Mr Rogerson and Ms Sanders, Fergus's PA, would keep an eye on me . . . blah, blah . . . I didn't really pay much attention.

All I could think about was trying to make up with Ketty.

I woke early the next morning and – unheard of for me – was the first person to arrive for our first class of the day – maths, with Mr Rogerson.

I kept an eye open for Ketty as everyone else arrived, but she didn't turn up. At one minute to nine, I scurried over to Lola and Lauren and asked why she wasn't there.

'She's gone off to that marathon in Scotland,' Lauren explained.

My mouth fell open, I'd forgotten all about the marathon.

'Yeah, Mr Fox got permission off her parents to take her. He's, like, signed up as her mentor and she's staying with him in his house in Edinburgh.'

What? My head spun. I knew about that house, though I'd never been there. It was Fergus's parents' old house – left to Fergus last year when his dad died. Why hadn't Fergus told me he was going there? And why hadn't he explained he was taking Ketty?

'Ketty's staying with *Fergus*?' I stared at Lola, shocked.

'Yeah.' Lola made a face. 'Rather her than me. After that, she's off to her parents' for the rest of the holidays.'

Ketty was going to Singapore for the next three weeks? No *way.* I let out a groan.

'Sorry, Nico, I forgot he's your stepdad.' Lola smiled

119

apologetically, misunderstanding the look of horror on my face.

'I wish he wasn't,' I muttered, my stomach turning somersaults as I anticipated the next few weeks without Ketty . . . without any chance to get her to change her mind about me.

'*I'm* around this weekend, though.' Lauren looked up at me from under her eyelashes.

'Yeah, me too,' Lola giggled.

'Right, er, thanks.' I made my way back to my desk.

Ketty was gone. And there was no way I could reach her. Fergus had not only grounded me, he'd taken that hundred pounds from the casino off me too.

As Mr Rogerson strolled into the room, I sank down in my chair, defeated.

By the end of the morning I'd decided to try and call Ketty in the house in Edinburgh. Fergus said he'd left the details with Ms Sanders. I wandered over to his office during the lunch break. Ketty might not be answering her mobile when she could see it was me ringing, but if I called her on Fergus's landline she'd *have* to come to the phone.

The office door was unlocked, but Ms Sanders had gone for lunch. I could see the Edinburgh phone number and address written on a notepad on her desk. As I copied them down, I glanced through to the inner office. Fergus's own desk was in plain view, his PC a slim, silver oblong beyond the big leather chair he sat in.

I wandered in. I was still supposed to be keeping my eyes

open for information on Viper, the fourth teenager with the Medusa gene. This was the perfect time to have a look on Fergus's office computer. Fergus himself was away and Ms Sanders wouldn't be back for at least thirty minutes.

Fergus's office was a total reflection of his personality – all neat and ordered. Every book was positioned in alphabetical order, by author, and the files on the bottom shelves were clearly dated and labelled. I switched on his PC.

As it buzzed into action, I wondered if Fergus still used my mum's name as a password. When the log in command appeared, I tapped it in: *LuciaRafael*.

A spread of folders appeared on the screen. Heart racing, I scanned them fast. Everything was labelled with predictable neatness. Files on everything school-related from pupils' academic records to their fee payments. Nothing remotely connected to the Medusa gene. I searched Fergus's documents folder. Nothing there, either. So where did he keep the information?

I logged into Fergus's main email account using Mum's name as a password again and did searches under 'Medusa' and 'Viper' and 'William Fox'. Still nothing. Apart from a few, vague legal exchanges about William's estate, most of which Fergus had apparently inherited, there was no information at all.

Frustrated, I sat back in the big leather chair. Ms Sanders would be back soon and I was no wiser about who Viper might be than I had been before. I stared at the open email account on the screen . . . Wait a minute. These emails only went back a couple of years. Fergus must have used an account before that – so where was it?

I checked his hard drive to see if he'd saved the emails there. *Yes.* My eyes lit on a folder called *Windows Live Hotmail.* I looked at the inbox and the sent items, searching under the terms I'd used before. *Nothing.* On the verge of giving up, I opened the deleted files and searched again.

Yes.

A short list of emails met my eyes. They had been deleted just two days ago.

I opened the top email. It was from William and dated a few months before I was born – presumably just before he died.

My throat felt dry as I read the message, and the email that had proceeded it. They'd been sent over a single evening:

William to Fergus:
Medusa info I told you about locked up – safe in our library at home. You know the number if you need it. Remember your promise. W.

Fergus to William:
No one will ever know.
Fergus

I stared at the emails, my heart thudding. This was it. This *had* to be it. The 'Medusa info' Fergus was talking about *had* to mean the identities of the babies with the Medusa gene. Which included the identity of Viper, the missing girl. And the 'promise' that William referred to must have been Fergus's promise to keep the data secret.

I read the messages again. William said in his email that the information was locked up in 'our library at home'. But I was certain that Fergus and William hadn't lived together since they were children.

And then it hit me: *that* was the 'home' William meant – his and Fergus's parents' house in Edinburgh . . . the very one that Fergus had gone to today. That was why William had written '*our library*' and '*you know the number*'. Of course Fergus, as his brother, would know the library and the phone number . . . they belonged to his childhood home too.

And *that* was why this email account had only recently been deleted. Knowing that Jack and Geri had come after me and Ed, Fergus must have decided to remove all reference to Medusa in his records, in case they came looking for more information.

It all fitted. Now I understood why Fergus had gone away . . . he wanted a chance to get hold of the locked up 'Medusa info'. Maybe even destroy it. Mentoring Ketty through her marathon was the perfect cover.

I turned eagerly to the next email in the inbox. But at that point Ms Sanders bustled into the outer office.

Damn.

I ducked down behind the desk, but it was too late, she'd seen me.

'Nico, is that you?' Her flat Yorkshire accent sounded in the doorway.

'Hiya.' As I sat up in Fergus's leather chair, I switched off the hard drive under his desk.

'What are you doing in here?' Ms Sanders asked suspiciously.

I thought fast, turning off the monitor as I stood up. 'Fergus said he'd left some money for me in here.'

Ms Sanders raised an eyebrow. 'Nice try.'

I shrugged. 'Maybe it's in the flat.'

'More than likely, love.' Ms Sanders went back to her own desk and picked up the piece of paper containing the Edinburgh phone number and address. 'You can call him and ask him, if you like.'

I shoved my hands in my pockets, feeling for the crisp edge of the notepaper on which I'd written those details earlier. 'No worries, thanks.'

'All right, love. Well, look after yourself.'

I threw her another smile as I sauntered out of the room. As soon as I was out of sight, I hared down the corridor. The bell was about to go for the end of lunch break and I needed to get somewhere quiet to call Jack.

My long shot at getting money off Ms Sanders had failed, but once Jack knew that the information on Viper was locked up in Edinburgh, I was sure he'd pay for both of us to get up there.

We'd have to move fast, though. Ketty's marathon was tomorrow, Saturday. I had no idea how soon after that she'd be flying off to see her parents. I needed to get to Edinburgh as soon as possible.

I couldn't believe my luck. If I played my cards right, I'd get to see Ketty, face to face, after all. And if I could see her I'd surely be able to explain everything I needed to . . . and ask her out.

I dashed outside and round the back of school, into the Tranquillity Gardens. In the distance I could hear the bell for afternoon lessons ringing. I dug my phone out of my pocket and called Jack.

His mobile was switched off. *Damn*. Without hesitating, I scrolled to his home number and tried that. It rang twice. I fidgeted as I waited for Jack's easy 'Hi'.

But it wasn't Jack who answered.

17: The break-in

I recognised Dylan's drawled 'hey' straight away.

'Is Jack there?' I asked.

'Nah.' I could hear she was chewing gum. 'He's not around. D'you want his cellphone number?'

'No, I've got it.' I hesitated. 'So, how come he's not there but you're in his house?'

'I just came by after going to the store,' Dylan said, breezily. 'Jack gave me keys – he said he'd be out most of the day . . . maybe overnight.'

'Oh.' I'd been so fixated on speaking to Jack, I didn't know what to say. 'I thought you were only here for a fortnight.'

'Yeah, well, I'm staying longer now,' Dylan said dismissively. 'So, why were you calling?'

'Er . . .' I didn't want to tell her, but it wasn't like I had time to mess around. I explained I was sure Fergus had the information about Viper, the fourth person with the Medusa gene in his house in Edinburgh.

'Wow. Okay, I'll tell Jack when he's back,' Dylan said.

'No, that's no good. I need to get up there straight away.'

'Why?'

I hesitated. The last thing I wanted was to explain about Ketty. 'I'm, er . . . I'm worried Fergus might have gone there to destroy the information.'

'Really?' Dylan sounded excited. 'Okay, then you and I should go there now. How soon can you get to the station?'

'What? You want to come? Right now?'

'D'you have a problem with that?'

'No,' I said, floundering. 'But it's the middle of school and I'm grounded and I don't have any money.'

'Well, if you can get away, I can supply the money.' Dylan's American accent got stronger as she spoke more intently. 'I'll sort the tickets and meet you at whichever station it is. I'll text you the time and place.'

'Er . . .' There wasn't time to think about it. Anyway, I could always ditch Dylan once we'd found the information on Viper. 'You realise we're going to have to sneak into Fergus's house . . . I mean, I'm supposed to be grounded, so he's not exactly going to welcome us in and—'

'Yeah.' I could hear the grin in Dylan's voice. 'I figured that. No sweat, it'll be fun. I've always wanted to go there.'

'Why?'

There was a pause.

'Didn't Jack explain?' Dylan said. 'It's the reason he found me so easily. I'm William Fox's daughter. That house is where he grew up . . . I've never been there.'

'William Fox was your *dad*?'

'Well that's usually what being someone's daughter means,' Dylan said, drily.

I stood, mouth open, on the other end of the line, taking in this information. A succession of realisations hit me. If Dylan was William's daughter, that meant her own father was responsible for her mother's death. It also meant she and I were virtually cousins.

I realised neither of us had spoken for several seconds. Dylan appeared to be waiting for me to say something. I didn't feel I could say either of the two things that had occurred to me. They both seemed way too personal.

'But that means you're Fergus's niece,' I said in the end.

'Yeah.' Dylan gave a light sigh. 'Though I haven't seen him since my mum died and I got sent to America.'

I shook my head. Yet another little detail Fergus had kept hidden from me.

'Didn't you ever stop and wonder why Jack was my godfather?' Dylan said, a slightly haughty tone in her voice, as if I was a bit thick not to have made the connection.

'Well, no, actually.' Truth was, I'd forgotten Dylan had ever told me Jack was her godfather.

'Jack worked with my dad, remember? He told you. He liaised between my dad and Geri Paterson, sorting out the finances for my dad's research.'

I nodded. 'Yeah, I remember.'

'I know what you're thinking,' Dylan snarled. 'And you can stop right now.'

'What?' I said, startled.

'You're thinking that I must be really screwed up because my dad killed my mom when he injected me with the Medusa gene.'

'No.' I frowned. Why would she think that? 'I mean, obviously that's got to be weird for you but then the whole thing's so bizarre that—'

'My dad didn't know what injecting me with the Medusa gene would do to my mom, okay?'

'Sure, but all our mums died. You're not the only one who—'

'So this is all about *you*, is it?' she snarled.

God she was annoying.

'No,' I snapped. 'By the way, did you sue them?'

'Who?'

'The teachers at whatever charm school you went to. Because if you didn't, I reckon you could make a fortune. You could certainly get your money back.'

There was a short silence. Then Dylan laughed – a quick, apologetic chuckle.

'Sorry,' she said, softly. 'I guess I have some issues about my mom and dad.'

Another short pause. I had no idea what to say.

'So . . .' Dylan cleared her throat. 'How soon can you meet me?'

*

I got away from school without much trouble. I was present for afternoon registration – then snuck out at the end of the first period. Hopefully it would take a few hours before anyone noticed I was missing.

I met Dylan at King's Cross about an hour later and we took a crowded, early evening train to Edinburgh. I thought Dylan might tell me more about her past, but once we'd found some seats on our train, she settled back and jammed in her earphones. She fell asleep after a couple of hours. I took a sneaky picture of her in her jeans and cropped top and texted it to Tom:

Heres y im gone 4 w/end. cover 4 me if u can.

At least that would throw everyone at school off the scent. I was expecting angry calls from Mr Rogerson – and Fergus – any minute. I waited for Tom's text back – which was a predictable mix of crudeness and envy – then switched my phone off.

Several more hours – and a long taxi ride later – and we were there.

It was almost midnight and freezing.

'It's not exactly a *house*, is it?' Dylan whispered, as we stood in the dark, peering in through the gates.

She was right. Mansion would have been a better description. Fergus's family home was enormous: a huge stone building covered in ivy and built over four floors – and

130

counting – with at least six windows across the front of each one.

I sighed, my breath misting into the cold, dank air. At least there was no sign of any lights on. Still, having seen the size of the house it was quite possible the whole of the back could be lit up with fairy lights and we wouldn't be able to tell, here at the front gate.

'Maybe they're out,' I said.

'Let's hope they're in and sleeping.' Dylan pointed to the burglar alarm box over the front door. 'If they're out, that alarm will be switched on. And the alarm on a house this size is bound to be connected to the local police station. Our one at home is.'

I glanced sideways at her, hoping for a bit more information. 'So where's home?' I asked. 'I mean you said America, but . . .?'

'Philadelphia.' Dylan took a black cap from her bag and set it on her head, shoving her red hair inside. She glanced sideways at me – her expression guarded. 'When my mom died I went to live with her sister . . . my aunt . . . okay?'

I nodded. It was funny, despite the aggressive way Dylan spoke, there was something really vulnerable about her too. I couldn't quite explain it to myself, but it had definitely been there in the soft apology she'd given me earlier, and in that wary look just now. Like a kid expecting to have its sweets taken away any second.

'When *my* mum died I got to live with Fergus Fox,' I said.

131

'I know,' Dylan whispered. 'Now, are we going to break into this place tonight or not?'

'I was waiting for you.'

We shoved our rucksacks under a bush by the gate. I took out the torch Dylan had brought with her and tucked it inside my jacket. The wrought iron gates were bolted and pad-locked, but it was easy enough to climb over them. We crept up the gravel drive, still scanning the house for signs of life.

Nothing. Two high walls prevented us from checking for lights round the back but, from here at least, the house looked completely deserted.

I switched on the torch and shone it along the front of the house. I was hoping to find an open window on one of the lower floors, but they were all shut.

'Can't you open one using telekinesis?' Dylan whispered.

I slowed my breathing, then focused on the nearest frame. It didn't move. I tried another, then another – but they wouldn't budge.

'Must be locked,' I whispered back.

The wind whistled past us. Dylan shivered. 'I guess we could break one, but it'll make a lot of noise.'

I gritted my teeth. 'There's got to be another way . . .'

'Look. Up there.'

I followed Dylan's gaze to the very top of the house. A little attic room poked up from the main part of the house – one of those pointy-roof jobs. It had an old-fashioned leaded-light window – which was open a fraction at the bottom.

'If we can get up there, we should be able to push the window open and get inside,' Dylan whispered.

'Good idea.' I tested the ivy on the wall in front of me. It was tough and thick, but I had no idea if it would be strong enough to take our weight all the way to the top. Still, I didn't have much choice. I'd have to take the risk.

'You don't have to come too,' I said. 'I can try and let you in once I'm inside.'

Dylan rolled her eyes. 'What, and miss all the fun? Anyway, you might need my help.' She grabbed a handful of ivy and hauled herself up.

I shoved the torch into my jeans pocket and clambered after her. The ivy sagged as I stepped on it, but was so tightly woven into itself, that it didn't break or tear under my weight. I reached for a handhold, grabbed more ivy above me, and drew myself up after Dylan. I soon overtook her and climbed on past, hand after hand, trying not to think about how high we'd have to go before we reached the top of the house.

The ivy grew patchier as we got higher. My heart pounded. Would it hold us both all the way up? Dylan was directly below me.

'Let's separate out a bit,' I said. 'Less weight on the ivy in one place . . .'

'Okay,' Dylan whispered.

The rustling noise beneath me told me she was shuffling sideways. I carried on climbing up. Clouds hid the moon and

I didn't want to let go long enough with my hands to reach for my torch, so I couldn't really see inside any of the rooms we were passing. I had a vague sense of a shadowy living room on the first floor and I could definitely make out the outline of a bed on the second. The combination of the darkness and the silence made the whole house seem more than a little creepy. I shivered.

As I reached the third floor, I looked down. Dylan was now some way beneath me and to the left. The ground below her was enveloped in darkness. Beyond were the iron gates we had climbed over and the road stretching away into the distance.

With a delicate patter, it started to rain.

I heard Dylan swear below me. I grinned. Then the rain got harder, which made the ivy more slippery, and the smile fell from my face. I sped up, pulling myself up past the top of the third-floor window on my right without even looking inside. I was almost there. I could see the little attic window ledge jutting out above my head.

One more step up. And another. *There.* I gripped hold of the sill and peered into the attic room. I could make out the shadowy outline of a wardrobe in the corner, and a narrow bed by the door. No one was inside.

Not wanting to let go of the sill and push the window by hand, I tried to shift it using telekinesis. It was stuck fast. No wonder someone had left it slightly open. It probably didn't move in *either* direction any more.

I redoubled my efforts. Carefully, I let go of the sill with one hand and used it to push the sash. Maybe the combination of telekinesis and brute force would work.

Dylan was almost with me. I could hear her hands reaching for ivy holds below my feet. The rain was still drizzling . . . trickling down the back of my neck.

Damn. This window was a bitch.

I kept pushing, trying to increase the telekinetic force I was using on the frame at the same time.

Breathe. Focus. Move.

With a resentful creak, the window rose. *There.* Enough space for us to crawl through. I turned my head so Dylan could hear me over the pounding rain. 'I'm going in. Come on up and I'll help you through.'

'Okay.'

I hooked my leg over the sill. As I took a breath, balancing myself ready to haul myself up, I wondered how close I was to Ketty. The thought made my stomach tighten into a knot.

I suddenly realised what an overwhelming task I'd set myself here – finding her *and* the Medusa information, and all without Fergus catching me.

Well, I was here now, I might as well get on with it. With a grunt I heaved myself up. The torch fell from my pocket.

No. I tensed, listening out for the crash.

Splat. The sound of plastic shattering on concrete rose above the rain.

Shit. That was really careless. Now we had no light.

I scrambled into the empty attic room – no alarm went

135

off. Well, that was a relief. I looked back out of the window. It had stopped raining now, but the ivy glistened, wet, in the moonlight. I could just make out the top of Dylan's head, she was right beneath me. She looked up.

'Was that our flashlight?' she said.

'Yup.'

'Awesome,' she said, sarcastically.

'Just get your arse in through this win—'

'Aaagh!!' Dylan gasped as the ivy ripped from the bricks.

No. I stared, helplessly, as one of her arms swung free. Her hand was still clutching the ivy she'd been hanging on with. She clawed at the wall again, but she was panicking too much to get a hold.

'Nico, help!' she hissed.

I reached out, but she was just too far below me. I could only touch the top of her head. 'Grab the ivy again.'

Dylan flung herself at the wall and reached for more greenery. She missed. She swung away from the wall, losing her balance and her footing.

For a second her whole weight appeared to be hanging off her right arm. And then the ivy she was clutching tore completely. She hung in mid-air for a moment. Then her body crumpled and fell, in slow motion, into the shadows.

My yell masked the thump of her fall.

'Dylan!' I didn't care who heard me now. I leaned right out of the window, straining to see her. But the moon had gone behind a cloud and the ground was shrouded in darkness. 'Dylan!'

136

Nothing.

My first instinct was to get out of the window and climb back down the ivy. But it was slippery from the earlier rain and the night was so dark now I could barely see.

Maybe I could see if I lit a match. I patted my pockets, but the matches I'd packed were still inside my rucksack, on the other side of the main gate.

Find the stairs, you idiot.

I raced across the attic room, my hands shaking, and pulled open the door. I pelted down the corridor, searching for stairs.

Down. Down. I had to get down and outside. Dylan had fallen, what, three floors? Three and a half? People could survive that.

Not without breaking something. Like their neck.

You don't know, you don't know. Just go down. Go and see.

A set of narrow iron stairs led down to a huge carpeted corridor. More stairs, much wider, twisting around each other. I flew down them to the second floor, barely noticing the fading brocade wallpaper and the oil paintings that hung like something from a stately home along the hallways.

I reached the second floor. The stairs stopped. Cursing my head off I ran along another corridor. Rooms led off on either side.

Stairs. There must be more stairs.

And then footsteps sounded, running towards me. I stopped, too shocked to move. I'd been panicking so much

I'd completely forgotten that Ketty and Fergus were almost certainly somewhere inside the house.

I just had time to hope it wasn't Fergus, when someone flew round the corner and skidded to a halt in front of me.

Ketty.

18: The meeting

Ketty's mouth fell open. Her hair was loose round her face and her eyes were round and shocked – though they still had a sleepy look about them.

She looked unbelievably pretty. I took in all this – and her blue and white check pyjamas – in a glance.

'Nico?' Her voice croaked. 'What are you doing here?'

My stomach was doing cartwheels. I wanted nothing more than to stand here and explain everything, but Dylan was lying . . . possibly dying . . . downstairs . . .

'Ketty, I . . . I really want to talk to you,' I said, speaking fast, 'but I have to go outside and—'

'Don't go.' Her voice was clear and insistent.

I stared at her. She smiled.

'I was asleep and I heard your voice calling out. I thought I was dreaming. I've been having these terrible dreams . . .' Ketty's voice tailed off into a whisper. 'Oh, Nico, I thought about what you did, entering me for the marathon up here, and I know that you told lies and did a whole bunch of

139

stupid things, but maybe there was a reason . . .' She looked up at me, questioningly.

'There was . . .' My stomach was knotting and unknotting now . . . I *so* wanted to stand here and talk to her. There was a softness in Ketty's eyes I'd never seen before . . . and a definite question . . . about us. But the image of Dylan's face – bloodied and bruised on the gravel drive – kept driving itself into my mind.

'How did you get in?' Ketty's forehead wrinkled with a frown. 'It's the middle of the night.'

'I climbed in through a window,' I explained. 'Listen, will you promise to wait here for me, while—'

'Thanks for coming to check if I was okay.' Dylan's ferocious drawl made us both jump.

She was standing, panting for breath at the end of the corridor. Her jeans had a mud stain on them and her black cap was gone, but she didn't appear injured in any way.

I stared at her in amazement. 'Are you all right?'

'Yes.' Dylan's voice was cool. She glanced at Ketty who stood, open-mouthed, beside me.

'I was on my way down to find you, I just . . .' I frowned. 'Are you *really* all right?'

'Yeah, my Medusa kicked in fast.'

Of course. Dylan could protect herself from harm she saw coming – including a fall from height onto a gravel drive, apparently.

Dylan jerked her thumb at Ketty. 'Who's this?' Her pale green eyes glinted.

140

Ketty stared at Dylan. 'Who are *you*?' she said.

Dylan raised her eyebrows. Her lips pursed in a haughty 'O' shape. 'I think you'll find I'm a friend of Nico's,' she said coldly.

The atmosphere tightened like a noose round my neck. I turned to Ketty. 'Dylan's Fergus's niece,' I said quickly. 'Sort of like my cousin. I came here with her.'

'Oh.' A look of disappointment flashed across Ketty's face. Then she pulled herself upright and tilted her chin up. 'So why have you both turned up in the middle of the night?'

'We might ask *you* the same question,' Dylan drawled.

'Excuse me . . .?' Ketty clenched her teeth.

Bloody hell.

'This is my friend . . . my *really good* friend, Ketty,' I said emphasising the words. 'She's staying here because she's running in a local marathon tomorrow.'

From the expression on Dylan's face I might as well have said Ketty was planning on visiting an alien spaceship. She shrugged.

'Whatever. Will she keep quiet?'

'Will you stop talking about me like I'm not here?' Ketty snapped. 'Nico, what's going on?'

Dylan's face flushed with impatience. 'We don't have time for this. Look, I don't mean to be rude, *Ketty* – or whatever you're called – but would you mind going back to bed? Nico and I have a job to do.'

Ketty turned to me. 'What does that mean?'

141

I glanced at Dylan. 'Give me a minute.'

She nodded. I took Ketty's arm and led her a little way down the corridor. I stopped and looked at her. All the softness in her eyes had gone. Her lips were pressed firmly together.

What on earth was I going to say to her? I thought back to what I'd decided when I'd realised flashing money about and showing off my telekinetic skills didn't impress her. The truth hadn't gone down particularly well when I'd told her about the Medusa gene, but it had to be the best option now.

'I came here for two reasons,' I said. 'One: I didn't want to leave things like I did with you. And two: I have to find something in this house and Dylan is helping me. That's the truth.'

Ketty looked over her shoulder. I followed her gaze to where Dylan was leaning against the wall, twisting her long red hair round her hand. The knots in my stomach tightened as I saw her through Ketty's eyes – the almond eyes, the perfectly oval face and those long, slim legs that seemed to go all the way up to her elbows.

Ketty crossed her arms. 'And what, *exactly*, is that girl helping you do?'

I stared at her . . . was she *jealous*?

Ketty narrowed her eyes. 'It's something to do with that Medusa gene, isn't it? She mentioned it earlier.'

'Yes, but . . .'

'Isn't that nice, you two having a lovely psychic gene in common?' she hissed. 'I'm going to get Fergus.'

'No.' I grabbed her arm. 'You don't understand.'

'Oh, I think I do.' Ketty tore her arm away from me. 'When Fergus told me about Jack Linden . . . how he couldn't be trusted . . . I didn't believe you'd be so stupid as to let him con you.' She glanced at Dylan, still waiting up the corridor. 'Now I see why you've gone along with everything he asked you to do.'

'No.' I followed Ketty's gaze towards Dylan, who was staring down at the carpet, her loose hair tumbling round her face. 'It's not like that—'

'I don't believe you,' Ketty whispered angrily. 'And I'm going to get Fergus. Wait here.'

She pelted away round the corner. I stared after her, my head spinning.

'Girlfriend trouble?' Dylan said, drily. 'Where's she going?'

'To get Fergus,' I said.

What the hell just happened?

'What?' Dylan's eyes widened. She pushed herself off the wall. 'Why didn't you stop her?' She ran to the corner.

I followed. But Ketty had already vanished down a maze of corridors.

'There's no point going after her,' I said. 'She knows the house and we don't.' My mind was working overtime, trying to make sense of Ketty's behaviour. She *had* to be jealous . . . that was the only explanation for the way she'd changed when Dylan had shown up.

'Nico.' Dylan was shaking my arm. 'Come on, we have to

143

move fast. She could be back here with Fergus in a few minutes. What did that email you found say exactly?'

I forced my mind back to the message. 'It was something like: "*locked up – safe in our library at home. You know the number if you need it.*"'

'So where's the library going to be?'

I shrugged. I didn't care about that now. I just wanted to sort things out with Ketty.

'I ran past a room that had a bunch of books in it on my way in,' Dylan said. 'Let's try that.'

I hesitated. Ketty could be anywhere in the house by now. *And* she was fetching Fergus. Dylan was right – we had to find the information on Viper before Fergus found us. I could go back for Ketty afterwards.

We sped off down the corridor.

'How did you get into the house?' I hissed as we ran.

'There was a dog door downstairs,' Dylan said. 'I saw it after I fell and came in through it.'

'A dog door? You mean like a pet flap?' I said. 'I haven't heard any dogs barking – did you see any on your way up?'

'No. I think it's old,' Dylan hissed. 'My dad had dogs when he was a kid – I've seen pictures.'

We reached another staircase and scuttled down to the ground floor. As we reached a tiled passageway, I decided what to do about Ketty. Once we had the Viper information, I was definitely going to find her again and talk to her.

If she was jealous of Dylan then that meant she liked me.

At least I hoped it did.

144

'The library's this way.' Dylan pointed to a door opposite that led into a room lined floor to ceiling with books. 'Come on.'

As we ran into the room, Fergus's roar sounded in the distance.

'NICO! WHERE ARE YOU?'

19: The kiss

We ran through the library. The curtains were drawn and moonlight flooded in, brightening the whole room. Apart from a single, shabby couch, all I could see were rows and rows of bookshelves.

'There's nothing—' Dylan began.

'Wait.' I pointed to a winding staircase in the darkest corner of the room. We raced over. I peered up the stairs. They disappeared into darkness. 'Up here.' I led Dylan up the narrow stairs. Our feet echoed softly on the iron steps.

'NICO!' At least Fergus's muffled shout sounded further away. Hopefully he was going in the wrong direction. It would take ages to search the whole house properly. After all, he had no idea I was looking for information on Viper.

As we climbed, my mind ran over how Ketty had looked when she'd first seen me. That soft look in her eyes . . . the way she'd smiled. The more I thought about it, the more certain I was.

She likes me back.

I grinned to myself, as we climbed on. It got darker for a minute, then lighter again. At last the stairs opened out into another room. This was also a library, but much older and dustier than the one downstairs. And the books were different too – children's encyclopaedias and large, colourful picture books were crammed into three wooden bookcases lined along the far wall. There was a window to the left and an old-fashioned fireplace in the corner with two small, faded armchairs in front.

I remembered William's email: . . . *our library at home* . . .

Our library meant his and Fergus's library – a children's library.

'We're in the right place,' I said.

'Good.' Dylan had crossed the room and was gazing up at the large photograph that hung above the fireplace, lit up by the moonlight from outside. It showed a middle-aged man and woman standing proudly in front of a lake. Beside them were two boys. One was a sullen teenager with a shock of red hair. He looked like he'd been forced into the picture. Beside him stood two large dogs and a younger boy – maybe eight or nine years old. He was holding a bicycle and grinning.

'Who are they?' I asked, looking round the room for any sign of a locked cupboard.

Dylan clasped her hands together. 'My grandparents and . . . and my dad when he was young.' She pointed to the red-haired teenager, her voice thick with repressed emotion.

'I've never seen a picture of him when he was my age before.'

'Who's the kid with the bike?' I said.

'That must be Fergus.' Dylan turned away. 'Come on, we're wasting time.'

I stared at the boy for a second. Had Fergus really ever been that young? Another yell shook me out of my thoughts. It was still muffled, but then we were up a long flight of stairs. Fergus was probably closer than he sounded.

I glanced round the room. A child's desk stood to the right of the bookcases. Two slim, marble candlesticks were the only items on top of the desk. There was no cupboard in the room. Nowhere to lock anything away at all.

'Maybe there's a closet behind those.' Dylan looked at the bookcases.

'Let's check behind the desk first.' I dragged it away from the wall.

'Look,' Dylan gasped.

A steel safe was set into the base of the wall behind the desk. A round knob surrounded by numbers was on the safe door.

The words from William Fox's email flashed into my head.

Locked up – safe in our library at home. You know the number if you need it.

He hadn't meant locked up *and* safe. He'd meant locked up *in* the safe. And the number he'd said Fergus would know must be the combination.

'This is it . . .' My heart skipped a beat.

'NICO!' Fergus was definitely closer now. 'COME HERE. NOW!'

Dylan and I exchanged glances.

'We haven't got time to mess around trying to open it,' Dylan said.

'I know.' I squatted down and examined the safe. It was small – about the size of a shoe locker at school – but set firmly into the plaster. It looked impregnable.

'We're going to have to break into it,' I said.

'How?' Dylan twisted her hair round her hand, frowning.

I looked round the room. There was absolutely nothing we could use to try and prise the safe door open. Not that I could see anything short of a customised crowbar and a lot of muscle working. And the room was all bookcases and dust.

Dust. Everything was so old. I reached over and scraped at the wall beside the safe. The plaster crumbled under my fingers. I tapped next to the small dent I'd made. The sound was light. Hollow.

'We don't break into the safe,' I said. 'We take the whole thing with us.'

'What?'

I grabbed one of the marble candlesticks off the desk, bent down and drove it into the wall beside the safe. More plaster crumbled away.

I thumped the candlestick harder against the hole. *Yes*. I was through. The plaster was only a centimetre or so thick.

'If we break through the wall all round the safe,' I explained quickly, 'we'll be able to pull it out and take it with us.'

Dylan nodded. She picked up the second candlestick and heaved it against the wall on the other side of the safe.

Thump. Thud.

We worked fast. In less than a minute the wall above and beside the safe was gone.

I reached down and tugged at the safe. It was incredibly heavy . . . impossible to lift, let alone carry.

'Jesus, what's this made of?' I said.

Dylan tried to help, but even with her holding the safe as well, we couldn't budge it a centimetre.

'I'll have to teleport it,' I said.

Dylan stood back while I focused on my breath. It was fast and jagged. *No good.* Panic rose inside me. I'd never lifted anything this heavy. Except . . . there was that bench in the school grounds. I'd moved that without even trying. Yes, this wasn't about how heavy the object was. It was about me . . . about how deeply I focused.

I breathed out again, slowly.

'NICO!' Fergus's shout was definitely closer now.

'Hurry,' Dylan hissed.

'Bugging me doesn't help,' I snapped, closing my eyes.

Focus. Breathe. Move.

I opened my eyes and positioned my hands on either side of the safe. I could sense Dylan hopping from foot to foot beside me but – unlike when Ketty was nearby – it wasn't so difficult to shut out the distraction.

Move.

The safe floated up and towards me.

Yes.

I drew it closer. It was just out of the hole when I felt it resist. I frowned, mentally tugging at it harder. But it was stuck.

'What's the matter?'

'I don't think it's me,' I said.

Dylan darted round behind the safe. She knelt down and peered into the hole in the wall the safe had just come out of.

'Shit,' she said. 'It's attached to something with two wires.' She peered more closely. 'The wires go into some kind of panel.'

For a second I hesitated. 'Pull them out,' I said.

'But . . .'

'It's the only way.'

'Okay.' Dylan grasped a wire in each hand and yanked, hard.

I felt the safe move freely again – but, in the same instant, an alarm screeched into the air. Unbelievably loud.

'No!' Dylan leaped to her feet

I stood too, the safe still floating just above my hands, the two red wires trailing from it. 'Run!'

We raced back to the stairs. Down. Round and round, down the spiral staircase. My entire focus was on the safe in the air in front of me, but in the back of my mind I knew

Fergus must be able to hear that alarm. He would know where it came from. He would be running here, too.

We reached the ground floor. Footsteps running towards us. No way back through that dog flap door.

We raced in the other direction. *There.* A window leading out to the front.

'Through here.' I hurled the safe through the glass. With a crash it landed outside. Dylan grabbed at the jagged shards of glass left in the frame, yanking them out with her bare hands.

'Stop,' I cried, horrified.

'Medusa gene,' she hissed, pulling out another sharp pane. 'Remember? It's fine.'

I stared at her hands. They should have been covered in blood, but they didn't have a scratch on them.

'Wow, that's *amazing*.' I stared at her. 'You didn't even have to psych yourself up.'

'Will you hurry up?' Dylan pointed at the window.

I hesitated. What about Ketty? I *had* to see her again. And she wanted to see me too. That look in her eye when she'd first seen me . . .

'Nico!' Dylan said furiously, crawling through the window. 'Come *on*.'

It was okay. I'd go back for Ketty as soon as I'd helped Dylan get away. I hauled myself up and out through the window. With a thud I landed heavily on the cold, damp ground, beside Dylan. The safe was just in front of us. I reached out my hands and tried to focus on my breath again.

'Hurry up.' Dylan swore.

'I'm going as fast as I can,' I hissed back.

Shouts sounded inside the house.

'Oh, crap,' Dylan said.

'It's okay, I can do it.' I breathed out and focused again. The safe sailed upwards. 'Let's go.' Behind us lights were going on inside the house, spilling out onto the stone path.

We ran, hard. Seconds later we reached the steel gates. I teleported the safe up and over the top as Dylan climbed. I held it for a second, then hurled it down with my mind. It landed with a soft thud in some bushes.

Dylan leaped after it like a cat. I followed, up and over the gate in a few swift moves. I jumped down and pulled Dylan into the bush that hid the safe.

I peered over the top of the bush, just as the side door to the house opened. Light spilled out. Fergus appeared, his silhouette dark in the door frame.

Beside me, Dylan stiffened.

'Nico!' Fergus looked round. 'Dylan . . .? Ketty said you were here too. Please . . . we should talk.'

I could feel Dylan trying to peek through the bushes at him. I pushed her down.

Ketty rushed out beside Fergus. 'I thought he would wait.' Her voice broke as she spoke.

My heart leaped into my throat. Ketty looked round. The light from inside the house lit up her hair like a halo. The wind ruffled the top curls.

Fergus shook his head and muttered something I couldn't

153

hear. He went back inside and the door swung shut. Ketty wandered further away from the house, towards the gates. She was coming closer. This was my chance to speak to her again.

'You go on ahead,' I urged Dylan.

'No way,' she whispered. 'Fergus could be calling the police right now.'

'I don't think he'd—'

'You don't *know* what he'll do,' Dylan insisted. 'Come on. We need to run and I need your help with the safe.'

I bit my lip. 'You can manage.'

'I *can't*. You saw. It's too heavy.' Dylan swore. 'Nico, will you—'

'Sssh.'

The side door was opening again. A different silhouette. Male, but shorter and younger than Fergus.

I strained my eyes, trying to see who it was. The boy walked towards Ketty. As he moved away from the house and into the moonlight I recognised him. Ed.

What was *he* doing here?

Ketty was almost at the gates now. As Ed reached her, he put his arm round her. She broke down, sobbing, and he pulled her into a hug.

Jealousy coursed through my body.

I gritted my teeth as he whispered something in her ear.

Ketty looked up at him. 'I'm so glad you're here,' she sniffed.

What? My throat constricted.

'Yeah, well, me too,' Ed said gruffly. He put his hands on her cheeks, wiping away her tears. Then he lowered his face. I held my breath. *No.*

They kissed.

A light, soft, sweet kiss.

I stared at them, forgetting the safe at my feet, the wind in my face, even Dylan, crouching beside me.

Ed lifted his head and smiled. Together, he and Ketty walked back into the house.

I couldn't register what had just happened. Ketty and *Ed*?

'Nico.' Dylan tugged at my sleeve.

I barely heard her. I was still numb, unable to take it in.

'Nico, there's every reason to go, right now. And there's no reason to stay. Come *on*,' Dylan insisted.

I stared at her. Her green eyes glittered in the moonlight, all concern and confusion.

She was right. There was no longer any reason to stay.

I nodded. 'Let's go.' The numbness I felt curled itself round my heart. I switched my focus back to the safe.

Dylan crept out of the bushes and, keeping close to the trees that lined the road, she broke into a jog.

Without looking back at the house, the safe hovering just above my hands, I followed.

20: The disk

The safe – apparently made from a steel alloy containing both tungsten and lutetium – was finally open and Jack and Dylan were examining the contents at the kitchen table.

It was late Saturday afternoon and the light was fading. I stood by the window, watching a steady rainfall in the courtyard. The mews house was silent, apart from the occasional excited exclamation from Jack.

'Look at this bit,' he kept saying, and: 'This is fantastic. Far more than I expected.'

It had been a long and mostly silent journey home from Scotland. Dylan and I had grabbed a few, unsettled hours' sleep at Edinburgh station, then caught an early-morning train back to London. We'd kept a lookout for Fergus – or the police – the whole time, but no one stopped or even approached us.

'I don't get it,' Dylan had said. 'Why hasn't he come after us?'

I thought about it. 'Maybe he tried and Geri Paterson stopped him. Everyone says how powerful she is.'

'Everyone's right.' Dylan looked away. 'I met her months ago, when Jack found me. She flew out to Philadelphia to talk to me. I mean, Jack was great – he was my dad's friend and I wanted to get to know him – but Geri just has this air about her – like whatever she wants, she gets. I was desperate to get away from my aunt anyway, but Geri made it sound like coming here would be the most exciting thing that would ever happen to me . . .' She tailed off.

I frowned. 'How was visiting your relatives in London for two weeks and hanging out with Jack a few times going to be so exciting?' I said.

There was a long pause. 'I can't explain . . .' Dylan hesitated.

'Can't explain what?'

She shook her head. I stared at her, an uneasy feeling in the pit of my stomach. There was something Dylan wasn't telling me. Something to do with Jack and Geri and the arrangement she'd made with them.

Something to do with why she'd come to London.

'So where do these relatives you're staying with over here live?' I asked.

But Dylan closed her eyes and turned, pointedly, away from me.

We didn't speak much for the rest of the journey. Most of the time I laid my forehead against the cold train window and stared out at the changing landscape, while Dylan slept – or pretended to.

As we travelled on, my thoughts drifted away from Dylan and whatever she was hiding from me back to Ketty and Ed. As I remembered their kiss, the reality of it gripped me like a claw, piercing through the numbness I'd felt earlier.

The pain got worse and worse. Whatever I saw – fields, trees, houses – the only image on my brain was Ketty and Ed kissing. Even the sound the train made seemed to mock me.

Ketty and Ed, went the engine. *Ketty and Ed . . . Ketty and Ed.*

By the time we got to King's Cross I was in such a state I couldn't begin to lift the safe any more. Dylan had to get a porter with one of those flat trolleys to get it off the train. She threw me a few weird looks, but said nothing as the porter loaded us and the safe into a taxi.

When we reached the mews houses, I'd recovered enough to teleport the safe inside, though I was scared I'd lose my focus at any moment.

Jack didn't seem to notice the mess I was in. He was there when we arrived – Dylan had phoned ahead to tell him everything – and full of praise for us both. A week ago I'd have lapped this up, but right now all I cared about was Ketty.

What was she doing with a geek like Ed, anyway? I mean, Billy Martin had been bad enough. But what on earth did she see in Ed?

I pressed my fingers against the French windows that led

from the kitchen to the courtyard, tracing the outline of a raindrop that was trickling down the outside of the glass.

'Come and see this, Nico.' Jack's insistent voice brought me back to the kitchen.

I wandered over to the table. It was covered with the papers from inside the safe. There were masses of them . . . some typed, most handwritten. Loose pages had been shoved inside notebooks. I opened one at random. The handwriting was that old-fashioned sort with big loops hanging off every letter. The words were clear enough but the meaning was way beyond me. I scanned the page quickly, picking up only a few recognisable words: *maternal . . . blood pressure . . . strand . . .* in amongst all the bewildering jargon. The file kept referring to *low molecular weight proteins* and *antigen processing genes.* What on earth were they?

'Not that, this.' Jack pushed another notebook under my nose. It was typed. The open page was headed: *Cobra. 07/08. Third recipient of Gene DR61-alpha. Processed: 08/Dec. Live birth 10.18 a.m., 07/August.*

Cobra. That was the code name Geri had told me I'd been given. And *07 August* was my birth date. I read down the page. It was a list of dates – medical appointments by the look of it – with a record of blood pressure and temperature readings – plus a bunch of other medical data that I didn't understand.

I looked up at Jack. 'This is all about me being implanted with the Medusa gene, isn't it?'

He nodded, all excited. 'Yes, plus William's record of

159

his check-ups on your mother. Both William and Fergus Fox claimed William destroyed all this. It's an amazing find.'

'Great.' I tried to summon up some enthusiasm. 'So is the information on Viper here?'

Jack's face fell. 'I haven't found much about her identity yet, other than that she was female, which we already knew. At least I have a birth date for her now. That's more than I had to go on when I was tracking Ed.'

'What's his code name?' I asked, interested.

'Sidewinder,' said Jack. 'It's a kind of rattlesnake.'

I nodded. That figured. Ed *was* a snake, too. Stealing my girl from under my nose.

But even in the midst of my misery I knew that wasn't fair. Ed had no idea how I felt about Ketty. In fact . . . with a jolt I remembered how I'd told him she liked *him* the evening we all went to the casino bar. He would probably never have had the confidence to talk to her if I hadn't encouraged him. Which meant . . . *oh my God* . . .Ed and Ketty being together was *my* fault.

'Hey, Jack.' Dylan held up another dog-eared notebook. This one had an old-fashioned computer disk taped to the page. It was square and made of black plastic. Nothing like the CDs or mini-disks I was used to. Dylan peeled the disk off the notebook and turned it over.

The word *Medusa* was written in red felt pen along the back. 'D'you think this'll have anything on it about Viper?' Dylan asked, eagerly.

Jack leaped up. 'I'm going to try it in my old PC.' He glanced down at the papers spread over the table. 'Don't move a thing.' He rushed off.

I wandered back to the window. The rain was still beating down outside – the only other sound was the low hum of the fridge in the corner.

Dylan cleared her throat. 'So, Nico . . . that girl in Fergus's house . . . Ketty. Does she know how much you like her?'

I turned round. Dylan was leaning back in her chair, head tilted to one side. As I stared at her, she raised her eyebrows.

'Well?'

I hesitated. I was so miserable that part of me was actually tempted to tell her the whole sad story. And yet that sardonic glint I'd seen before in Dylan's eye made it impossible.

'I don't know what you're talking about,' I said evenly.

Dylan rolled her eyes. 'For God's sake. I saw the way you looked at her yesterday. And you've been acting real lame ever since we left that house.'

I shrugged and turned away again. A rustling of papers told me Dylan was, once again, looking at her dad's notebooks.

I don't know how long I stood at the window. It was certainly at least half an hour before Jack reappeared. His mood had changed from excited to edgy. He paced round the kitchen as he spoke.

'Okay, well the disk's got the information we need. Er . . .

161

unfortunately it looks like Viper will be harder to track down than I thought.'

'Why?' I asked.

'I don't have time to explain,' Jack said. 'I'm taking the information to Geri now. Will you guys be okay till I get back?'

Dylan stretched her arms and yawned, catlike. 'Sure.'

I looked up. 'I think I'm going to go back home . . . to school . . .'

Jack frowned. 'Okay, if that's what you want. But I'll be back in a couple of hours. We could go out for a meal, later, the three of us?'

I shook my head. Eating out with Jack in this edgy mood and Dylan casting me sly, knowing glances about Ketty was the last thing I wanted.

Anyway, I'd been away over twenty-four hours, with my phone switched off that entire time. I was in enough trouble as it was . . . not only had I run away when I was supposed to be grounded, I'd also stolen those notes from Fergus's safe.

At least if I got back before Fergus returned, maybe I could talk my way out of the worst.

'Er . . . sorry, but could you lend me a few quid for the tube?' I said. 'I used the last of my cash getting to the station to meet Dylan yesterday – and Fergus took away my Oyster card when he grounded me.'

'Fine, I'll leave some money for your journey back on the hall table,' Jack said distractedly. 'I'm going to dash, it's going to be impossible getting a taxi at this hour. Just pull the door shut when you leave.' He locked the Medusa papers away and rushed out.

Seconds later Dylan called from the hall. 'I've taken the cash on the table, but there'll be more on Jack's desk in his room.'

'What? *Wait* . . .'

But the front door slammed shut. Muttering to myself about Dylan muscling in on my cash, I gathered my stuff and went upstairs to Jack's room. I hadn't been in there before, but it was exactly as I'd expected – all pale wood furniture, and designer chairs. A couple of modern prints hung on the wall over the white-sheeted bed. No photos, though. In fact, no individual touches of any kind. It was more like a hotel room than someone's personal space.

I wandered over to the desk. It was the most cluttered area of the room, full of CDs and notebooks and scraps of paper – with a half-drunk mug of coffee in the corner. A pile of coins lay by the mug. I stared at it, wondering how much it would be okay for me to take. I reached out to pick up a couple of pound coins and some small change . . . and knocked the coffee mug over. It fell to the ground with a smash. Coffee splashed onto the wooden floor.

Crap. I'd broken his mug.

I bent over to pick up the pieces. As I leaned down, I noticed a little ledge under the desk. Something black was wedged inside. I peered closer, then pulled it out. It was the computer disk we'd just found – the one with *Medusa* written in red on the back.

My heart skipped a beat. How come Jack had left it behind?

I stared at the disk, the broken mug forgotten. If Jack turned up to his meeting with Geri without this he'd look really stupid. I grabbed a handful of coins off the pile and raced to the door. Jack had only been gone five minutes. He could easily still be on Long Acre, waiting for a cab. If I hurried, I should catch him.

21: In the park

I caught sight of Jack at the corner of the street. He'd obviously given up on finding a cab and was disappearing into Covent Garden tube station. I pelted down the road and dived in after him. I had to buy a ticket and by the time I reached the lift, there was no sign of him. He must have already gone down. I got in the next lift.

As I reached the platform, a westbound train pulled in. The doors slid open. I could see Jack right at the other end of the platform, stepping inside. I hesitated for a second then, as the doors beeped their about-to-close warning, I leaped into the nearest carriage.

I tried to walk through the train, but the doors between the carriages were locked. I got out at the next station – Leicester Square – but I couldn't see Jack on the platform. I nipped back on the train a few carriages along but I was still only halfway down when I saw Jack get off at the next station, Piccadilly Circus. He was right next to the way out and, again, had disappeared before I had time to call out his name.

I followed him up the stairs but could see no sign of him at the ticket barrier. There were a number of exits out of the station – I darted up the nearest one. Surely I'd see him at surface level. I looked round. People everywhere. *Yes.* There he was, across the road from me, walking in the opposite direction.

Fingering the disk in my pocket, I crossed the road and followed him. He was walking fast – too far ahead for me to catch him, or for him to hear my yells. He reached the bottom of the road and crossed into the park opposite. St James's Park.

I raced after him, worried I'd lose him in the trees. He hurried across the grass, finally stopping at a bridge over-looking a long stretch of water. Trees and bushes were planted on either bank and families of ducks swam up and down the stream.

'Jack!' I ran over.

He jumped when he saw me. 'Nico, what are you doing here?'

I held out the black disk. 'You forgot this.'

Jack frowned. 'Oh, right. Where did you find that?'

I explained what had happened, feeling more than a little embarrassed. Jack maintained his frown throughout my story, looking edgily round every now and then.

As I finished speaking he checked his watch. 'Okay, you're right, I'd have looked ridiculous without this. Er . . . You'd better get off.' He took the disk and slipped it into his jacket pocket.

Now it was my turn to frown. I hadn't expected Jack to gush heartfelt thanks all over me, but I was saving his bacon here, for God's sake. I'd thought at least he'd be grateful.

'Okay.' I slunk off. As I reached the path leading up to The Mall I turned round. Jack was watching me go. I walked on up the path, feeling uneasy. Was he making sure I left? And how odd had his behaviour been? It was almost as if I was bringing him something he *didn't* want, rather than something that he desperately needed.

In fact . . . I stopped. Wasn't it kind of weird that Jack should have forgotten the disk in the first place? I mean, that ledge under his desk looked more like a hiding place than somewhere a disk might fall, unnoticed. And, now I came to think about it, the whole meeting was about handing it over and yet he'd clearly got all the way to the handover site without noticing he didn't have it.

I turned on my heel and headed back towards the bridge where I'd left him. Jack was still there, but he was no longer alone. He was talking to a tall, thin man with cropped black hair. So where was Geri? I couldn't hear what the two men were saying out there by the water, but it didn't look like a discussion on the best way to feed ducks.

I crept along the row of trees lining the path. The thin man's voice was raised now, but I couldn't make out individual words. I edged closer, into the undergrowth that fronted the water. I climbed over the low fence that separated the path from the stream and crawled from bush to bush until I was close enough to listen in.

'You're sure this is the Medusa gene formula?' the thin man said.

'Yes.' Jack sounded tense. He held out his hand. There was something in his palm. 'It's all here. The whole thing.'

I crouched, stock-still, behind my bush. Jack had said the computer disk contained information about Viper. Not the gene formula. In fact, it had never occurred to me that there *was* a formula for the Medusa gene.

'And this also explains how the gene code for Medusa causes whatever virus it's implanted in to mutate and cause cancer in the mothers?'

'Yes, though there's no explanation as to *why* that happens,' Jack said. 'But all the important details are in there. Everything you need to know. And remember, Carson, the gene might kill the mothers, but it leaves the babies unharmed and fully skilled. Still, you know that from the recordings of Dylan and Nico that I sent you.' Jack held out his hand again.

Recordings? When had Jack recorded me using my telekinesis? My stomach twisted over as I remembered that first day in the garage at the mews house – and how Jack had filmed me moving that tyre around.

Carson took what Jack was holding out. It wasn't the disk we'd found in William Fox's notes. It was much smaller. Like a memory card for a phone or a camera.

He peered at the tiny card more closely. 'This can't be the original,' he said.

'It's not. I downloaded it from a disk I found in William Fox's files.'

So that's why Jack hadn't needed the disk. He'd copied the formula onto the memory card. And now he was giving the card to this man, Carson. But why? Did Carson work for Geri too? What about Viper? I thought that finding her was what Geri and Jack were interested in?

'I'll need the original, too.'

'Sure.' Jack nodded, but he didn't take the disk I'd brought him out of his pocket.

The man took out some kind of hand-held device and inserted the tiny memory card Jack had given him into the machine. As he pressed buttons and stared at the screen he spoke again, but more quietly. I could only catch the occasional word.

I waited, frozen to the spot, as Carson took the card out of his device. He nodded and said something else I couldn't hear.

'That's not what we agreed.' Jack's voice rose, bitter. He snatched the memory card back and shoved it into his wallet.

'Give that back,' Carson said.

'Not until you agree to wire me *all* the money. *Now.*'

'No,' Carson snapped. 'You'll get the rest when I've verified the formula.'

'I'm taking a huge risk bringing this to you.' Jack was almost shouting now. He tucked his wallet, containing the memory card, into his inside jacket pocket. 'I want my payment in full. Now.'

Payment? *Money?* My head spun as it sank in. Jack was *selling* the formula. But . . . but . . . how did this tie in with everything he'd said about wanting to find Viper?

And then I realised. It didn't. Jack had *never* really been interested in finding Viper – or in helping any of us develop our abilities. He'd obviously only worked with me on my telekinesis for one reason – to win my trust so that I'd help him find and steal Fergus's Medusa files.

He had used me. He had used Dylan and Ed too. He didn't care about us. All he cared about was finding the formula that – at a terrible cost – had given us our special abilities. And now, even though he knew that this formula would kill any pregnant mothers whose babies were implanted with it, he was trying to sell it.

He had lied and cheated and betrayed my trust.

Bastard.

22: The betrayal

I felt like I'd been chucked out of a plane and was freefalling through a storm.

A red haze coloured the park. Rage boiled inside me . . . anger twisting and roaring . . . I held out my hands, pointing at the trees and the benches and the flower beds around me, my only thought to tear and destroy.

Branches swayed violently . . . a bench flew several metres across the ground . . . flowers ripped themselves out of the earth . . . Out of the corner of my eye I could see people in the park gathering . . . staring . . . and Jack and the other man, Carson, looking round, eyes wide.

A dead branch, hanging from a tree just above my head, tore off. In a second I'd transported it across the bushes to the path where the two men stood. Without thinking about it, I flung the branch as hard as I could against Jack. He stumbled sideways to the ground. The computer disk that I'd brought him fell out of his pocket and onto the grass. I summoned it straight into the stream and heard its dull plop into the water. I knew my priority should be getting hold of the tiny memory card which Jack had placed in his wallet, but all I really wanted to do right now was get even with him. As Jack struggled to stand up, I raised the branch again and hurled it towards him.

I missed Jack. The branch whacked Carson round the stomach. He fell to the ground, then looked up. Gasping, he saw me . . . pointed at me. *Crap.* Jack turned. I ducked back behind my bushes, then peered out. Furious I tried to lift the branch again, but now I was consciously trying it wouldn't move. *Damn.*

Jack's face filled with alarm. He said something I could-n't hear to Carson, who was still doubled over on the ground, then ran towards me.

'Nico.'

I turned and fled, racing past the bushes, up over the low fence, along the path. I glanced at an overflowing litter bin ahead of me. I held out my hand and made a twisting motion to pull the rubbish out. Crisp packets, ice cream wrappers, plastic bags, bottles all flew up, into the air. I directed them behind me into what I hoped was Jack's path.

I heard him yell and gritted my teeth as I ran. I pounded on, swerving past a rollerblader coming up the path. Just ahead was a woman with a pram. As I noticed it, the front wheels of the pram rose a fraction into the air.

Baby. There's a baby in there!

As suddenly as it had started, the rage inside me vanished. I froze with terror. In a few more seconds my out-of-control

172

telekinesis would have tipped that pram over, spilling the baby onto the ground.

The pram settled back onto the ground. The woman pushing it stopped for a second, clearly bemused by what had just happened. She frowned, then started walking again.

I stopped running and forced myself to focus on the stream that drifted alongside me. I was terrified that if I looked at the pram it would start to rise up again. My heart drummed against my chest. I stood, waiting for the woman to pass. *Don't look. Don't look.*

Seconds later, Jack grabbed me. He swung me round to face him. I looked up. He was panting, his forehead shining with sweat.

'You little idiot,' he spat. 'What the hell were you thinking?'

'You were selling the Medusa gene formula.' The accusation ripped out of me. 'Even though it kills people.'

Jack tugged me onto the path. 'Come on,' he said. 'Carson's only winded, he'll be right behind us. And believe me, you don't want him to find us until he's calmed down.'

We ran up the path to The Mall. Buckingham Palace was on the left, but Jack swerved to the right, then took a series of twists and turns until he was satisfied Carson was not following us. He hailed a black cab, pushed me inside, then slumped against the back seat.

'What got into you, Nico?' he panted. 'Why did you do all that . . . the park, chucking the original computer disk into the water?'

I stared at him. I couldn't believe he couldn't see it.

'You used me.' I tried to keep my voice steady. 'You told me a bunch of lies about helping me develop my abilities but all along what you really wanted was for me to steal that formula off Fergus so you could sell it.'

'No.' Jack ran his hand through his hair. 'I *did* . . . I *do* want to help you make the most of the telekinesis. And when I met you I had no idea Fergus even *had* the formula. Both he and William told me that William destroyed it just before he died.'

'You're lying.' I hesitated. 'Anyway, even if it's true, you were still prepared to sell the secret of the Medusa gene when you know that it killed my mum. And you met her . . . you said you *liked* her . . . you . . .'

My voice cracked as a huge sob built up in my chest. I'd *trusted* Jack. I thought he cared about me.

'There are things you don't understand,' Jack said wearily.

'Really?' I turned away.

'Yes, and one thing you don't understand is just how dangerous Carson – that man I was meeting – is.'

I shook my head. 'I don't care. Let me out of this cab.'

'No.'

I looked out of the window. We were almost back at Jack's mews house. My panic levels suddenly ratcheted up. I wanted to get home. To see Fergus. Call Ketty.

The doors of the cab were locked. I felt for my phone.

'I'll take that,' Jack said.

'I—'

'You'll do what you're told.' Jack opened his jacket just enough to reveal a revolver in a small holster.

The atmosphere immediately tightened. I stared at the gun.

Jack glanced at the cab driver, presumably to check he was unable to see the revolver from where he was sitting, up front.

'This gun is real.' Jack's voice was low and tense. 'And I know how to use it.'

I stared at him. *Surely* this was a bluff. Jack might be a liar and a conman, but he wasn't capable of hurting anyone. Was he?

'You wouldn't . . .' I stammered.

'Don't try me.' Jack smiled – a mean, thin smile. I realised, with a jolt, that I wasn't sure whether he would use the gun or not. Feeling sick, I handed Jack my mobile.

'You don't understand what you've interfered with here, Nico. Carson is a dangerous man. Capable of anything. He makes Geri look like a pussycat.'

I stared at him. 'I thought you worked for Geri?'

'Not now.' Jack's smile broadened. 'Carson pays more.'

'I don't understand.'

'It's simple. Geri was paying me to round up the four teens affected by the Medusa gene – you, Dylan, Ed and Viper, whoever she is. But when you and Dylan discovered William's research hadn't been destroyed after all, I knew that I could make twice as much money from selling the Medusa gene formula itself.'

175

'Why not sell it to Geri? Surely she'd be interested.'

'She would, but I'd have a massive job getting any extra money out of her for something I just stumbled across. Anyway, when it comes down to it, the formula's only of limited value to Geri. She would never invest in something that kills innocent people. Carson, on the other hand . . . '

'So you're going behind her back?' I said. 'And not looking for Viper any more?'

Jack shrugged. 'It has to be done.'

'But why sell to Carson?' My mouth felt dry.

'I've known him for years – no details of his actual deals, of course, but the rumours about him are legendary. He buys and sells biological weapons. I knew he'd love Medusa. Imagine the power that psychic abilities would give an army.'

'But it doesn't work like that – we didn't get our powers until we were fourteen or fifteen years old . . .'

Jack laughed. 'Only because William and Geri refused to experiment on adult humans. They said it was too risky. But Carson won't care – he'll have a team of scientists trying to make the formula work on all ages. And if he can't, he'll still be able to breed kids like you. Some third world dictator'll be up for that, I'm sure. Fifteen years isn't as long as you think it is, if you're going to own an army of brainwashed child soldiers with psychic powers at the end of it.'

My breath caught in my throat. 'But don't you care about all those people getting hurt?'

Jack shrugged. 'I'm not doing any of the hurting, am I? If it wasn't me, Carson'd be paying someone else . . .'

'But you're hurting me,' I said. 'Why don't you just let me go?'

Jack shook his head. 'Not until my deal's gone through with Carson. I can't risk you telling anyone. Anyway, Carson saw you in the park. He knows you've seen his face *and* he's furious with me for being followed. If I'm going to convince him to go ahead with the deal he'll want to know I've got you under control. At least I still have the formula.' He patted his pocket where he'd put the memory card.

The cab braked. We were at the mews house.

I was still fixed on the gun. My heart pounded.

'Out.'

My legs shook as we got out of the cab. Jack paid the driver quickly, then dragged me inside the house. Dylan obviously wasn't back from her shopping trip yet. Jack walked me through to the kitchen and opened the utility room door.

'Inside.'

I stumbled into the tiny utility area. There was nothing in here except a washing machine and a freezer on either side of the door. Barely room even to sit down. Jack shoved me inside and slammed the door.

Before I could believe what was happening, the key had been double-clicked in the lock, then removed.

I was a prisoner.

23: Trapped

Dylan came in from her shopping trip about an hour later. As soon as I heard her footsteps tap across the hall floor I yelled her name.

The footsteps stopped. 'Nico, where are you?'

As I shouted back, Jack came thundering down the stairs. He was talking fast, his voice too low for me to make out what he was saying. I caught snatches of Dylan's reply.

'But why . . .? When did . . .?'

Then Jack must have dragged her upstairs, because the house fell silent. I sank back against the washing machine. There wasn't even enough room in the utility area to sit on the floor and stretch out my legs. I'd already checked the window. Like all the downstairs windows in the mews house, it had bars over the glass. No hope of me getting past them, with or without telekinesis.

How was I going to get out of here?

The day stretched on and the light started to fade. If Dylan didn't manage either to get me out or to get help, my

178

only option seemed to be to tackle Jack whenever he next appeared.

A chill snaked down my back as it occurred to me he might, simply, just leave me here to die of starvation. But, no, that didn't make sense. Hadn't Jack said he needed me alive? That he had to prove to Carson that I was under control in order to reassure him it was still safe to buy the formula? Jack was still planning to use me.

One way or another, his plan had always been to use me.

I was lost in thoughts of how I was going to hurt him when I got the chance, when there was a light tap on the door.

'Nico?'

'Dylan?' I pressed my hand against the door. 'Listen, I don't know what Jack's told you but he's selling the formula, the one for the Medusa gene that killed my mum . . . and yours. That was what was on that disk . . .'

'I know, Jack just told me, sssh,' Dylan hissed. 'Listen, Nico, you're in big trouble. That man you saw Jack with in the park. His name is Cars—'

'I know. Look, can't you find the key to this door and get me out of—'

'You *don't* know.' Dylan's voice was insistent. 'Carson is ruthless. He saw your telekinesis in action and now he wants you as *well* as the formula.'

My breath caught in my throat. 'He wants me? But that doesn't make sense.'

'Yes it *does*. Think about it. The formula alone is valuable, sure. But you're the proof that it works. The living proof.'

There was a short pause while this sank in. Once Carson had me, I reckoned, he'd never let me go.

'Listen,' Dylan hissed urgently. 'You've got some time to get out of here. Jack's no killer. I mean I wouldn't put it past him to shoot you in the leg to stop you running away, but he won't kill you in cold blood.'

'Then . . .?'

'Will you *listen*. Carson's insisting if they're going to rescue the deal, Jack has to hand *you* over as well as the formula. There's a heliport round the corner. He's getting a helicopter from there first thing tomorrow morning. And you're going with him.'

My mind reeled.

'I have to go,' Dylan whispered. 'If he hears me, he'll think I'm helping you.'

'You *have* to help me.' Panic clutched at my guts. 'Dylan you have to find some way—'

'I'll do what I can, but it's dangerous. If Jack thinks I'm helping you then he'll tell Carson about me too.' She hesitated. 'You shouldn't have let on that you were against him going behind Geri's back and selling the formula.'

'I *had* to,' I hissed. 'That formula *kills* people. Dylan, please . . .'

But all that came back was the sound of Dylan's footsteps, softly padding into the distance.

I slumped, defeated, to the floor. Dylan was too scared to defy Jack. Which meant escaping from here and getting help to stop Jack was down to me alone.

Fear and misery welled up inside me. How stupid was I, not to have listened to Fergus's warnings? He had told me Jack was untrustworthy.

But I'd refused to listen.

I sank to the floor, my head in my hands, trying to work out what to do.

Hours later, when it was pitch black outside, the key turned in the lock and Jack opened the door.

I scrambled to my feet, ready to fight.

Jack set a tray of food on top of the washing machine. I resisted the impulse to hurl it into his face. I needed to get closer to the front door before I caused any kind of distraction.

'I need to go to the bathroom,' I said.

'Find a bucket.' Jack scowled.

'Please.'

He hesitated, then conceded. 'Okay, but no telekinesis.'

'Fine.'

I walked through the kitchen, Jack right behind me. There was no sign of Dylan. The ground floor of the mews house just consisted of the kitchen, hallway and a small bathroom by the front door.

I glanced at the front door.

'It's double locked and bolted,' Jack said. 'Now go and pee.'

I nodded. With a jolt I noticed Dylan's phone, sitting on the hall table.

With all the locked doors and barred windows, a call for help was going to be my only chance of getting away.

Playing for time I turned to face Jack, leaving my back to the mobile.

'So what's Geri going to do when she finds out you've double-crossed her?' I asked.

'When I get my hands on all the money Carson promised me, hiding from Geri'll be a cinch. I'll be able to go anywhere in the world,' Jack boasted.

I held my hands behind my back at what I hoped was the same level as the tabletop. *Focus. Breathe.*

'And what if Carson doesn't pay up? He didn't sound like he would back in the park.'

'He will.' Jack shook his head. 'No more questions, Nico. Get in the bathroom, if you're going.'

Move.

A second later the phone zoomed into my hands. I clutched it tight and slid it into my pocket.

'Keep your hair on.' I walked into the bathroom and shut the door.

'Don't lock it,' Jack instructed. 'You've got two minutes.'

The bathroom was tiny – just a loo and a sink and a shower. I stood in the shower cubicle, hoping the additional wall would reduce the sound of my voice when I started talking.

I got out the phone. Who to call? Geri Paterson was the obvious choice – she'd want to know Jack was double-crossing her – but neither her name nor the codename 'Medusa' were listed on Dylan's phone. I could just dial

999, but everyone, from Fergus to Jack, had told me that Geri was 'above the law', and – as long as she still thought Jack was working for her – she'd still be protecting him. Anyway, I didn't have enough time to start explaining about the Medusa gene over the phone – even if anyone would believe me.

I could have called Fergus, but I didn't know his mobile off by heart. And by the time I'd got the number for school and tracked him down, Jack would be breaking the bathroom door down to get me out.

I stood for a second, riven with indecision. *Come on.* Dylan could come downstairs at any moment and see her phone was missing. *Hurry.*

And then it struck me. The obvious person to call.

Ketty. I'd memorised her phone number almost without trying, weeks ago.

Hands trembling, I dialled.

Ketty answered on the third ring. 'Hello?' Her voice sounded strained.

Something squeezed tight in my chest. *God*, it was good to hear her voice.

'It's me.' I stopped. All the emotion of the past day welled up again. For a second I was on the verge of tears.

'Nico?' Ketty's voice rose. 'Are you okay? I—'

'Sssh. You have to listen to me,' I hissed. 'I'm trapped. Jack Linden's holding me prisoner. I nicked this phone but I'll have to put it back before they see it's missing.'

'They?' Ketty said anxiously. 'I don't under—'

'It's too complicated to explain but you have to tell Fergus. He knows Jack . . . he'll be able to—'

'But what's happened? Where are you?'

Outside the door Jack shouted, 'Thirty seconds.'

'Who was . . . was that Jack Linden?' Ketty sounded frantic.

'Listen.' I whispered the mews address. 'Just get to Fergus. He'll know what to do.'

I rang off, hoping that what I'd just said was true. I switched off the phone and flushed the loo. As I opened the bathroom door, I saw Dylan coming down the stairs. She was frowning . . . preoccupied – like she'd lost something.

Shit. She must be looking for her phone.

Hands sweating, I slid it back onto the hall table before she reached the bottom step. To my relief, neither she nor Jack noticed what I was doing.

'Come on,' Jack said.

I let him lock me into the utility room again and sat, waiting.

Night fell and the house grew quiet. I slipped into a broken sleep, where I woke every few minutes, cramped and aching and cold.

And then a shout woke me. My head jerked up. Another shout. 'Oy.' Deep and male. Jack. I twisted round to look out the window. It was dark night outside. I had no idea what time it was . . . my heart thumped.

A light went on outside. More shouts. Seconds later I heard the kitchen door outside flung open. I pressed my eye

184

to the gap between my utility room door and its frame, trying to make out who was stampeding into the kitchen beyond. Then someone slammed on the light switch and the shadows became real people. Jack stood by the kitchen door, his face twisted with fury.

In front of him were Ketty and Ed.

24: Viper

I stared at Ketty's face. Well, the half of it I could see through the crack in the utility room door. Her eyes were storm clouds – sullen and resentful. It was unbelievably good to see her.

Actually, it was scary how good it felt.

But why was Ed here? In fact, why were either of them here? I'd asked Ketty to tell *Fergus* to get help, not to come herself.

Dylan flew into the room, red hair streaming out behind her. 'What's going on?'

'I heard a noise outside,' Jack growled. 'Found these two trying to force the front door lock.' He turned to Ed.

'What are you doing here, Ed?' Jack stared at Ketty. 'And who's this?'

Ed's arm moved protectively round Ketty's shoulders.

I watched, torn between annoyance at Ed and concern for both of them.

'I'm Ketty,' she said icily. 'From the pub the other day, remember?'

186

Jack frowned. 'How did you know where we were?'

'Nico must have called them on my phone,' Dylan said quickly. 'I left it on the hall table by accident.'

Crap. Jack glared in my direction.

'Where *is* Nico?' Ketty said.

'Here.' I banged, hard, on the utility room door.

Ketty jumped. 'You have to let him go,' she said, her voice rising.

Jack ignored this. 'Did Fergus Fox send you?'

'No.' Ed spoke for the first time. 'Mr Fox is in Scotland. He doesn't even know we're here. I mean, Ketty spoke to him but he told us to wait at school.'

I closed my eyes. Giving that much information away was a mistake.

'Does anyone else know you're here?' Jack asked.

Silence. I couldn't see Ed's face, but I could imagine it – all open and earnest. He muttered something in a low voice.

'So no one knows where you are?' Jack said, triumphant. 'Good, well as you're here you might as well join Nico.' He unlocked the utility room door and shoved Ketty and Ed inside. The room was so small we were all forced to stand right next to each other.

Ketty didn't meet my eyes. I didn't know what to say to her, so I turned on Ed.

'Why didn't you wait for Fergus?' I snapped.

'Because Ketty wanted to find you,' Ed explained, a hint of exasperation in his voice.

187

'What happened, Nico?' Ketty looked up at last. 'Why did that man – Jack Linden – lock you . . . us . . . in here?'

I explained about finding the disk in William's files and how Jack had copied the formula onto a memory card and tried to sell it to Carson. I didn't mention that Carson now wanted me *as well* as the formula. I couldn't see any point in Ketty worrying about that on top of everything else. She looked freaked out enough as it was.

'Dylan says Jack's taking me to meet Carson in a helicopter tomorrow morning,' I said. 'He'll probably let you go first – then release me when the deal's gone down.'

Ed leaned against the washing machine, his face deeply troubled. Could he tell I was lying? I tried to catch his eye, to warn him that if he could, he shouldn't say anything. I didn't want Ketty more upset than she was already. But, as usual, Ed was carefully avoiding making eye contact.

Ketty herself was looking round. Her eyes flickered past the barred window. She gasped.

'I know.' I grimaced. 'It's a prison.' I soaked in her face, pale in the street light that seeped into the room.

'It's not that,' she whispered. Her eyes filled with tears.

I stared at her, helplessly. 'What?'

Ed looked at her, his face tense. 'Did you see this before?'

Ketty looked away. She nodded. 'The window,' she whispered. 'I saw the window.'

'What are you talking about?' I said.

There was a long pause. Ed reached out and squeezed Ketty's hand.

'I keep having dreams . . .' Ketty's voice was barely above a whisper. 'I told you at Mr Fox's house. It's horrible. There's one in particular. I get snatches of this cliff top – really clear. And then . . . it's like I know something bad's about to happen. I don't know what exactly, it's like a warning . . .'

I frowned. 'They're just nightmares.'

'No,' Ketty said. 'The one of the cliff started that night you broke into Mr Fox's house with that girl. Afterwards we came back to school . . . I missed that marathon because Mr Fox insisted we left Scotland straight away, then—'

'Because I broke into the house?' My mouth fell open. There was a tight knot in my chest. I hadn't meant anything I did to stop Ketty from running. 'I'm so sorry, babe.'

She shrugged. 'Anyway, that night was when I started dreaming about the cliff. I'd had other visions before, but that was the first scary one. That's why I didn't go to Singapore to see my parents. I wanted to stay here with people who understood what I was going through.'

Ketty and Ed exchanged a knowing glance.

The knot tightened. If I'd had any doubt that they were a couple, these looks they kept giving each other made it plain.

'What exactly d'you mean by "visions"?' I asked.

Ketty took a deep breath. 'Remember that night we went to that pub, when those pills were found in my bag and you tried to do that juggling thing?'

I nodded.

'Well, when I got back to school, Mr Fox found me and he saw I was really upset. Ed had told him what happened . . .'

I glanced at Ed, but he was staring determinedly at the floor.

'Anyway,' Ketty went on. 'Mr Fox took me into his office and we talked and when I told him what you'd said about the Medusa gene, he explained that . . . that it's in me, as well. I'm the fourth person with the gene – the one Jack Linden's looking for.'

I stared at her. *Ketty* was *Viper*?

'Except that from what Nico's just told us, Jack's decided to double-cross Geri so he's not looking for you any more.' Ed frowned. 'Is there any way we can get word to Geri herself, let her know what's happened?'

'I don't see how. Jack's the only person who's got her number,' I said, only half paying attention. '*You're* Viper?' I stared at Ketty, my mind whirling. 'But . . . but you can't be.'

Ketty shrugged. 'Well I am. I can see into the future . . . it's called precognition, Mr Fox said.' She glanced at the barred window above our heads. 'I dreamed that exact same window a few nights ago.' She sighed. 'It's not the first time . . . I've dreamed things that came real later a couple of times, I just thought it was a weird coincidence before.'

'But you never said anything.' I couldn't believe it. How could Ketty have kept all this from me?

'Well you didn't tell me about your abilities, either.' Ketty flushed.

'But you have a mum,' I said, still completely bewildered. 'I've heard you talk about her. The Medusa gene would have killed her.'

Ketty's flush deepened. 'It did,' she said softly. 'My mum died just like yours and Ed's. But she was on her own so I went into care. Then, later, when I was seven or eight, I was adopted by my new mum and dad. They'd already adopted Lex a few years before . . .'

I shook my head. How come I didn't know any of this?

'So how far into the future can you see?' I said at last.

'I don't know.' Ketty frowned. 'It only happens when I'm asleep . . . like dreams, but different. I see bright lights and there's a smell too – like a sweet, heavy perfume. And then these little flashes of the future just flit in front of my eyes. The past few days I've seen this cliff top . . . there's a dead tree near the edge and the sea beyond, but I don't know where it is or when I'm going to go there. I just know something terrible is going to happen there.'

'Wow.' I realised my mouth was open and closed it.

'It makes sense, if you think about it,' Ed said earnestly. 'From what Mr Fox told me about William Fox's work, it's likely that the Medusa gene would develop in different ways in different people – like an extension of their basic personality.'

I remembered Jack saying something similar, but I didn't see how an ability to predict the future was in any way an extension of Ketty's personality.

191

Ketty looked equally confused. 'So, how come I developed precognition?'

'Maybe because you're quite goal-oriented,' Ed said eagerly. 'You know . . . focused on where you're going, like with your running.'

'You're kidding,' I said scornfully.

'No,' Ed insisted. 'I mean, look at me. I'm always thinking and analysing things. So it makes sense I can read minds.'

'I guess that does make sense,' Ketty said slowly.

'Yes,' Ed went on, 'while Nico—'

'. . . while I like to destroy my surroundings on a daily basis and therefore was born for the psychic gift of telekinesis.' I rolled my eyes. 'I think you're over-analysing this.'

Ed shrugged. 'What about that girl who was here earlier – the one who was with you in Mr Fox's house? What's her ability?' he said.

I could feel my face reddening – more because Ketty's eyes were fixed on me than for any other reason. I hoped it was too dark in here for either of them to notice.

'Dylan can protect her body from harm, if she knows it's coming,' I said.

'So . . . maybe she's quite a private person . . . possibly a bit shy, or defensive?' Ed mused. 'What d'you think, Nico?'

That didn't sound like Dylan at all, but I didn't want to say so. 'I don't actually know her that well,' I mumbled, unable to meet Ketty's eyes.

192

'*Really?*' There was a tartness to Ketty's voice. 'Well, d'you know if she'll help us get out of here?'

'No, she's too scared of Jack,' I said. 'We're on our own.'

Several hours passed. I sat up, cross-legged, on the washing machine, while Ed and Ketty slumped down onto the floor. I kept running through our options. There must be some way to use my telekinesis to escape this little room, but I just couldn't see a way past the lock on the door and the bars on the window. I didn't sleep, though the others seemed to drift in and out of an uneasy slumber. At one point, Ed gave a series of little snores. I glanced up. Ketty was watching him, a soft smile on her face.

She likes him.

Jealousy twisted like a knife in my guts.

'So . . . you took Ed with you to Fergus's house in Edinburgh?' I said, trying to keep my tone light.

Ketty looked up at me.

'My mum and dad agreed to Fergus mentoring me, but they wanted me to take a friend. None of the girls in our class wanted to go, so I asked Ed.'

Right.

I lowered my voice, not wanting to wake him. 'But he's more than a friend now?'

Ketty nodded. We both glanced over at Ed. He was breathing steadily, his head slumped to one side.

'You're way too cool for him, Ketts,' I said.

'No.' She sighed. 'Don't you get it, Nico? I'm *not* cool. I spend all my spare time going running instead of talking about music and boys . . . I mean, I don't like make-up and jewellery; I don't care about clothes and my hair's all frizzy. Look at me.'

'I am,' I said. 'I do. I think you look great.'

Silence. The tension between us grew.

Then Ketty's eyes flashed up at me. 'What about Dylan?'

There it was again – that fierce look of jealousy I'd seen before.

'There's nothing going on between me and her. *Nothing*. I promise.'

'Don't lie to me,' she hissed. 'Tom forwarded your text *and* that picture to everyone. Lola says he told her you'd been seeing her for *weeks*.'

I stared at her. I'd completely forgotten how I'd told Tom I'd been dating Dylan – or the text I'd sent him from the train to Edinburgh.

'That was just a cover, babe.' A slow grin spread across my face. If Ketty was this annoyed about me seeing Dylan, it could only be because she liked me herself – whatever was going on between her and Ed.

'I'm *so* fed up with you lying to me.' Ketty's voice rose as she spoke.

'I'm not ly—' I started.

A loud grunt issued from Ed. Ketty immediately turned to him. He opened his eyes and stared blearily round him.

'Must have fallen asleep,' he said croakily.

'Are you okay?' Ketty put her hand on his arm and smiled.

Ed sat up. 'Hey, I have an idea.' He stretched, wincing as he moved his neck. He peered through the crack in the utility room door. 'I thought so . . . there's a knife block in the corner,' he said. 'I don't want to ask, but this is really important. Nico, d'you think you could teleport one of the knives over here?'

'Yes.' Ketty clapped her hands together. 'Then we can pick the lock.'

I slithered down off the washing machine. I didn't much like Ed taking the lead like that – or Ketty being so excited about his suggestion after calling me a liar. Still, it *was* a good idea.

'I guess I could try,' I said.

I peered through the crack in the door. The street light from outside was casting long shadows across the kitchen, but the sky was starting to lighten outside. It must be nearly dawn.

The knife block was, as Ed had said, in the corner. It took me a moment to focus, my head full of Ketty's accusation. The worst thing was that it was true. Even though I wasn't lying about Dylan, I *had* lied to Ketty before.

I concentrated on the knife block, breathed in and out . . . and brought a knife zooming through the air to the floor in front of the door. There was just enough gap under the door in front of me to slide it through.

Yes. I snatched the knife up.

'Great idea, Ed,' Ketty said, giving him a hug.

What about me? I was the one who actually transported the knife over here . . .

Disgruntled, I tried to pick the lock with the tip of the knife. It didn't work, so I started carving at the wood around the lock. It took another thirty minutes and a lot of force before I'd managed to chip away enough wood to stop the lock catching in the door frame but, eventually, I did it.

The door creaked open. I wiped the sweat off my forehead and followed the others into the kitchen. The French doors out to the courtyard were covered with one of those concertina iron grilles. Ketty rattled the bars gently. 'Can you see a key for this anywhere?'

We looked round, but there was no sign of any keys.

'What about the front?' Ed asked.

'That'll definitely be locked,' I said. 'Jack has all the keys.'

Crap. I looked round. The kitchen – the whole ground floor, in fact – was as much of a prison as that tiny room had been.

'At least there's more space out here,' I said.

'Well that's a comfort,' Ed muttered under his breath.

Ketty suppressed a giggle.

Great. A new, confident, sarcastic Ed. That was all I needed.

'Ha-ha.' I looked at the French doors again. Those sliding metal bars over them were just so solid. There was no way we could break them down. Anyway, the noise would bring Jack running. Which was the last thing we wanted. Except . . .

I went over to the cooker and switched on the hob. The

electric ring glowed red – a spooky circle in the dim light of the kitchen.

I grabbed a tea towel from the hook by the sink and held the end against the electric ring.

'What the hell are you doing?' Ketty hissed.

'Playing with fire, babe,' I whispered back. 'It's our only way out of here.'

25: Fire

'What?' Ketty looked appalled.

'There won't really be a fire,' I said. 'I'm just going to make some smoke and set off the fire alarm so that Jack has to open the back door and let some air in.'

'But how . . .?'

'We hide while Jack and Dylan open the door,' I explained. 'While they're busy checking out what's causing the alarm to go off, we get out. If there's enough smoke they won't be able to *see* us escaping. And even if they do, they'll be too surprised to stop us.' I turned my attention to the tea towel. It was singed already – a dark burn mark spreading across the fabric.

'I don't think that's a good idea,' Ed whispered urgently. 'Fire spreads really fast and the smoke is more dangerous than—'

Too late. The tea towel burst into flames. Holding it at arm's length I looked up at the ceiling. The smoke alarm was just above a cluster of bottles and jars on the counter by the utility room door. I flicked it under the alarm.

'Stop,' Ketty squealed. She jumped back, knocking over one of the bottles. It smashed onto the floor in front of the utility room door, just as the flames from the tea towel licked at my hand.

'Ow.' I dropped the tea towel.

It fell onto the smashed bottle, lighting up its contents – some sort of cooking oil. The flames flared in the oil.

A proper fire. *Shit.* And I'd just set light to the only thing to put it out with. Smoke poured upwards. A moment later, the alarm erupted into a drawn-out screech.

'Come on!' I grabbed Ketty's arm. 'Jack'll be here any second.' Coughing, I dragged her into the hallway, with Ed right behind. Footsteps pounded across the landing above . . . and down the stairs.

I opened the bathroom door, shoved Ketty inside and pulled Ed in after us. I pushed the door to, just as Jack leaped the last few steps into the hallway. I could see him through the crack in the door. He raced past us towards the kitchen, his eyes fixed on the fire ahead. He swore, then disappeared from view.

'Dylan, get down here!' he shouted.

I could hear Jack fumbling with the kitchen door. Smoke was pouring into the hallway now.

'I *told* you a fire wouldn't work,' Ed hissed.

'Sssh.' I hissed back.

Coughing, Jack re-emerged from the kitchen, just as Dylan

199

flew down the stairs and into the hallway. Dylan's hair was messy round her face while Jack's shirt was buttoned up all wrongly – like he'd dragged it on in a hurry.

'What's . . .?'

'They've got out of that utility room – door's wide open – and set a bloody fire in the kitchen.' Jack was still coughing. The smoke swirling at his feet was dark and toxic-smelling.

'Where are they now then?' Dylan shouted.

Jack looked round. His eyes stopped on the bathroom. 'They must be in here . . .' He flung open the door and Ketty, Ed and I spilled out into the hallway.

'What the hell were you doing?' Jack snarled.

Ed doubled over, coughing.

'Making sure we left,' I said, coughing now too.

Jack swore. 'Come on.' He grabbed Ketty's arm, then unlocked the front door.

'Don't even *think* about running.' He tapped the inside of his shirt – the place where I knew he kept his gun.

We stumbled outside. My eyes were watering. Smoke was pouring out of the house. We stood on the street, coughing, gulping in the fresh air. Fire engine sirens sounded in the distance. Lights were on in the rest of the mews . . . Jack's neighbours raced out of their houses, talking in anxious voices. The smoke alarm still screeched.

I glanced over at Jack. He was gripping Ketty's arm tightly.

How were she and Ed and I going to escape?

'Let's go,' Jack said.

We set off up the little street, all bunched together. It was light outside, almost morning. Jack's neighbours were staring and pointing at the smoke that poured out of his house. A couple of them came over. Jack gave them smiling reassurances that we were all okay. I thought about running up to one of them and asking for help, but what good would it do? Jack was adult, charming and persuasive. Plus, he had that gun – and, whatever Dylan said about him not being prepared to go as far as killing us, I didn't want to hang around and take the risk.

No. We had to find some way of getting away from him on our own. I looked round. There had to be something here that would help our escape. A large stone urn in the front yard of the mews house on the end of the row caught my eye. If I could crash that into Jack, he'd have to let go of Ketty. Then I could grab her and run.

Ed walked beside me, still coughing. I poked him in the ribs to get his attention. His eyes turned on me straight away. With that, now familiar, rushing sensation, he was inside my head.

What? His thought-voice was curt.

I hesitated. I wasn't sure how to tell him my plan without him seeing *all* my thoughts.

If you don't want me to pry into everything you've been thinking, then just think the thought you want me to see.

I thought my plan in words in my head, like I was speaking, but making no sound.

Ed's eyes burned into me. *Okay, but make sure Ketty doesn't get hurt.* He broke the link, then looked back at me. As usual, when he wasn't trying to read my mind, he didn't make proper eye contact, but I could still feel the warning intensity of his gaze.

I resisted the temptation to roll my eyes. We had almost reached the stone urn and I had to focus. This had to be fast. There was no time to think. With an in-breath, I brought the urn a fraction above the ground. It hovered in the air, just a centimetre above the tarmac. Jack was right beside it now. He hadn't noticed. I breathed out, bringing the urn towards Jack. He caught sight of it out of the corner of his eye. Jumped back. Tripped. Stumbled into Ketty. She twisted and fell, heavily, on her ankle.

'Ow!' She screamed out in pain.

Shocked, I lost my focus. The urn thudded onto the ground.

Dylan dropped to her knees. 'Are you okay?'

Ketty clutched her foot. 'It hurts. My ankle.'

'What the . . .?' Jack's gaze raced from the urn . . . to me. He reached to help Ketty up, still glaring at me. She struggled to her feet. Tested her ankle.

'Ow.' She looked up, tears in her eyes. 'That hurts.'

I stood, staring helplessly at her.

'Brilliant,' Ed muttered beside me.

'Nico, I swear,' Jack hissed. 'If you try anything like that again, I'll . . .' He let the threat hang in the air and turned to Ketty again. 'Can you walk?'

202

Tears in her eyes, Ketty put her weight on her ankle again. 'Yes, but it hurts.'

Jack swore under his breath. A chill wriggled down my spine. Before, all I'd had to worry about was distracting Jack, so that we could escape. But now how were we going to get away? Ketty could barely walk, let alone run.

'We have to go.' Jack checked his watch. 'I can't afford to miss my flight.'

Ed put his arm round Ketty. She leaned into him and limped slowly off, just as a fire engine roared into the mews street.

'She's not walking fast enough.' Dylan glanced at Jack.

'You're right. Nico, you help too.' Jack looked over his shoulder at the fire engine. 'Christ, I hope they can contain the fire.' He shot me another furious look, as one of the fire-fighters leaped down from the machine and started yelling at the onlookers to move back, away from the fire.

I wandered over to Ketty's other side and reached for her arm. The three of us set off in an awkward huddle, Jack just behind.

Behind us, more firefighters were leaping down, shouting out to find out if there was anyone left in the house. I could hear Dylan telling someone that the house had been empty . . . that there was definitely no one inside.

'Dylan!' Jack yelled. 'Hurry.'

As we reached the main street, Dylan caught us up. She and Jack began muttering in low voices behind us. A small crowd had gathered, surging forwards to see the fire. As we pushed our way through, I glanced over my shoulder. Smoke was still billowing out of Jack's front door, but there was no sign of any flames. The firefighters were unfurling a long hose.

I glanced across at Ed and Ketty. I was sure Ed and I could get away now, if we ran hard enough. But I couldn't leave Ketty. I had to make sure she escaped too.

We turned onto Long Acre. Most of the shops were still locked up, just a few newsagents with the owners outside, removing their shutters. The sky was bright and the air cold. I guessed it must be gone 6 a.m.

Ketty limped on, with Ed and I on either side.

'Nice work, Nico,' Ed said, his voice dripping with sarcasm.

Irritation snaked into my throat. 'Well, what's *your* plan?' I hissed.

Ed glanced over his shoulder. Jack and Dylan were still deep in conversation.

'See that scaffolding up ahead on the corner?' Ed whispered. 'First level up?'

I looked up. Several buildings away, at the corner of a narrow alleyway, a network of scaffolding poles criss-crossed half the way up the front of a shop. A long line of bricks sat in piles across the planks laid along the first level up. More planks were laid against the side of the building, clearly waiting to be used further up the scaffolding.

'I see it,' I said, tersely.

'Well, I can hardly believe I'm asking after what just happened,' Ed went on, 'but d'you think you could manage to bring the bricks and planks down? If you caused a distraction I could probably get Ketty away. I'm sure I could carry her for a few streets.'

I looked back at the scaffolding. There was a lot of material up there, but nothing I couldn't teleport easily.

Ketty squeezed my arm. 'It's a good plan.'

I nodded. 'Yeah,' I said, 'but I've got a better one.'

'Oh, God,' Ed groaned. He glanced over his shoulder at Jack again. 'What d'you mean?'

'Well, if you just take Ketty and run, Jack'll follow you – I mean, even if I distract him for a few seconds, he'll notice you running off. But if you, me and Ketty run into the alley together and I bring those bricks and stuff down between us and Jack he won't be able to follow us and we'll *all* get away,' I whispered. 'There's a lot of stuff piled up on the scaffolding and it's a narrow alley. I'm sure I can do it.'

'But you might hit me or Ketty,' Ed said.

'Or yourself,' Ketty added.

'I'll aim carefully,' I said. 'Let's go.'

Ed opened his mouth, as if to say something else, then shut it again. We shuffled on for a few more metres. I looked up at the bricks, getting ready to move as many as possible, as fast as I could.

'Hurry up,' Jack called from behind us. I looked over my shoulder. He was frowning, his eyes fixed on the three of us ahead of him. 'We need to get a move on,' he went on. 'I

205

have to catch that chopper. If I miss my slot at the heliport I won't get to the meet with Carson in time.'

We were almost at the alleyway. I focused on the nearest pile of bricks. We reached the entrance. And then everything happened at once.

'Now,' I said.

Supporting Ketty round the waist, Ed darted sideways, into the alley. I followed, teleporting a brick down behind me. It landed at Jack's feet. He jumped. Swore. I turned and hurled another brick. But this one missed Jack. It swerved out of control and skimmed across the ground – into Ed's shin.

'Ow.' With a yelp he stumbled, letting go of Ketty.

No. As Ed fell towards me, I turned back to the bricks and plates, desperately trying to bring them down between me and Jack. But they were out of control, raining down in all directions as the others ran – or, in Ketty's case, hobbled – away as fast as they could.

I cast my eyes down, praying it would stop, but the bricks had a momentum of their own now . . . one pile tipping into the next, cascading down.

Finally it ended. I looked up.

Shit. I had indeed formed a wall of rubble and Ed and I were certainly on the alley side of it. Unfortunately, Ketty was still on the other side – with Jack and Dylan. All three were hidden from view.

'*Nico? Ed?*' she called, as the sound of Jack, swearing, rose up above the wall.

'We're okay,' I yelled back, tugging Ed away from the mess.

He turned on me, furious. 'Can't you do anything right?' he hissed. 'I *warned* you that you might hit me.'

'It's not that easy to control,' I snapped, pulling him further away. Jack's voice echoed from the other side of the wall of rubble.

'We don't have time to chase them,' he said.

Ed and I glanced at each other.

'But . . . but what about Carson?' That was Dylan.

'I'll tell him Nico's locked up at home – that he'll get the boy when my money's safe.'

'What about me?' Ketty's voice shook.

There was a short pause. I held my breath.

'You'll have to come with us to the meet,' Jack said.

'No,' Ketty sobbed. 'Please, *no*.'

'Come on.'

Their footsteps echoed away.

Ed stood, head bowed. 'Oh, God,' he said.

I grabbed his arm. 'Come on, if we run we can reach them. Get to the heliport first.'

'How?' Ed looked wildly up at me. 'We don't even know where the heliport is.'

'Have you got a phone . . . any money?'

'No. Jack took it all.'

I thought fast. 'We need to see an A-Z.'

'What? How will that . . .?'

'Come on.' I grabbed his arm and dragged him through the alley. More shops were opening up now. We passed a corner store. I darted in and rifled the shelves. There was a stack of

207

A-Zs to the left. I took one and thumbed through the index, my hands shaking.

'There.'

Ed peered over my shoulder as I pointed to the page. The only heliport in the area was clearly marked. Raven Street Pier, just north of the river. It looked like a fifteen-minute walk or so.

'We'll have to go the long way round to get there, but if we run we might beat them,' I said. 'They'll have to go slower because of Ketty.'

Ed nodded.

I stared again at the map, making sure I had the route firmly fixed in my head. I put the A-Z back and we raced off, the shopkeeper muttering crossly as we left. We ran hard, swerving round bends and down turnings.

Ten minutes later we reached the heliport. It was a modern building with glass-fronted doors and a large outside tarmac area on which two huge helicopters stood idle. The sun emerged from behind a cloud, warming the cold morning with an orange glow.

I peered inside. A reception area with sofas and a desk. No sign of anyone except a security guard, leafing through a magazine at the desk.

For a second I thought we'd got here first. And then a door to the outside area opened and Jack, Dylan and a limping Ketty appeared, walking towards one of the helicopters with another man.

We ducked back, into the shadow of the wall. I watched,

uncertain, as the other man, presumably the helicopter pilot, opened up the doors. Jack stood back to allow Dylan and Ketty to get in first.

'No,' I breathed.

'We have to do something,' Ed moaned.

But the helicopter's engines were already whirring. I focused on the blades, trying to calm my breathing. Maybe I could stop them using my telekinesis.

But the force of their spinning was too fast and hard for me to control. There was nothing I could do. A black misery filled my head as I watched the helicopter rise up into the sky, bank, then whirr off into the distance – taking Ketty far away from me.

26: Helicopter ride

Ed looked across at me. The fury in his eyes was unmistakable.

'She's gone,' he said. 'Jack's going to take her to Carson and Carson's going to use her like he was going to use you.'

'What d'you mean?' I stammered.

'Did you really think I wouldn't work it out?' Ed gritted his teeth. 'Carson wants you because you've got the Medusa gene – he can use you to demonstrate that it works. That's what Jack meant when he said Carson would get *you* when Jack got his money. But now you've gone, so Jack will have to give him Ketty instead.'

'You're being ridiculous,' I snapped, suddenly filled with panic. 'Jack and Carson don't even know Ketty has the Medusa gene. They'll just let her go.'

'You don't know that,' Ed said coldly. 'For all you know Jack or Dylan could have overheard us talking about Ketty being Viper. Or they might force the information out of Ketty herself.'

'They wouldn't—'

'You don't *know* what they'd do,' Ed insisted. 'But you should know this . . .' He paused. '. . . If anything happens to Ketty, it's all down to you. You're the only reason Ketty's mixed up in this – the only reason she's here.'

I stared at him. 'I didn't think—'

'You never *do* think, do you?' Ed clenched his fists. His normally eager, open face screwed up into an angry frown. 'Ketty was so right about you.'

'What?' My chest tightened. 'What did she say?'

'That you only care about yourself,' Ed snarled. 'That you're selfish.'

I reeled back like he'd punched me. Had Ketty *really* said that?

'That's not true,' I said. 'I *do* care about her . . . I . . .'

'Well, she's going out with me now, and I'm telling you to stay away from her.'

He stood glaring at me for a second. I could feel he was itching to make proper eye contact and punish me somehow. I looked away, wanting to complain this wasn't fair. But in my heart I knew he was right.

I *had* been selfish. It made sense that Ketty wouldn't like me any more.

Unable to bear these thoughts, I focused on the phone box at the end of the street. Where could we get help?

'Maybe we should try Fergus again?' I said.

Ed shrugged. 'There's no point. He was adamant we should stay at school. He said there was no point calling the

211

police . . . that *he* would find you and rescue you, but Ketty didn't want to wait.'

'But he doesn't know where Ketty's gone.' My voice rose. 'We should tell—'

'Nico, *we* don't know where Ketty's gone.' Ed's voice was heavy with contempt.

Ignoring him, I walked to the phone box and reversed the charges to Fox Academy. The switchboard put me through to the flat. Fergus's answerphone kicked in.

Sorry we can't get to the phone. If you have a message for Fergus Fox or Nico Rafael, please speak after the tone . . .

A lump rose in my throat. I hadn't realised Fergus still kept my name on the answerphone.

'Hi, it's me. Er . . . Ed and Ketty came to get me out,' I stammered into the phone. 'Don't be cross with them, they were trying to help. But Jack's taken Ketty—'

'Nico?' The phone picked up and Fergus' anxious voice cut across me. 'Where are you?'

'Ed and I got away, but Jack took Ketty somewhere in a helicopter. They set off five minutes ago from Raven Street Pier heliport.' My voice cracked. 'I'm going to try and find—'

'No.' Fergus's voice cut me off again. 'No. You and Ed must come back to school. I'm going to call the police. Let them handle things. I should have done it when you took the papers from my safe, but—'

'You *can't* call the police. Geri Paterson is too powerful. *You* told me that. So did Jack.'

'I know, that's why I didn't go to them before,' Fergus

212

sighed. 'But this is too big for me to handle anymore. I have to trust the authorities will know what to do, it's—'

'The police won't know where Ketty is,' I said.

'They can track the helicopter,' Fergus said. 'That'll be a start. Now promise me that you and Ed will come straight back to school?'

'We don't have any money . . .'

'Go to the police yourselves, then. Say you've been . . . mugged or something. Just get off the streets. Get to safety. I'll find you.'

I agreed, half-heartedly. I didn't want to go back to school and leave Ketty. But what else could we do? As I walked back down the road to where Ed was leaning against the wall by the heliport, my mind went over what he'd said before.

If anything happens to Ketty it's all down to you.

I gritted my teeth. That was true. And it meant I couldn't leave Ketty. Whatever I did, I had to at least *try* to save her.

I told Ed what Fergus had said. 'But it's a big risk,' I added. 'Remember, Geri doesn't know Jack's double-crossing her by selling the formula to Carson. She still thinks Jack's working for her – which presumably means she'll be keeping the police off his trail.'

'You're right.' Ed looked at me, not quite meeting my gaze as usual. His dark blue eyes were far older than the rest of his face. 'But what can we do?'

As I stared at him, a plan formed in my head. *God*, it was dangerous – beyond dangerous in fact.

I took a deep breath. 'The first thing we have to do is find

213

out where that helicopter went,' I said, looking in through the heliport entrance, where the security guard was still reading his magazine, feet up on the reception desk. The clock on the wall above the desk said it was 7.08 a.m.

'How?' Ed asked. 'We can't just go in and demand they tell us.'

We peered in at the security guard.

'We could read his mind, find out where the flight info is kept,' I suggested.

'We?' Ed raised his eyes. '*We?*'

'Okay, would you rather I teleported that chair and hit him over the head with it?' I said.

'I told you, I don't—'

'Sssh, he's seen us.'

The security guard was crossing the foyer. He was a hefty, balding man with a slow, easy swagger.

I stood, waiting, my heart pounding.

'All right, lads?' The security guard opened the door. 'You with that school party we've got this morning? Bit early, aren't you? They're not due in for another twenty minutes.'

Ed froze.

'Yes,' I said, buying time. 'We're meeting the teachers here.'

I nudged Ed. He needed to do his mind-reading thing. Fast.

The security guard looked down the street. 'Where are your parents?'

Crap. 'Er . . . they're not here. We came on our own,' I said as smoothly as I could. I smiled. 'It's just we love heli-copters . . . er . . . we got up early to get here. Any chance we could look around?'

The security guard chuckled. 'No chance in a million,' he said. 'Come in if you want, though. It's warmer in here.'

He turned and headed back to his desk. Ed and I fol-lowed. Ed still looked frozen with fear. I poked him, hard, with my elbow. I couldn't keep my helicopter-geek act up much longer . . . Ed had to get it together.

As we followed the security guard inside, his desk phone rang. He spoke quietly for a second. All I could make out was a lot of mumbled 'yes, sir's'. After a second, he motioned us to wait in the chairs by the desk, then put down the phone and pressed an intercom button.

'Sorry to disturb you, Mr Parks, but I just had a code S.' He lowered his voice. 'They said that a Geri Paterson wants all records of the last flight out scrubbed. Everything deleted – paper, screen – I just wanted to . . . oh, okay, Mr Parks, of course.'

The hair on the back of my neck stood on end, as the security guard stood up.

'Now where's the frigging shredder got to,' he muttered.

'He's going to destroy all the details of their flight,' I hissed.

Ed's eyes widened. 'How did Geri Paterson know Mr Fox had called the police so fast?'

'Jack must have rung her – told her that we were on the

215

loose and likely to go to Fergus for help,' I said. 'Which means that following that helicopter is up to us and finding out where it went is up to *you*.'

'What?' Ed's mouth trembled. 'I can't.'

I glared at him. 'Go on, it's for Ketty. Hurry.'

Ed took a deep breath, then sidled up to the desk. 'Sir?'

The security guard looked up. His eyes glazed over as Ed stood in front of him and pushed his way into the man's mind.

Seconds ticked by like hours. 'Well?' I said, impatiently. 'What have you found out?'

'There's a log on the desk,' Ed said, not taking his eyes from the guard. 'No details, but it'll give the time of take-off and expected arrival and the destination heliport.'

I raced round the desk and started pulling at the files.

'It's blue,' Ed went on. 'With a black spine.'

I found the file and opened it . . . whipping through the pages to today. Three flights were logged since midnight. The copter Jack and Ketty were on had left just before 7 a.m. I ran my finger across the page.

Departure 6.56 a.m., ETA Penhagen House, Penhagen, 8.45 a.m.

'Where's Penhagen?' I said.

'Cornwall, I think. Are you done?' Ed said, still staring at the guard.

'Sure.'

'So what do we do now?'

'Get to Penhagen ourselves,' I said, scanning down the list

216

of upcoming flights. 'There're three flights in the next hour. That school trip the guard was talking about, but that's a bit later . . . er . . . yeah, before that there's a private helicopter leaving for Petherton Bridge – which it says is in Devon – in five minutes. Devon's right next to Cornwall, isn't it?'

'Yes.'

I looked over at the security guard. He was clearly unable to move his eyes away from Ed's gaze. I knew how that felt – like your mind was pinned against a wall. However, I also knew that the guard would still be aware of everything going on around him. And, as soon as the link with Ed was broken, he'd be free to tell whoever he wanted what had just happened.

'Can you wipe this guy's memory so he doesn't remember we were here?'

'No! *Jesus*,' Ed said impatiently. 'And I wouldn't even if I—'

'Well, you'd better think of something to stop him blabbing,' I snapped. 'At least for the next few minutes.'

There was a pause. 'Okay,' Ed said. 'He's tired. I think I can make him sleep. That'll give us however long he stays asleep for.'

'Do it.'

I walked to the door that opened out onto the helipad. There was only one helicopter on the tarmac, its doors open. Two men were standing beside it, chatting and laughing. I glanced over my shoulder. The security guard was sitting down, his head lying on the top of the desk. As Ed walked away from him, a series of gentle snores burbled out of the man's mouth.

'My turn,' I whispered.

Ed muttered something under his breath. I ignored him.

The heliport concourse was a square of concrete surrounded on two sides by walls with rolls of barbed wire along the top and a line of sheds at the far end. Hiding behind the building door, I focused on a line of luggage carts in the darkest corner, by the sheds. I took a breath and concentrated on tipping over the cart furthest away. It fell onto the one next to it, which cascaded onto the next . . . and the next. A second later all four carts crashed to the ground.

Even from inside the heliport building you could hear the smash.

The two men standing beside the helicopter spun round and raced towards the cart.

'Come on.' I ran over to the open helicopter door, Ed at my side. We hurled ourselves into the machine just as two more men emerged from the shed at the end of the concourse.

'What's going on?' one of them yelled. The four men stood, staring at the carts. There was so obviously no way anyone could have tipped them over and got away without being seen, you could almost see their confusion.

'Must've been cats.'

'Yeah, or a fox, maybe.'

Inside the helicopter, Ed had pulled out a crate and hidden behind it. I crouched behind another, then peered out of the window. Two of the men were walking towards the helicopter. I looked round. We were in the back row of the helicopter, two rows behind the pilot's seat. A coat was draped across the seat in front of me. I slid it between the seats and pulled it over our heads.

If he looked . . . if he checked . . . if the guard at the front desk woke up, we'd be found.

I held my breath. Voices came from outside.

'Okay, Terry, you'd better get off.'

'See you later.'

Men were stomping round the helicopter, slamming doors. One got in, whistling. Then the engine roared and all other noises were drowned out. A minute later the helicopter lurched, and we were in the air.

27: The journey

The flight took about two hours. In spite of my constant,
nagging anxiety about Ketty, I loved the swoop and sway of
the helicopter in the air. From the greyness of Ed's face,
peeking out from behind one of the crates, I guessed he
wasn't enjoying it quite so much.

We landed more gently than I'd have thought possible.
The whirring slowed and the engine cut out. I stayed completely still, very aware that now he'd reached his
destination Terry, the pilot, might well reach for his coat –
and see me cowering underneath it. But instead he opened
the door.

'Hey, Terry, how you doing?' A man's voice.

'Good, thanks. Knackered, though.'

Ed nudged me. His eyes bored into mine. This time I
knew what was coming and was ready for the *whoosh* of his
thoughts rushing into my head.

How are we going to get out without anyone seeing us?
Wait a sec.

Ed looked away, breaking the connection. He peered out from behind his crate. I shifted the coat off me and peeked out too. Terry, and the other man were busy in the helicopter doorway, chatting. I glanced round. The helipad we were in couldn't have been more different from the one in London. It was basically just a circle of tarmac in the middle of a huge field. A small shed stood to one side, with a van parked next to it. Otherwise there was nothing but moorland for miles.

Forget how we were going to get away without anyone seeing us.

How were we going to get away at all?

I sank back down, defeated.

Ed pulled me round. His eyes were wild with panic now he'd seen what we were up against. He looked as if he were struggling to get inside my head. Maybe he needed to be just as calm and focused as I did before he could make his psychic ability work properly. He gave up and leaned right into my ear.

'What are we going to do?' he hissed.

I thought fast. 'Plan B,' I whispered back.

'What the hell is Plan—?'

'Time to go,' I said loudly, standing up and pushing my way towards the front of the helicopter.

'Nico?'

I ignored Ed's desperate voice behind me and kept my eyes on Terry and the man he was talking to. 'Hi,' I said.

They both spun round. Terry's jaw dropped. 'What the . . .?'

221

I jumped down from the helicopter. 'Thanks for the ride, Terry.'

'Oy!' Terry's large hand grabbed my arm. He stared at me, his face a total picture of shock.

The other man peered into the helicopter and spotted Ed. 'Hey, there's another one. Get out of there!'

The two men stared at us, then each other, in shocked silence.

Ed stumbled out of the helicopter, his face bright red.

'What the . . .? How did you get in there?' Terry frowned.

'Actually it was quite easy,' I said. 'We were really careful – just wanted the ride. We didn't damage anything.' I smiled at him, hopefully.

Terry's face clouded. 'Well, you're nicked now. Trespassing little bastards.' He turned to the other man. 'We should take them to the police.'

Crap. I could feel Ed's angry glare, burning into the back of my head.

'Yeah.' The other man nodded. 'But after they've helped us load up.'

Five minutes – and some seriously back-breaking work – later, Ed and I had loaded the crates into the van and were locked into the back section, speeding across the scrub towards the main road.

'What the hell did you do that for?' Ed hissed as soon as we were alone.

'It was the only way we were going to get out of there,' I said.

222

'But he's taking us to the *police*,' Ed said indignantly.

'I don't think so,' I said. 'I mean, what kind of helicopter lands its deliveries in the middle of a field? Whatever's in these crates has got to be well dodgy. They're just trying to frighten us.'

Ed shook his head. 'It's a big freaking risk, Nico.'

'Well, if it doesn't work you can always put him to sleep while we run away.' I chuckled. 'Can't you . . .?'

Ed looked out of the window and swore under his breath.

We were soon on the main road, after which the moorland around us quickly turned into a series of small towns and villages. Terry finally pulled up outside a hardware shop. He said goodbye to the other man, then came round to the back and opened it up.

'We're unloading the first four crates here. Then the other three somewhere else,' he said, 'then I'm taking you to the cops.'

My heart sank. I was still sure Terry was bluffing, but we didn't have time to go to another place after this one and unload more crates. We had to get to Ketty.

'You sure you want to involve the cops?' I said. 'You'll just end up filling in a bunch of forms.'

Terry shot me a nasty grin. 'It'll be worth it. Now pick up a crate and get ready to hump it where I tell you.'

Beside me, Ed groaned.

I grabbed the nearest crate and hauled it into the shop. Terry stood, holding the door open for first me, then Ed. As I walked back to the van I thought about making a dash for

223

it, but Ed was still inside. I took another crate and walked back. The shopkeeper was handing Terry a bundle of notes. As I passed him, Terry shoved the money into his back trouser pocket.

I grinned to myself. *Of course.*

Ed made a face at me as he walked back to the van for the last crate. I deposited mine in the corner of the shop, then glanced over at Terry. He was by the till, next to the door, still talking to the shopkeeper. Six crisp fifty-pound notes peeked out of the top of his back pocket.

I took a breath and focused, mentally tugging the money towards me. The notes slid easily out of Terry's pocket. As they zoomed across the shop into my hands, Ed reappeared, the final crate in his hands.

He saw the money flying through the air and nearly dropped the crate.

'Is that the last of the four for here?' Terry asked.

Ed nodded, his face burning red.

'Come on.' Terry beckoned me outside. 'It's a half-hour drive to the next drop.'

Ed groaned.

I scrunched the cash up in my hand and followed. Terry opened the van doors. 'Get in,' he said.

'Er, please don't do this, sir.' I dug my hand into my jeans pocket, pretending to rootle around inside it. I drew my hand out and opened it up. Terry's own money – all three hundred pounds of it – sat screwed up in my palm. The crumpled notes didn't look anything like the crisp bills he'd just been given. I prayed he wouldn't make the connection.

'I'm really sorry we stole a ride in your helicopter. Please, just take this – it's all the cash we've got – please, let us go.'

Terry stared at me for a second, his head tilted to one side. Then he sighed and took the money. 'Well . . .' he said. 'All right. Hop it.'

I turned and ran fast down the street before he changed his mind. Ed pounded along beside me. I took a left and two rights, heading into what seemed the busiest part of town. At last we reached a street full of shops. I stopped.

'I suppose Jack taught you that trick.' Puffing, Ed came to a halt beside me.

I shrugged. 'Don't tell me you wouldn't have done the same thing if you could.'

'You know I don't think we should use our . . . our abilities unless somebody's *life* is at stake.'

'You're just jealous that you don't have my smarts,' I said.

'I'm *not*—'

'Oh, give it a rest.'

We walked on in silence, past a Starbucks and a WHSmiths. It was starting to rain as I asked an old lady where we were.

'Southbarton, love,' she said, tugging her scarf round her neck.

'Is that near Penhagen?' I said.

'Where, love?' The old lady frowned.

'It's in Cornwall.'

'Why don't you ask at the bus station.' She pointed to the end of the street. 'Just round that corner.'

We found the bus station easily enough. A coach direct to Penhagen was leaving in thirty minutes. We scraped together the money we each needed for the fare from some loose change in our pockets and the emergency tenner Ed had tucked into the lining of his shoe.

The journey took just under an hour. I slept for most of it. Ed shook me awake as we rolled into Penhagen. The place was much smaller than Southbarton – a collection of squat grey little houses with a single row of shops. The rain had stopped, but the sky was still the colour of steel.

As we got off at the bus stop, my stomach rumbled.

'We'll have to ask someone where Penhagen House is,' I said, glancing over at Ed's watch. 'God, it's almost midday. Jack and Ketty must have got here hours ago.'

'Yeah.' I could hear my own concern echoed in Ed's voice.

We looked up and down the street. There was no one about and only two shops and a pub in sight. I glanced at the shops. One was a newsagent with a closed sign hanging on the door. The other was a bakery with fresh pies and tarts in the window.

'I'm starving,' Ed said, eyeing the bakery.

'We've got to ask directions anyway,' I said. 'Maybe we can get some food too.'

'We don't have any money.'

'That doesn't need to stop us. I mean, if we're going to

help Ketty we've got to eat.' I threw Ed a sideways glance. 'You do the talking. I'll grab what I can, yeah?'

Ed said nothing. I knew he didn't like the idea of me using my telekinesis to steal food. Still, what choice did we have? Neither of us had eaten in over twelve hours.

We walked across the road. While Ed asked the girl at the counter for directions to Penhagen House, I fixed my gaze on a tray of pasties in the shop window. They were too far away for me to reach without leaning right over the counter. I held my jacket over my arm for cover, and motioned two pasties into my hand. I covered them with the jacket as we left the shop.

'It's the next right, then the left-hand fork at the end of the village.' Ed glanced at where the pasties make a bulge under my jacket. As we turned the corner I held one out to him.

He shook his head. 'I can't,' he said. 'It's just wrong.'

I sighed and bit into my own pasty. It tasted delicious, all light crisp pastry and thick meaty filling.

As we hit the main road out of the village, we started jogging. I wasn't sure what time it was but Ketty must have been here for hours now. I swallowed down the last of my pasty and sped up.

'Why d'you hate your abilities so much?' I said.

Ed shrugged as he kept pace beside me. 'I told you . . . it's wrong to look inside people's heads. Apart from the fact that it could put me in danger, Mr Fox says it's . . . it's an invasion of privacy. '

A few days ago I'd have dismissed this as typical Fergus

uptightness. Now, after Jack's betrayal and nearly hurting that baby in the park, I considered it carefully.

'Sometimes it might be wrong to mind-read, sure,' I said. 'But, sometimes, it's justified. Sometimes – like you said before – if it's going to save someone's life – you *have* to. Like you did back at the heliport, for Ketty.'

Ed looked at me. His eyes were intense, for once almost meeting mine.

'Okay, but where do you draw the line?' he said. 'How do you know when it's okay to mind-read and when it isn't? Who decides?'

I didn't have an answer for that. And, just then, the road out of Penhagen narrowed into a single-lane country road. Cars were whizzing past, so we fell into single file, running harder now, both of us lost in our own thoughts.

After about five minutes, we reached a gleaming iron gate and a sign which read: *Penhagen House.*

My heart leaped into my throat. Ketty was in here.

'This has to be it.' Ed's low whisper spoke my own thoughts. 'We've found her.'

28: Penhagen House

I peered over the gate at the house beyond.

Dramatic wasn't a big enough word to describe what I saw.

A sprawling, ultra-modern mass of glass and metal, it stood at the end of a long, sweeping driveway and was set into the hill, like a series of shelves, on three levels. Beyond was the cliff edge – bleak and bare, apart from a single dead tree – and past that was the sea. Nearest us, at the end of the first 'shelf' of house, a helipad jutted out. But there was no sign of the helicopter which had ferried Ketty, Jack and Dylan here earlier.

'D'you think they're still here?' Ed said. 'What if Carson's already come and taken the formula . . . and Ketty?'

'We can't think like that,' I said. I glanced up. The sun was high now, blazing down from a clear blue sky.

'Where d'you think Ketty is?' Ed said.

I looked at the building. 'We're going to have to get inside and look around.'

'What about those?' Ed pointed to a set of security cameras on the roof. 'And there're probably others.'

I nodded. 'I'll take care of them. Let's get a bit closer.'

Keeping close to the line of trees we edged down the hill so we were more on a level with the house. From here I could see three sets of security cameras. Only one, though, was pointing towards us.

At that moment Jack came out of a door in the house, just under the camera. We both shrank back behind our trees, but Jack didn't even look in our direction. He walked purposefully across the patio and round the corner to the back of the house. The camera followed him until he disappeared from view. Then it swivelled back into position, trained towards us again. I glanced at the door Jack had come through. It had swung to, but was not properly shut.

'At least we have a way in now.' I took a breath in and focused on moving the camera myself. It shifted a centimetre or so, but as Jack paced into view again, a phone clamped to his ear, it trained itself back on him.

I tried to move it again, but my telekinesis wasn't powerful enough.

Crap. 'It's really hard for me to move anything that resists,' I whispered.

'So how are we . . .?'

'No problem.'

Jack disappeared round the front of the house again. I picked up a stone.

'I'm going to smash the camera lens above that door. It should buy us enough time to get inside.'

'I don't think you'll be able to send a stone that far.' Ed screwed up his forehead, clearly trying to work out what he thought I was capable of. 'Not fast enough to smash the lens, anyway.'

I gritted my teeth. What did he know? 'Watch me.' I focused on the stone, letting it hover in the air for a second. Then I let it fly. The stone whizzed through the air. *Yes.* It was soon soaring past the helicopter pad, but, the further it got away from me, the slower it travelled. I urged it on, but I could feel my power draining . . . the stone was losing height . . . *crap* . . . it was going to fall on the concrete and Jack would hear.

'Nico!' Ed whispered urgently beside me.

With a huge mental effort I swerved the stone sideways so that it fell, noiselessly, on the grass.

I sat back, panting.

Ed raised an 'I told you so' eyebrow at me. 'Plan B?'

He sounded so like Ketty it made me wince.

I shrugged. 'Got any suggestions?'

Ed thought for a minute. 'What about a decoy?'

'How would that work?' I said.

'You go over and draw the camera's attention away, while I slip through the door.'

I wrinkled my nose. 'But then they'll know we're here. I'll be captured.'

'It's the only way.'

231

'Really? Well how 'bout *you* let yourself be captured while *I* find another way in.'

'But . . .'

Jack reappeared, hands in pockets, his phone call clearly over. He stood on the edge of the patio, looking out to sea. And then Dylan stepped out of the house. As she walked across to him, the camera above the door swivelled after her. So did Ed's eyes.

'I thought you were all into Ketty,' I said, accusingly.

'I *am*.' Ed glared at me. 'It's just . . . I've never really looked at her properly . . . Your girlfriend, I mean.'

I glanced over at Dylan again. She was wearing jeans and a tight black jumper. Her hair was loose, blowing in the wind like red silk. She looked like a model taking a break from some photo shoot.

'She's not my girlfriend,' I said. 'Anyway, she might *look* fit, but she's kind of useless underneath. I know she's scared of Jack and Carson, but she could still *try* and help us.' I paused. 'I mean, the Medusa formula – which she's basically helping Jack to sell – killed *her* mum too.'

Ed watched Jack and Dylan talking for a second. 'I was thinking,' he said hesitantly, 'we came here for Ketty, but we do – also – have to stop Jack selling that formula.'

'I know.' All the way here, underneath my overriding desire to rescue Ketty, the same thought had been running through my mind. I glanced up at the camera above the door again. It was focused on Dylan and Jack. They were still deep in conversation, looking out towards the dead tree on the cliff edge.

It was as good a chance as we were going to get.

'We have to go now. Make a run for it.' I looked round at Ed.

He blinked back at me. There wasn't time to persuade him.

'Come on.' I raced off.

'Wait,' Ed whispered, furiously, behind me.

But I ran on, only pausing when I reached the cover of the house wall. I peered round. Dylan and Jack were still talking. Ed caught me up.

'You have to stop going off on your own like that,' he hissed.

I shrugged. 'Sssh.' The wind was fiercer here, closer to the sea. It whistled round my ears, stinging my cheeks. It carried Jack and Dylan's voices towards me.

'Carson will be here soon,' Jack was saying, sounding tense. 'As soon as we've done the handover, we're out of here.'

'What about Ketty?' Dylan asked, twisting her hair round her hand.

Jack shrugged.

Ed's face paled. 'He *is* going to hand her over,' he breathed.

'Hurry.' It wasn't far to the door now and Jack and Dylan were still talking. I crept round the wall, praying neither of them would look round. Just a few more strides . . . *There*.

233

I tugged the door open. We were inside.

We tiptoed quickly down the corridor. The house was so designer it made Jack's mews house look like some old lady's home. Wooden floors. White walls. Strange, iron ornaments. But I wasn't really thinking about the décor at that point. I was all focused on Ketty – on how I'd failed her . . . on how we had to find her . . .

There were no cameras that I could see inside the house, but it was large and sprawling and we had no idea if anyone, other than Jack or Dylan, was here. We crept along a series of identical corridors, passed a few empty rooms, but no sign of Ketty – or anyone else.

'Let's try up there.' Ed pointed to a short flight of stairs.

We walked up. Another corridor. Most of the doors were open, leading into more smart, bare rooms. Ed stopped outside the third door on the left. It was shut. He pointed to a keypad and a row of lights on the wall.

'It's an electronic lock,' he whispered.

I hesitated. None of the other doors we'd passed had been locked. Surely that meant Ketty *must* be in here . . .

I knocked lightly. 'Hello?' I hissed. 'Ketty?'

There was a scuffling noise on the other side of the door. Then the sound of footsteps, rushing across the room.

'Nico?' The voice said. 'Is that you?

I started, then glanced at Ed. He looked as shocked as I felt. Because the voice belonged to the last person I was expecting to find here.

Fergus Fox.

29: The formula

My chest tightened. Fergus was here. *He'd* come for Ketty too. A mix of emotions swirled through me: relief that we weren't on our own any more mingled with anxiety that Fergus was locked up.

'Mr Fox?' Ed said uncertainly. 'Is that you?'

'Ed?' Fergus's voice grew alarmed. 'I told you to go back to school. What are you doing here?'

'Rescuing you, apparently,' I said.

'Nico?' Now Fergus sounded really panic-stricken. 'Are you both all right?'

'We're fine. Have you seen Ketty?'

'No, but she's here somewhere.' Fergus paused. 'After I spoke to you I called the police. But they claimed no helicopter had left Raven Street Pier heliport at the time you said early this morning.'

'We know,' I said. 'Geri Paterson got the heliport people to destroy all the info on the flight.'

'I guessed something like that must have happened . . .' Fergus tailed off.

'So you came here by yourself?' I said.

'I called Ketty's phone,' he said. 'Dylan answered. I realized it must be her straight away.' He tailed off again.

'So did she tell you where she and Jack and Ketty were?'

'Yes, but I think it must have been a trap because Jack saw me as soon as I arrived and I didn't see Dylan at all. God, I thought I could talk Jack out of selling the formula . . . that I could get him to let Ketty go. Anyway . . . listen, boys, you must get yourselves out of here. I can take care of myself . . . and Ketty.'

I looked round. 'Maybe there's some way we can get the door open.'

'Not without this.' Jack's mocking voice came from behind us.

I spun round, ready to fight.

Jack held up some sort of key fob. His gun was in his other hand. 'Talk about walking into the lion's den,' he said, shaking his head. 'I've got to hand it to you two, you're certainly brave. I thought I'd have to chase after you once I'd given Carson the formula.' He walked over and swiped the key fob past the narrow row of lights on the wall. The door clicked open. 'Inside.'

As he pushed Ed and me into the room, my mind raced, trying to work out if I could lift the gun from Jack's hands. But he was holding it too tightly.

The room we'd walked into was a bedroom. Small and

bare, with a single bed against one wall and a wooden wardrobe in the corner. Fergus was standing by the window, his face white and strained.

'You can't keep us here, Jack,' he said. 'Think it through.'

'Shut up.' Jack pointed the gun at Fergus. 'Sit on the bed.'

Fergus sat. Jack turned to me and Ed. I noticed he avoided looking Ed directly in the eye, presumably to protect himself from any mind-reading. 'You came here alone, I hope?'

I pressed my lips together, unwilling to give anything away.

'Yes we did, but Mr Fox called the police,' Ed squeaked.

I rolled my eyes. Jack just grinned. 'Thanks for filling me in,' he said. Keeping his gun trained on us, he backed out of the door.

As soon as he'd gone I turned on Ed. 'Nice one, truth boy,' I hissed. 'Jack knows Geri Paterson controls the police. Now you've told him we came here alone, he knows we've got no back-up.'

'What do you need back-up for?' Ed snapped. 'You're the bloody Lone Ranger.'

'Stop it, boys.' Fergus sighed. 'This is bad enough without you two squabbling.'

Irritation surged through me. 'Don't tell us what to do,' I said. 'If you'd told me the truth about the Medusa gene, we wouldn't *be* here.'

'If you'd *listened* to me, we wouldn't be here,' Fergus insisted. 'Don't you understand even now, Nico? Everything I've done has been about trying to protect you.'

237

I looked away, not wanting to admit to myself that he had a point.

'So how are we going to get Ketty?' I said.

Fergus walked across the room and stared out of the window. We were only a floor or so off the ground, facing out from the side of the house, and the view only reached as far as the trees, with just a hint of the rough, dark, choppy sea round the corner. 'I don't know.' He sighed.

I went over to the door. There was no way on earth I could get through an electronic lock – with or without telekinesis. Lying, on the other hand, was simple.

'I've got an idea.' I banged on the door. 'Jack! Help!'

'What are you doing?' Fergus looked up, bewildered.

'Pretend you've collapsed or something,' I said. 'Help! Come here!'

'*What?*' Fergus glanced at Ed. 'What's he talking about?'

'He does this.' Ed rolled his eyes. 'The Lone Ranger . . .'

Footsteps pounded down the corridor outside.

'Sssh.' I pointed to Fergus' stomach. 'Pretend you've got an ulcer or something.'

'What's up?' It was Dylan.

'Open the door,' I said. 'Fergus is ill.'

I glared at Fergus, who rolled his eyes, but gave a fairly convincing moan.

'Dylan, please. He's your uncle, for God's sake.'

'I can't.' Her voice was as guilty as it was suspicious. 'Jack has the key fob.'

'He has an ulcer,' Ed shouted.

238

'Yeah, he needs his medication,' I added.

'I'll get Jack.' Dylan's light footsteps retreated along the corridor.

Damn.

'Never mind, so long as they open the door that's all we need.' I glanced at Ed. 'When Jack gets here you'll have to do your weird-eye shit on him, find out why he's keeping us here.'

'It's not *weird-eye*—'

'Boys!' Fergus hissed.

Ed turned sulkily away and slumped to the ground by the window.

I waited next to the door for Jack. If he came in alone, maybe Fergus could keep him talking while I took the gun. I wasn't sure having the gun would do me much good, though. I mean, it wasn't like I had any idea how to use it.

Which Jack undoubtedly did.

'Jack's coming.' It was Dylan, outside the door again. 'I have to go keep watch for Carson up at the gate. Listen, there's something you—'

But before she could say any more, Jack was back, stomping and swearing down the corridor. He ordered her away. Dylan left.

Jack flung the door open. He stood in the doorway, holding his gun in front of him. His face was twisted with fury.

'What?' he said to Fergus.

'I'm ill.' Fergus doubled over. 'It's my ulcer.'

'Does it hurt?' Jack said.

239

'A lot.'

Jack sucked in his breath. 'Good.' He turned to me. 'Now, where is it?'

I stared at him. Any thoughts I'd had of taking the gun with telekinesis had gone. Jack was too alert.

'Where's what?' I said.

Jack strode over to me and grabbed me round the throat. His fingers clutched roughly at my neck. There was a tiny fleck of spit in the corner of his mouth. I could see the fear, deep in his eyes. 'The memory card, you little bastard.'

I stared up at him. What was he talking about?

'*The memory card* . . .' Jack repeated. 'The one that I copied the Medusa gene formula onto. You took it out of my pocket as you snuck into the house, didn't you?'

'No.' I tried to pull away from him, but Jack was too strong. His free hand reached into my pockets. Searching . . . finding nothing.

'Leave him alone,' Fergus shouted.

Jack backed away, the gun waving dangerously in his hand. His breath was heavy and ragged.

'I'll be right back.' He left the room, slamming the door behind him.

I felt my bruised throat.

'Are you okay?' Fergus asked, anxiously.

'Yes.' I stared at Ed. 'What's he talking about, though? I didn't even know the memory card was in his pocket when we passed him outside.'

Ed shook his head bewildered. 'I don't—'

240

And then the door slammed open again and Jack pushed Ketty in through the door.

She stumbled into the room, her curls falling over her face. My heart raced as she looked up. She saw me. She smiled.

'Nico?' she breathed.

My heart was thumping hard now. I'd almost forgotten Jack and the others were still in the room.

And then it all fell apart.

Jack seized her arm and pulled her towards him. He pointed his gun at her neck. 'I know how much you like this girl, Nico.' His face twisted into a cruel smile. 'But I *really* need that formula. If the deal goes wrong a second time I'm not just broke . . . I'm dead.'

I was dimly aware of Fergus and Ed, standing horrified on either side of me, but all my focus was on Ketty. Her eyes were wide with fear, her chest heaving as she gasped for breath. Her gaze slid from me to Ed, then glazed slightly. I glanced at him. He was communicating with her, his eyes alive and intent.

'Nico?' Jack said.

'I told you, I don't know where the formula is.' My voice was high and strained. My stomach twisted over.

'Wrong answer.' Jack shook his head. He cocked the gun and pressed it against Ketty's neck. 'Now tell me where you put the memory card. Or Ketty dies.'

241

30: Outside

Ketty gasped. Ed's face went as white as the bright wall behind him.

My chest constricted. My mind went blank.

Do something.

Fergus clenched his fists. 'Let the kids go, for God's—'

'Shut *up*.' Jack glared at him. He turned back to me. 'Nico, you have three seconds.'

I looked straight into his eyes. What on earth could I say to convince him I didn't know where the formula was?

'One.'

Jack's bright blue eyes pierced into mine.

'Two.'

I was going to have to make something up.

'Three.'

'Okay, I took it,' I blurted.

Jack eased the gun off Ketty's neck, though he still held her tightly by the arm. 'Where is it now?'

'Let Ketty and the others go, and I'll tell you.'

Jack shook his head. 'No deals, Nico. Talk.'

'Nico doesn't *know*,' Fergus said, his voice stretched with tension. 'It's—'

'Shut up.'

I thought fast. We'd have the best chance of escape if we left the house. 'It's outside,' I said.

I could feel Ed shuffling beside me. I prayed Jack wasn't going to look at him and see my lie in his face. But Jack kept his eyes fixed on me.

'Outside?' he said slowly. 'Where?'

'Yes.' I tried to remember what the outside of the house had looked like. Only one distinctive feature came to mind. 'I teleported it near that dead tree on the edge of the cliff.'

Jack backed away, through the open door and into the corridor, pulling a limping Ketty after him. I suddenly remembered that she'd twisted her ankle when we left the mews house. Had that really been only a few hours ago? I forced my mind to focus. At least if Jack was threatening to kill Ketty, he couldn't know she had the Medusa gene – which meant she was safe from being part of his deal with Carson.

All I had to do was make him let her go.

Jack held up his gun. 'Everyone . . .' He pointed along the corridor. 'Outside, and don't think about running.'

I left the room, with Fergus and Ed beside me. As the five of us trooped down a series of corridors, Fergus drew Jack into a hushed conversation. I glanced round. Jack had his gun pressed against Fergus's chest as they talked, but his eyes were darting from me to Ed to Ketty as we walked on ahead.

243

My stomach twisted over. What the hell was I going to do when we got outside?

As we reached the side door that led out to the helipad, Ketty drew close to me. 'I don't want you to tell him where you hid the formula, Nico,' she whispered. 'It doesn't matter what happens to me. I don't want that formula getting out to kill more people.'

I glanced at Jack. He was still deep in angry conversation with Fergus.

'As it happens you're in luck, babe,' I whispered back. 'I can't tell him because I didn't actually take the formula . . . I have no idea where it is.'

The look of horror on Ketty's face deepened. 'But then he'll kill all of us!'

'No. So long as he doesn't know you're Viper he'll let you go—'

'What?' She frowned.

'It doesn't matter. You're going to be all right. *That's* all that matters.' I tried to smile reassuringly, but my lips trembled. I looked away.

'Open the door, Nico,' Jack ordered.

I stepped out onto the helipad and walked towards the cliff edge at the front of the house. It formed a sheer drop to the sea, hundreds of feet below.

I stood beside the dead tree, looking down at where the dark water crashed against the rocks. The wind roared past my ears. I shivered.

What the hell was I going to do now?

244

I turned back to Ketty, hoping she was looking at me . . . hoping I'd see some kind of understanding of what I felt in her eyes.

But she was standing a few metres back, staring at the tree beside me and the sea beyond, her hands clapped over her mouth.

'No.' A low whimper. 'No.'

'What is it?' I said.

I looked round. Fergus and Jack were still deep in their argument, but Jack was watching us now. Ed walked up next to Ketty.

'Ketts?' I whispered. 'What's the matter?'

Ed touched her arm. 'Ketty?'

'I didn't notice when we arrived, but this is from my nightmare,' she said hoarsely. 'That dead tree . . . its branches and the sea beyond. Oh, Ed, something really bad is about to happen – like someone's going to die. I can *feel* it.'

He put his arm round her and she buried her face in his shoulder. I stared at them, as the fear I felt about what was going to happen to us mingled with the dull, heavy weight of knowing that Ketty had chosen Ed.

I'd lost her.

'Right, we're here,' Jack barked. 'Now, where did you put the memory card?'

I dropped to my knees at the base of the tree. Suddenly what I had to do was clear. Ketty was everything and Ketty needed Ed. Which meant I had to save Ed for her.

245

I had to save them both.

I scrabbled in the earth, then stood up, my right hand holding a small stone. I held it towards Jack.

'The memory card is in my hand,' I lied, taking a step backwards, towards the cliff edge. 'Let Ketty and Ed go, right now, or I'll jump.'

'No.' Fergus and Ketty spoke together.

'Quiet.' Jack pointed his gun at Fergus. 'Don't be so melodramatic, Nico,' he snarled. 'Just give me the card.'

I shook my head and took another step closer to the cliff edge. The earth crumbled under my left foot. Despite the freezing wind, a trickle of sweat ran down my neck. 'You don't need Ketty or Ed,' I said, trying to keep my voice steady. 'Neither of them could identify Carson. He doesn't even know they exist. You said all he wanted was me and the formula. Well, me and the formula are right here. Just let Ketty and Ed go and you can give Carson exactly what he wants.'

'No.' Ketty's voice trembled. 'No . . .'

Out of the corner of my eye I could see Ed staring at me. I glanced at him and in seconds his mind was inside mine, penetrating deep into my thoughts. I gasped at the force of it. This was *way* more powerful than when he'd read my mind in the classroom. In seconds his mind was shooting through my brain, darting in and out of my thoughts, my feelings, my memories. I was powerless to stop him. And then he slowed down and I heard his voice in my head:

We can't leave you, Nico.

I stared at him, willing him to understand. *Just look after Ketty. Please.*

Ed's eyes bored into mine. *You really care about her.*

It was a statement, not a question. As soon as he'd thought it, he looked away from me and the link was broken.

Jack sighed, his gun still trained on Fergus. 'Fine. Edward. Ketty . . . get out of my sight.'

'No.' Ketty sobbed.

'Leave,' Jack ordered. 'When you reach the gate, tell Dylan I said it was okay.'

Ed tugged at Ketty's arm. 'Come on,' he said, gently.

She glanced at him. They exchanged a look I didn't understand, though I was sure Ed was communicating with her telepathically. In spite of the terrible danger I was in, I felt a stab of jealousy.

Ketty looked up at me. She opened her mouth as if to say something, then closed it. Ed tugged her arm, pulling her round. They ran – Ketty limping heavily – across the field towards the gate leading back to the road. Dylan was standing there, beside a tree, still keeping watch for Carson. Her red hair was the only splash of brightness against the murky greens and browns of the earth and trees.

'Right,' Jack snarled. 'You've got what you wanted, Nico, now hand over the formula.'

'In a few minutes,' I said. 'I want to make sure Ketty and Ed get properly away.'

Jack swore. 'One minute and that's it,' he said.

I nodded, my mouth dry.

'Using kids, Jack . . .' Fergus said. 'It's beneath even what *I* thought you were capable of. I mean a liar, yes, but I never took you for a coward.'

Jack turned to him. 'You should leave too,' he said.

'What?' Fergus looked shocked.

'Go.' Jack checked his watch. 'Carson will be here in approximately three minutes. If he realises you know about our deal, I can promise you he won't think twice about killing you.'

'I'm not leaving Nico.' Fergus clenched his jaw.

'Then Carson will probably shoot you when he gets here,' Jack said.

The two men stared at each other. In the distance I watched Ketty stop running halfway across the field. Ed tugged on her arm, trying to make her move. I frowned. What was she doing?

'Fergus, go,' I said.

Fergus frowned. 'I can't . . .'

'Please.' My eyes were still fixed on Ed and Ketty. They had started running to the gate again. A few seconds later they reached Dylan. Ketty grabbed her arm, then pointed back in my direction. Dylan shook her head and pointed out to the street, as if urging Ketty and Ed to run away. I watched anxiously as the argument continued. What was Ketty *doing*? I needed to see that she and Ed were safe.

'Do what Nico says,' Jack snapped.

'But . . .'

'Please, Fergus,' I pleaded. 'Ed and Ketty need you. Make sure they're okay. You can come back for me.'

Jack cocked his gun again. 'Leave, now, Fergus,' he said. 'I'm not saying it again.'

'No!' Without warning, Fergus lunged forwards. He swung a punch. Caught Jack off balance. Jack staggered back.

In a split second all my focus was on the gun . . . if I could just get it out of Jack's hand . . . but Jack was gripping it tightly.

Fergus roared. His massive frame – all six foot four of it – lunged forwards again. With a yell, Jack skipped sideways. Off balance, Fergus lost his footing. Jack raised his fist – the one with the gun in it – then drove it hard down onto the side of Fergus's head.

Fergus crumpled onto the grass. I stared at his body, my heart pounding. Jack fell to his knees. He bent over Fergus, pressing his fingers into Fergus's neck, feeling for a pulse.

'Is he okay?' My words came out in a hoarse gasp. Fergus *couldn't* be dead. He just *couldn't*.

'He'll live.' Jack was staring at Fergus, his hand only loosely holding the gun.

A wave of relief washed over me. I stared at the gun. This was my chance.

Breathe. Focus. Move.

With a swift upward motion, I jerked the gun out of Jack's hand and sent it flying out to sea.

'STOP!' Jack roared.

'Sure.' I grinned, then let the gun drop. It fell down, down, into the black water.

Jack rose to his feet, eyes blazing.

Suddenly I remembered Ketty's nightmare about the tree and the cliffs. Her warning that something bad was going to happen. That someone might be going to die.

It had all come to this point . . . this moment . . . And, now, in that moment I was sure.

It was me. I was going to die.

31: The phone

'You little *idiot*!' Jack's chest heaved with anger. 'I needed that gun.'

We stood facing each other for a split second.

'Enough games,' Jack snarled. He strode over Fergus's body and thrust his hand out towards me. 'Give me the memory card.'

My fist tightened on the tiny stone in my hand. It felt hard and warm. I was going to have to show Jack what it was, that I didn't have the card. I just hoped the others had had time to get away. I glanced up.

A small figure was racing across the field, half-running, half-limping towards us. Ketty.

'Wait,' she shrieked. 'Wait!'

I frowned. What was she doing?

Jack saw her too.

'Nico doesn't have the memory card,' she panted, running up to us. '*I* do.'

'What?' Jack frowned. 'You're lying.'

No. I shook my head at her.

'Show him the stone in your hand, Nico,' she said, backing towards the cliff edge.

What? How did Ketty know what I was holding?

'What's she talking about?' Jack snapped.

'I don't know—'

'The memory card with the Medusa gene formula is in here.' Ketty drew her pink phone out of her pocket and showed it to Jack. 'I swear.'

'What?' Jack looked from Ketty to me and back again, an expression of bewilderment on his face. 'How did Nico get it in there? I gave your phone to Dylan when—'

'It wasn't Nico,' Ketty went on, breathlessly. 'Dylan stole the card off you about thirty minutes ago. She hid it in my phone, then called Geri Paterson and told her that you've been trying to double-cross her. Geri's dealing with Carson right now, then she's coming here to deal with you.'

My eyes widened. *Dylan* had taken the card? *And* got hold of Geri Paterson?

'I don't believe you,' Jack snarled. 'Dylan doesn't even have Geri's number.'

'She sneaked a look at it off your phone at the same time as she stole the memory card,' Ketty explained.

Jack glanced over to the gate, where Ed and Dylan were still waiting. 'If all that's true, why did Dylan let you bring the card over here?'

'She didn't want me to have it at first,' Ketty explained, pulling the back off the phone, 'but I made her see that we couldn't let you hurt Nico.'

Jack shook his head. He checked his watch and swore under his breath.

'There's no time for this,' he said. 'Nico, show me what you're holding.'

There was nothing else I could do. I opened my fist and the tiny stone and a trickle of earth fell out.

Jack gave a roar of frustration.

Ketty slid the back of her phone off and drew out a tiny memory card. She held it up. 'Look, this is it.'

Jack glanced from Ketty to me, then back to Ketty. 'That could be *any* memory card,' he said.

'No.' Ketty peered at the card. 'It's red and gold with the number 894410633 in the corner. It's yours. It's the one with the Medusa gene formula.'

A look of fury crossed Jack's face. He swore. 'I suppose it was *Dylan* who told Fergus where we were as well? Double-crossing little bitch. I *thought* it was strange him working that out when Geri had covered my tracks so well.' He held out his hand to Ketty. 'Give me the card.'

'Let Nico go and I will, I promise.'

'No.' I took a step towards her. 'Ketty, no.'

'No more bloody games,' Jack snapped. 'Hand it over.'

Ketty took a step away from him, towards the cliff edge.

'Once Nico's gone,' Ketty said.

253

'You shouldn't be doing this, Ketty,' I said. 'What about what you said earlier? If Jack sells that formula, more people will die.'

Ketty ignored me. She kept her gaze on Jack and stepped back again. Now she was as close to the edge of the cliff as I was, just a couple of metres to my side. The wind roared behind us. Waves crashed against the rocks beneath.

'Let Nico go,' she said, calmly. 'Then you can have the card.'

Jack gritted his teeth. He waved me away. 'Go.'

'No.' I turned to Ketty, my heart thumping. 'I can't leave you.'

She smiled at me. 'Yes, you can. This is how it's supposed to be. I've *seen* it.'

No. This was all wrong. Tears welled up behind my eyes.

'What about your mum and dad and brother? What about Ed?' I said. 'I thought you and he were like this big item? Aren't you going out together? You can't do this to him.'

Ketty shook her head. 'Ed and I are only together because you're with *her*.'

I stared at her, forgetting everything, even the fierce wind that whipped at my face. 'You mean *Dylan*? I told you there's nothing—'

'Go, Nico,' Jack ordered, clearly out of patience, 'or I'll kill her anyway.'

Ketty's gaze fixed on me. 'It's okay,' she said. 'Trust me.'

I took a step away. Then another. I was hardly aware

254

of what I was doing. My mind kept going over Ketty's words. Her eyes were still fixed on Jack . . . her arms outstretched, the pink phone and the memory chip clenched in her fist.

'Nico's not far enough away,' she was saying. 'Let him get further.'

A seagull screeched overhead. The wind roared in my ears. I took another step back, my head spinning.

Jack checked his watch again. 'Carson'll be here any second. Come on, let me have it.' He reached forwards.

Ketty stepped back again. She was right at the edge of the cliff now. Dangerously close. Her eyes swivelled to look at me, pleading with me to run. To escape.

'I'm not going any further away,' I said. 'I'll be fine.'

'I know.' Ketty smiled. And in that moment I understood what she was planning.

'Wait,' I said. 'I don't know if I can do it.'

'You can.' Ketty shuffled backwards. Earth crumbled under her feet. 'You *will*.'

She teetered on the edge of the cliff.

'NO!' Jack roared, fury consuming his whole body. He lunged forwards to grab her.

But Ketty took a final step backwards – off the cliff, into air.

Everything went into slow motion.

I could feel my mouth opening slowly to yell. Ketty seemed to stand in mid-air, like a cartoon, her arms windmilling.

255

I started running towards the cliff edge as Jack backed away.

But it was too late. *I* was too late.

Arms outstretched like wings, Ketty toppled and fell, towards the rocks.

Towards the sea.

32: Fall and rise

Everything was still happening in slow motion. I passed Jack. He was turning . . . running away. I hurled myself onto the ground by the edge of the cliff. Ketty was still falling, her body bumping against the rocky cliff face beneath. The phone and the card containing the Medusa gene formula flew out of her hands, into the sea.

'KETTY!' As I screamed, I focused on her . . . my eyes straining with the effort.

Breathe. Breathe. Breathe. I had to stop her . . . had to hold her. But the weight of her body resisted.

I'd *never* been able to control my telekinesis around Ketty. She didn't understand. I *couldn't* bring her back. I gripped the edge of the cliff. The ground was rough under my fingers.

'*NO!*' Every ounce of energy in my body concentrated on Ketty. But she was still falling fast . . . too fast . . .

The rocks, zooming up to meet her. I couldn't hold her. Gravity was pulling her away. Panic rose. I pushed it down. No.

This was it. This was everything. *Now*.

I breathed out – my hands reaching out over the cliff, towards her. I felt a surge of energy flow through me, down to my fingertips.

Ketty's voice sounded in my head: *you can . . . you will . . .*

Her body stopped in mid-fall. She was just centimetres above the rocks. Spray cascading over her. I held her, my focus intent. The energy was still coursing through my body . . . tingling into my fingers, my toes. She was limp. Was she even conscious? *Yes*, her eyes flickered open.

Slowly I turned my hands to pull her towards me. Gently, carefully, I hauled her up . . . up . . .

The wind roared around me . . . the sea smelled fresh and clean . . . all my senses were heightened as I held on, drawing Ketty closer and closer to the top of the cliff. As she got nearer I could see her jumper was torn and her jeans ripped. A thin trail of blood trickled down her left cheek. But her eyes were open, fixed on me now, holding me as I lifted her.

She looked at me and smiled.

Time zoomed back to normal speed as she rose up, past the cliff edge. I laid her onto the earth beside me. All the energy drained out of my body. I sank down, suddenly exhausted.

'Nico?'

I leaned over her body, trying to catch my breath. My head pounded like it was being machine-gunned.

'Ketty?' My voice was hoarse. 'Ketts, are you okay?'

258

'I knew you'd save me,' she whispered, her eyes shining. 'I saw it when you sent Ed and me away. It came to me while we walked across the field. Not a dream, but a vision. A really clear vision. I saw it all.'

I stared at her. 'I don't get it,' I said.

'There's nothing to get.' She smiled. 'I saw what was going to happen, and then I told the others. I made Dylan give me the phone and wait with Ed by the gate while I came over to you and Jack.'

I glanced across the field to where Dylan and Ed were still standing by the gate. They appeared to be arguing – Dylan had Ed by the arm, as if stopping him from running towards us.

'I told them to wait five minutes after you brought me back up and over the cliff,' Ketty went on.

'I don't think Ed's enjoying the wait much,' I said, drily, the pounding in my head finally easing.

'I know,' Ketty said quietly, her voice almost lost in the roar of the wind, 'but that's what I saw. That's what has to happen.'

I bent lower over her, trying to hear her better. 'Ketts, I know I've been selfish, but I *do* care and you've got it all wrong about me and Dylan—'

'Sssh,' she whispered. 'I know.'

I frowned, not understanding. I leaned even closer. For a second we were just looking at each other. I took a deep breath.

'It's you, Ketty,' I said. 'It was always you.'

259

'I know.' She smiled.

'Will you stop saying that?' I smiled back.

Ketty's smile deepened. 'Okay.'

And then the world spun inside my head and I leaned closer and closer and we kissed.

As we drew apart, I knew that everything was different now. The whole world was different. Ketty's eyes were closed, her mouth still curved in a blissed-out smile. I leaned forward to kiss her again.

'Stop.' Ketty's eyes snapped open. 'We don't do a second kiss yet.'

I frowned. 'Er . . . what? Well, when . . . er, *why*?'

Ketty wriggled away from me. 'Because of Ed,' she said. 'He didn't see us just now, but we can't risk it again. My vision didn't show me what happens after . . . er, this point . . .'

I stared at her.

'Nico?' Fergus's moan from across the grass tore me away from Ketty. He was sitting up. The wind whipped round my ears as I scrambled over to him.

'Fergus?' My throat tightened. 'Are you all right?'

He grimaced up at me. 'I'm fine,' he said, struggling onto his feet. 'What happened to Jack? Did he get the formula? Is everyone okay?'

'Jack's gone,' Ketty said, 'but everyone else is here. No one's hurt.'

Fergus stared at her, bleary-eyed. 'What about Carson? He'll be here any second. We have to go.'

Ketty shook her head. 'Dylan called Geri Paterson. She's dealing with Carson. It's over. We're safe.'

Fergus followed her gaze to where Dylan and Ed were still arguing by the gate. 'I don't understand,' he said.

'Dylan was standing up to Jack after all,' I explained. 'She was just doing it in secret.'

Fergus rubbed his forehead. 'I'd better make sure she's . . . that she and Ed are all right.' He set off unsteadily across the field.

'They'll be back here in a second,' Ketty said. She looked up at me hesitantly.

I shook my head. All I could think about was kissing her again. 'Ketty?' I leaned towards her.

She took a step away from me. 'I'm still going out with Ed,' she said.

My stomach twisted over. 'Then stop. I don't want you to go out with him any more.'

'Really?' Ketty bit her lip. 'Why?'

I took a deep breath. 'Because I want you to go out with *me*.'

There was a pause. Ketty's face split into a huge grin. 'Okay.'

I grinned back.

'But not right now,' Ketty went on. 'I'll tell Ed it's over, but you and me . . . that has to be a secret. At least for a while.'

'*What?*' I said, the smile sliding from my face. 'That doesn't make any sense.'

261

'Yes it does.' Ketty tucked her hair determinedly behind her ears. 'Ed's a sweet guy. But he's been bullied at every school he's ever—'

'That's not your fault—'

'Will you *listen* to me?' Ketty frowned. 'He'd never admit it, but Ed's a bit envious of you. I think it would really hurt him if he knew I'd started dating you straight after we broke up.'

Raised voices sounded from the field that led up to the gate. I glanced round. Fergus had reached Ed and Dylan and the three of them were talking loudly as they walked back towards us.

'Keeping it a secret's ridiculous,' I hissed. 'It totally sucks.'

'Well, it's your own fault.' Ketty's eyes flashed. 'If you'd asked me out sooner instead of saying nothing for months I'd never have looked twice at Billy Martin, and if you'd just told me how you felt instead of trying to impress me with money and flash juggling tricks . . .'

I gasped. 'You mean you'd have said "yes" back then?'

Ketty shrugged. 'Yeah, but you didn't ask and I figured you could have any girl you wanted so you couldn't be interested. Then, later, after you met Jack, it was like you'd changed and it didn't feel like we were friends anymore.'

A helicopter whirred high in the sky above us, but I didn't look up. My stomach twisted over. I couldn't believe it. All that time I'd had . . . all the opportunities I'd missed. If I'd been going out with Ketty when my telekinesis developed, maybe I could have controlled it from the start . . . maybe I wouldn't have been interested in meeting Jack . . .

'We'll just keep it quiet for a bit.' Ketty's face softened. 'Just till Ed's settled down at school. Deal?'

'Are you really all right?' Ed ran up, ahead of the others. He threw his arms round Ketty, his face white. 'There's blood on your face, are you sure you're not hurt?'

'It's just a scratch. I'm fine.' She hugged him back and smiled. 'Nico is too, aren't you, Nico?'

I stared at her. At them.

'Yeah, I'm good, babe.' I looked away. I had to give Ketty a chance to do things her way. I had to trust that she meant what she said. That we were together – even if it was a secret.

Fergus was talking to Dylan. I could see him trying hard to be nice, but coming over a bit stiff and formal. And I could see Dylan not knowing what to make of him – her long-lost uncle.

They walked over. Dylan pointed to the helicopter, still buzzing overhead.

'Geri said she was sending a car for us,' she said. 'Not a helicopter.'

'Well, it's definitely not Jack,' Ed added. 'He ran past the gate at about ninety miles an hour – but that was less than ten minutes ago.'

'D'you think it's Carson after all?' I said anxiously, as the helicopter lowered itself slowly to the ground.

'I don't see how,' Dylan said.

I was suddenly aware of Fergus by my side. He bent

263

down and whispered in my ear. 'Whatever happens next, I want you to know how proud I am of the way you tried to save Ketty and the others earlier.'

There was a pause, as the helicopter landed. 'Thanks,' I said. 'And I . . . er . . . I'm sorry I didn't listen to you before. You were right . . . about not trusting Jack, I mean.'

Fergus sighed. 'I should have told you more . . . realised that you're becoming a man . . . more able to make your own mind up about things.'

I stared at him. Fergus had never spoken to me like that before. There was some new quality I couldn't quite identify in his voice.

'What I can do – the telekinesis – it isn't evil,' I said. 'Not on its own. It's what I do with it that counts. Some of the things I did before . . . the cheating and stuff. I know that was wrong. But there are times . . . there *will* be times . . .'

He nodded. 'I know . . .'

I grinned, suddenly recognising the new quality in Fergus's voice.

Respect.

'Nico?' Ketty's voice made me turn.

She pointed to the helicopter. It was on the ground now, the blades spinning slowly to a stop. A fresh panic twisted at my guts. There was no time to run away. Who on earth was inside?

'We may have to fight.' I looked at Ketty. 'Okay?'

She nodded, pressing her lips together in a determined line.

'Ed . . . Dylan?'

They both nodded. I glanced back at Ketty, the memory of our kiss suddenly flashing into my head. Her face reddened and I knew she was thinking about the same thing.

We stood in a line, the four of us, with Fergus behind, as the helicopter door slid open.

A figure emerged.

'What's *she* doing here?' Ed said.

'You said she was sending a police car for us,' Ketty added.

'Whatever she wants,' Fergus added grimly, 'it won't be good news.'

We all watched, as Geri Paterson slammed the helicopter door shut and walked towards us.

33: The Medusa Project

Stony-faced, Geri approached.

'Are you guys all right?' she said, tucking her neat blonde bob under a beret. She took in the whole cliff top scene, then turned to Dylan. 'Where's Jack? Did you get the Medusa gene formula?'

'Jack ran away,' Dylan said quickly. 'And the formula's been destroyed.'

'Ah. Well, never mind. We'll catch up with Jack Linden – greedy, double-crossing idiot.' She glanced at Fergus. 'And perhaps that memory card didn't contain the only copy of the formula?'

'It did,' Fergus said, shortly.

Geri laughed her tinkly little chuckle. Her eyes flickered over Dylan, Ed and me. 'At least you're all safe,' she said.

I stared at her. 'Why would you want the formula anyway?' I said. 'It's lethal. Jack said you were too ethical to use it.'

Geri stared at me in surprise. 'I wouldn't use it on actual

people,' she said. 'But now you've all proved the gene works, I'm sure I could get funding for research into a new prototype – one that works more immediately and doesn't have fatal side effects.'

Funding from *who*? I frowned. Neither Jack nor Geri had ever properly explained who they worked for. I was determined to get some answers now, but before I could speak, Dylan had opened her mouth.

'Did you find Carson?' she asked.

'Yes, at least the police did. My priority was to get here and make sure you and Nico and Ed were all right. Lucky I wasn't too far away when you called.' Geri raised her eyebrows. 'Not that you needed me. It looks as if you've managed to prevent Jack from selling the formula *and* keep everyone safe. Well done.'

Dylan smiled modestly. 'It wasn't just me,' she said. 'Nico helped.'

'I could have helped more if I'd known you were planning to steal the memory card,' I said. 'Why didn't you tell me you were working against Jack before?'

'There wasn't time. Anyway, I didn't want Jack to know what I was doing and I wasn't sure you'd be able to keep quiet about it,' Dylan said, haughtily. 'I mean you're not trained or anything . . .'

Trained? What did she mean by that?

'But I left my phone out for you on the hall table, back at the mews house,' she went on. 'Didn't you realise I'd done that on purpose?'

267

'Er . . . no, actually . . .'

'*And* I told Fergus we were at Penhagen House. He rang Ketty's cellphone, which Jack had left with me,' Dylan went on. 'So you see, I was trying to help you, but I *had* to get that formula without Jack knowing. And Jack's the only person I know who knows Geri – so I had to wait until I could steal a look at his phone contacts list before I could get hold of her.' She turned to Geri. 'By the way, Ketty helped too. She's Viper.'

Geri's eyes widened. Her gaze settled on Ketty. '*Really*, dear?' she said. 'And what is Ketty's gift, I wonder?'

'She has precognition,' Dylan explained. 'She foresaw that Nico would save her if she fell off the cliff and that Jack would run away as soon as he'd lost the memory card and knew you were onto him.'

'Yeah, Ketty saved my life,' I added.

'Er, I can talk for my—' Ketty began.

'How *marvellous*,' Geri enthused. 'Precognition is a gift we can make *great* use of.'

'Mmm, I don't think what she can do is very sophisticated,' Dylan said, a hint of a sneer in her voice. 'She can't actually control what or when she sees anything.'

'Not to worry.' Geri smiled at Ketty, who was pointedly glaring at Dylan. 'A deeper gift may develop in time, dear.'

'I'm not worrying,' Ketty muttered.

She threw me a cross look. I winked sympathetically at her, then turned to Geri.

'You keep talking about "us" and "we",' I said. 'Don't

you think it's time you told us exactly who *you're* working for?'

'Absolutely,' Fergus agreed.

Geri and Dylan exchanged glances.

'Very well,' Geri said. 'I work for the state. A discrete part of the secret services.'

The wind whistling in from the sea suddenly dropped. I shivered.

'You mean the government?' Ed said slowly. 'Why is the *government* trying to track us down? How do they even know we . . . the Medusa gene . . . exists? '

'Okay.' Geri smoothed down her hair below the beret. 'D'you remember I told you my code name was Medusa?' she said.

Ed nodded.

'So?' I said.

'Well, I was given that code name years ago, when I joined a small team of government agents whose remit was to investigate unexplained phenomena,' Geri said. 'There were three of us – one agent's job was to look into the existence of mythic creatures, while the second had to analyse weird and unexplained events in the natural world. I was the third agent, code named Medusa, and tasked with investigating psychic phenomena.' Geri paused. 'For five years, I ran a secret operation through which I tracked and tested thousands of people who claimed psychic abilities such as mind-reading and telekinesis. But every lead I followed took me down a dead end, until I met Dr William Fox. He claimed that, given sufficient resources he could manufacture a gene for specific psychic abilities. His thesis made sense, so we invested money in his research. The result was the four of you.'

Dylan, Ed, Ketty and I all looked at each other, then back to Geri.

'The original investigative operation came to a close when we realised that Fox's Medusa gene had fatal side effects.'

'You mean it killed all our mothers,' Ketty said.

'That's right, dear. And very sorry I am about it too,' Geri said, quietly. 'Anyway, in response William Fox told us that all the research and gene engineering data on Medusa had been destroyed. We had no reason to doubt him – he was genuinely appalled by the cancer your mothers were infected by and particularly devastated that his actions were going to cause the death of his own beautiful wife.'

I glanced at Dylan. She was staring stonily at the ground.

'However, despite his anguish, William couldn't quite bring himself to destroy his research. Instead, he hid all his notes in his family home, only telling one person – his brother – where they were. We questioned Fergus after William's death, but he backed up William's story. And managed to make sure that Ed and Ketty's true identities were kept quiet.'

I stared at Fergus with a new respect.

Geri sighed. 'Without the state resources I'd enjoyed

270

before, my operation was closed down, there was no way I could find you. And – to be honest – little point in doing so at that time. William Fox had made it clear that the effects of the Medusa gene wouldn't kick in until puberty. And, of course, we couldn't be sure back then that the gene would really work.'

'So what changed?' I said.

'Last year, when I knew your abilities would be emerging, I got the government to fund a new project and set Jack to find you all. Dylan – as Fox's own daughter – and Nico – who we knew was living with Fergus – were the easiest to track down. The other two, as you know, took more time. And it would all have gone very smoothly, if Jack hadn't stumbled across the Medusa gene formula . . .'

'. . . and Carson hadn't offered him twice as much money as you were paying him,' I added.

Geri nodded.

'So what's the purpose of this new project that the government's agreed to fund?' Fergus asked.

'And how do the four of us fit into it?' I asked.

Geri was silent for a moment, the only sound the wind and waves raging. Then she spoke again.

'The four of you *are* the new project,' she said.

'What does that mean?' I said.

'That's up to you, dear,' Geri went on. 'There are three options . . .'

'Go on,' I said.

'Okay.' Geri cleared her throat. 'Option one. I call the

271

gutter press and tell them all about you. I make sure they know wherever you go and whatever you do. They hound you forever.'

'No!' Behind me, Fergus exploded. 'That's exactly what I've been trying to protect them from! That's . . .'

'Option two.' Geri continued as if Fergus hadn't spoken. 'We keep everything secret and I hand you over to a team of government scientists. They will keep you locked up in lab conditions, away from your friends and families, for the rest of your lives.'

'*What?*' Ketty said.

'You can't,' I said.

'These kids have rights!' Fergus was red in the face. 'You're not their legal guardian, you can't just whisk them away and turn them into . . . into . . .'

'Research experiments,' I finished for him. 'Those are crap options, Geri.'

Geri smiled at me. 'But you know I can make them happen,' she said. 'You saw how fast I was able to remove the records of Jack's helicopter's flight this morning. He called me on the way to the heliport, claiming he had new intel on Viper's identity. I didn't know he was double-crossing me with Carson at the time – so when he said he needed to throw the police off his scent I just assumed he'd broken some minor law to get a lead on Viper and covered his tracks as he requested. It was – literally – as easy as making a phone call.'

'You're still offering us crap options,' Ed stammered.

272

'Yeah.' I nodded. 'Media victims or lab rats isn't much of a choice.'

'You haven't heard the third option,' Geri said slowly. 'How would you like to go back to school and still stay in touch with your families? No press. No labs. A normal life. Your old life, in fact.'

'It wouldn't be an old life for Dylan,' I said.

'Dylan's already agreed to option three,' Geri said briskly. 'She did so months ago, when we first met in the States. You can ask her yourself, but I know for a fact she was – and is – very keen to leave Philadelphia and begin a new life here . . . at her uncle's boarding school.'

I stared at Dylan. 'So you were never staying with relatives,' I said slowly. 'You and Jack made that up because you didn't want to have to explain you were moving here.'

Dylan crossed her arms and gazed out to sea. I suddenly remembered what she'd told me on our train journey back from Scotland.

Geri made it sound like coming here would be the most exciting thing that would ever happen to me.

I frowned. How could she think joining Fox Academy would be exciting? There had to be something Geri wasn't telling us. 'What's the catch?' I asked.

'No catch,' Geri said. 'But we *will* need something in return.'

The wind died again. A seagull squawked overhead.

'And what's that?' I said.

273

Geri's high, tinkly laugh rang out. 'Every now and then, a difficult situation arises in the world which can't be dealt with by normal means. Your abilities will help.'

I narrowed my eyes. 'You want to *use* our abilities?'

Geri nodded. 'That's why we set up that elaborate con in the casino – to test out how well you performed under pressure. Unnecessarily, as it turned out. All four of you have had to work under far greater pressure today – and it has been a huge success.'

'Wait a minute,' Ketty said. 'You're saying you want us to form some kind of crime-fighting force?'

'To fight *criminals*?' Ed added. 'Using our abilities? *No.*'

'They're just kids,' Fergus pleaded.

Geri shrugged. 'You'll get relevant training and a proper briefing each time. And you'll be able to develop your team-working abilities too, under Mr Fox's guidance.'

Team-working? I made a face. That didn't sound much like fun.

'I want no part of this,' Fergus snapped. 'These are *children* whose lives you'll be risking.'

'Would you rather we went back to options one or two?' Geri sighed. 'Anyway, from what I've seen, the four of you work together very well.'

I glanced from Ketty and Ed to Dylan. My secret girl-friend, plus the boy who wanted her *and* the most arrogant girl on the planet, whom everyone appeared to think I was actually going out with.

Oh yeah. Loads of team-working potential there.

274

'There isn't a choice, then,' Ketty said flatly. 'We're part of this project whether we like it or not.'

Ed put his arm round her shoulders.

I looked away.

'We're agreed then.' Geri smiled. 'In that case,' she said, 'welcome to the Medusa Project.'

34: The beginning

Two weeks later and we were settled back at school for the start of the summer term . . . back to our old lives. Well, except everything was different of course.

Dylan was there for a start. I don't think she was very impressed that I'd spread a bunch of rumours about us going out together last term, but she didn't seem any more bothered by the gossip about us than she was by the legions of boys queuing up to get it on with her. She ignored everything and everyone – keeping herself to herself most of the time.

As for me, once it was obvious that Dylan and I weren't together I got a load of teasing, especially from Tom and Curtis. But I didn't care.

I had Ketty.

She did as she'd promised and cooled it with Ed straight away. But they still hung out a lot after school. I left them to it, knowing I'd see Ketty later. We met up – outside usually – for a couple of hours every evening. Those times were great. I just wished it didn't have to be this big secret, but Ketty kept saying Ed needed a chance to get used to them only being friends. Then she'd tell him, and everyone else, about us.

It was the end of the first full week of term. We were going to have our first team-working session the next day, Saturday. God knows what it was going to be like.

At least Fergus and I were getting on better. After that little chat we'd had back on the cliff top at Penhagen House, Fergus promised that from now on he would treat me like an adult. No hiding the truth from me any more.

And, true to his word, he told me as soon as Geri Paterson contacted him to say they'd captured Jack Linden.

That meant a lot.

Anyway, like I said, it was Friday afternoon, school had finished and I was outside, sitting on the low wall out the back of the main building.

I heard footsteps and looked up. Ketty and Ed were running towards me. Ketty reached me first.

'Mr Fox wants us in his office,' she said, catching her breath.

'Really?' I smiled at her. She looked beautiful, with the sun shining on her hair and her eyes all wide and excited.

Ed ran up and the smile fell from my face. I knew it wasn't really Ed's fault that Ketty was keeping our relationship a secret, but it didn't exactly make me like him any better. I almost wished he'd break his own rules about mind-reading – and find out the truth for himself.

'Hi,' I said.

'Come on.' Ed stared at me, as usual not quite making eye contact. 'Mr Fox says it's important.'

'Really?' I faked a yawn. 'What does he want us to do? Colour-code his paper clips?'

There was a pause. Ed and Ketty looked at each other, then back to me.

'It's our first mission,' Ketty said. 'For the Medusa Project.'

I sat bolt upright, all my bitterness at Ed forgotten. 'You're kidding.'

'No.' Ketty's eyes sparkled with excitement and fear. 'Come on, they're waiting.'

'Who?'

'Mr Fox and Geri Paterson . . .' she said.

'And Dylan,' Ed added

'Did Fergus say anything about what we were going to have to do?' I asked, jumping down from the wall.

'Only that the people we'll be dealing with make Carson look like Snow White.'

I turned to Ed. Despite the sunshine, his face was pale. 'So what d'you think about all this?' I asked.

Ed shuffled from one foot to the other. 'I don't like it,' he said. 'It's wrong and it sounds really dangerous. But if Ketty's up for it, then I am too.'

I nodded. As we set off, Ed started talking to Ketty in a low voice, clearly not wanting me to hear. I hung back a little, watching his sandy head next to her dark curls. Ed was right. Whatever lay ahead of us was going to be dangerous. But on the other hand . . .

This was my chance to spend more time with Ketty. And maybe if the mission went well, Ed would get more confident and she'd stop feeling she had to look after him quite so much. In fact, maybe I could use the mission like a deadline.

As Ed walked through the door into the school building, I grabbed Ketty's hand, pulling her back. 'Listen,' I whispered. 'I can see Ed's a bit freaked by having to do this mission, but once it's over – whatever happens – we tell him and everyone we're going out together. Deal?'

Ketty smiled at me. A big, beautiful, loving smile.

'Deal,' she said.

I let go of her hand and we walked on. That was good enough for me. As we stood, knocking, outside Fergus's office door, my confidence surged. So long as Ketty was by my side, I could handle anything.

Grinning, I followed the others into the room.

TO BE CONTINUED . . . in *The Hostage*

As well as writing the
Medusa Project series, Sophie McKenzie
is author of award-winning thrillers,
Girl, Missing and *Blood Ties*.

BLOOD TIES

READ THE EXTRACT NOW

Theo

I could see him waiting for me outside the steel school gates.

Roy.

He was leaning against a lamppost, his arms folded. From the second-floor window behind my desk I couldn't make out the expression on his face. But the way he was slumped against that lamppost suggested he was bored.

Good. Bored was good. If Roy was bored, he wouldn't be suspecting anything.

'Hey, Theo,' Jake hissed.

I turned away from the window. The last lesson of the day was almost over. History. Something to do with the Second World War. I wasn't really paying attention.

'Twenty seconds until Operation "Liberate Theo" commences,' Jake whispered. His eyes were fixed on the stopwatch function on his phone – he'd synchronised it with the school bell earlier.

I rolled my eyes, pretending I was way too cool to be excited. But the truth was my heart was pumping like it might burst. This was my first serious attempt to escape from Roy. I mean, I'd tried – and failed – to run away from him before. But this was the first time I'd planned out an actual escape route.

'Fifteen . . . fourteen . . . thirteen . . .' Jake said under his breath.

I glanced towards the front of the classroom.

'Eleven . . . ten . . .'

The teacher was writing on the white board.

'Eight . . . seven . . . six . . .'

My books were already in my bag. I picked it up off the floor and slid it silently onto my back.

'Three . . . two . . . one.'

The school bell cut through the squeaking of the white-board pen.

I leaped to my feet.

'You are go. Repeat. You are go.' Jake's voice rose above the commotion that filled the room.

I stormed towards the door. Wrenched it open. Sped down the corridor. Other doors were opening. Other classes spilling out. I pounded down the stairs. Down, down to the ground floor. A huge group of Year Sevens and Eights were jostling and shoving their way across the entrance hall.

But I was bigger.

Faster.

Stronger.

The younger boys shrank away as I barged through, my eyes on the fire door at the end of the corridor.

I reached it. Shoved it open. Burst into the tiny courtyard at the back of the school – a patch of concrete surrounded on three sides by the school building and on the fourth by a high brick wall. I raced towards the large tree next to the wall. As I ran, I glanced over my shoulder. No one was following me. I looked up at the windows overlooking the courtyard. No one was watching me.

I reached the tree. Jake and I had dragged a school chair outside at break and stashed it behind the trunk. I hauled it out and climbed up, steadying myself as the chair wobbled on the uneven tarmac. The nearest branch still looked a long way up. I bent my knees. Jumped. *Yes.* My hands gripped the branch. My arm muscles tensed, straining to hold my weight. I swung for a moment, the bark cutting into my palms. *Do it.* Using all the strength in my arms and shoulders I hauled myself up. Up. I gritted my teeth. Hooked one elbow over the branch. Then the other. I was scrabbling up with my legs now. Locking a knee over. Kneeling up. Reaching for the branch above. *Yes.*

I stood up, panting, catching my breath.

The air was cold, despite the sunshine. A gust of wind blew my fringe across my eyes. Mum's always nagging me to get it cut. It *is* sometimes a bit irritating. Still. Her being annoyed about it is worth any amount of irritation.

I took a deep breath and pushed the hair off my face. I gripped the branch above me more tightly. Hauled myself up again. *Jesus.* Even a few months ago, there was no way I could have done this. Back then my escape attempts

285

depended on distraction techniques. But now I was tall enough and strong enough to overcome any physical obstacle. Well, that's how it felt. That's how *I* felt.

Powerful. Unbeatable. Invincible.

I'm Theo Glassman. I need no one.

I scrambled up and up. It got easier as I climbed, the branches closer together. Soon I was level with the top of the wall. I looked down. My stomach tightened. The ground was a long way beneath me – maybe four or five metres. I edged across the branch until I reached the wall.

'Oy! You there! Boy!' The voice was deep and male. One of the teachers. Shouting from a school window.

Crap. I didn't have much time. If whoever that was realised it was me out here, he'd be straight down to tell Roy. I stepped onto the wall, carefully avoiding the spiky shards of glass poking up at intervals along its surface.

'GET DOWN FROM THERE!' the teacher yelled.

My plan exactly.

The wall was three brick widths across – enough room for me to stand on both feet and turn right round. I'm good at balancing, and I don't mind heights. But this was way high. I held tightly onto the branches above my head as I shuffled round. The grassy park on the other side of the wall was littered with heaps of blown leaves – all reds and browns. A long way down. *Don't think about it.*

I jumped. *Whoosh.* Through the air. Through the leaves. *Wham.* The impact jarred all the way up my legs. I fell over onto my side, breathing heavily for a second. Then I pushed myself up. Tested my legs. They were fine. I was fine. *Yes*, I'd done it.

I'd escaped from Roy. I'd escaped from my bodyguard.

I smiled to myself as I started running across the grass. My plan was to head for the nearby high street, meet Jake in Starbucks and go to the cinema.

Maybe that sounds weird to you. That I'd risk getting detention, falling out of a tree, cutting myself open on glass and the rest of it, just to hang out in the high street for a bit and catch a movie.

All I can say is: you'd understand if you lived my life.

Rachel

GODDESS STILL SAFE IN HEAVEN. RICHARD.

I had to read the text twice before I took it in. I'd been so sure it was going to be some toxic message from Jemima that it took a full minute before I realised it wasn't. I checked the caller I.D. – a number I didn't recognise. So, no one on my contact list.

I breathed a sigh of relief. Just some random message. A wrong number. Nothing that made any sense.

I almost skipped down to my piano lesson.

The lesson itself wasn't too bad. My fingers wouldn't move like they're supposed to, and the more they wouldn't move, the more embarrassed I got. Still, Miss Vykovski was really nice and we ended up having a laugh. So I was in a good mood when Mum called me for supper. Mum likes it when we eat together, though Dad doesn't often get home in time. He manages a cosmetic surgery clinic in central London. I reckon that's why Mum married him, to be honest, so he could get her free treatments.

288

'Richard!' Mum yelled up the stairs as I scurried past her to the dining room. 'Richard. It's on the table!'

I stopped, a spoonful of salad leaves midway between the bowl and my plate. *Richard*. My dad had the same name as on the text. It hadn't occurred to me the message could be from him. *No*, that didn't make sense – we'd been speaking just seconds before I received it. Anyway, why would my dad send me some weird text about goddesses in heaven? The name had to be a coincidence. Plus, surely he'd sign off *Dad*. Which also proved the message couldn't be from him – his number is logged on my mobile under *Dad*. So, if he'd called me, that name would have shown up.

Still.

'Hey, Dad,' I said as he sat down. 'I just got this weird text.'

'Mmmn,' Dad said, helping himself to a slice of chicken breast. 'Nothing X-rated, I hope.'

'Just weird,' I said. 'It—'

'How was piano, sweetie?' Mum bustled in, a bowl of potato salad in her hand.

'Fine.' I reached for the potatoes.

Mum gave a little cough. 'Are you *sure* you want to do that, sweetie?'

I stared up at her blankly.

'Carbs weigh very heavy on the stomach overnight,' she smiled. 'I'm just saying.'

My mind flashed back to Jemima's comment about my double-satellite-dish bum. I swallowed, torn between know-ing Mum was right and really, really wanting the food.

'Oh, let her eat a sodding potato.' Dad rolled his eyes at me and grinned.

'I'm not stopping her,' Mum snapped. She set the bowl down on the table. 'I'm just pointing out the consequences.'

The consequences: being fat. Being ugly.

This was about Rebecca too. That was what Mum was really saying. *Rebecca didn't eat too much potato salad. Ever. She had a marvellous figure, sweetie.*

I gritted my teeth and hauled as many potatoes as I could onto my plate.

'So tell me about that text, Ro?' I could hear the kindness in Dad's voice. It just made me feel worse.

I shook my head and stuffed a potato into my mouth.

Dad sighed, then started chatting to Mum about his day. Dad does that a lot – acts like a big cushion protecting me from Mum. I kept my head down, shovelling in one potato after another. After a couple of minutes I stopped. Now I'd made myself even fatter. I felt so miserable that, for a second, I seriously thought about going upstairs and making myself sick. Some of the girls at school have done that. Cassie Jones swears by it. *Eat what you like then just chuck it up before it makes you fat.*

She calls it: *Having your cake and hurling it.*

Cassie Jones is stupid though. I know that making yourself sick over and over is a majorly bad idea. It's bad for your body, bad for your heart, bad for your teeth even.

It's bad for your head, too.

And my head's screwed up enough as it is.

290

Anyway, I hate how it feels when you vomit. Maybe that's the real truth. I'm just too scared to stick two fingers down my throat and feel that acid burn up into my mouth. *Ugh*.

'Ro?' Dad's voice was insistent. 'Ro, earth to Ro!'

I jerked back into the real world. Mum had vanished into the kitchen. Dad was smiling at me.

I tried to smile back. Dad doesn't realise I know it, but he calls me Ro when he's trying to make me feel better about something. Trouble is, I'm sure that's what he used to call Rebecca, too.

'Hey, Ro,' he said. 'You were saying something before Mum came in?'

'It wasn't anything major,' I said. 'Just a text. A wrong number. It said something about a goddess being in heaven. From some guy with the same name as you.'

'Oh.' Dad paused for just a second too long. 'Well, that *is* weird,' he said.

'Dad?'

'What?' He smiled at me, but his eyes were all wary.

Mum bustled back in. 'Homework, Rachel, sweetie.'

'Yes, I've got loads of paperwork to check over.' Dad stood up so abruptly he knocked his chair and had to steady it to stop it from falling over.

He left. I helped Mum carry the plates and stuff out to the kitchen. She was chattering away about her tennis again, but I wasn't listening.

Why had Dad acted strange like that? Was I being para-noid or had he practically run away from me just then?

291

A few minutes later he was back, holding a bundle of papers, completely normal again. 'Hey, Ro?' He kissed my forehead. 'Give us a shout if you need any help with your homework.'

He wandered through to the living room and switched on the TV.

I trudged upstairs. Back in my room I pulled out my phone.

Dad knew something about the message, I was sure. But if he'd sent it to me by mistake, why not just say so?

My heart beat faster. Was I imagining this whole thing? Before I could think about it any more, I pulled my mobile out of my pocket and scrolled through to the last logged message. I clicked on the number and pressed *call*.

I wandered out to the landing. Dad was downstairs, through two open doors. If his phone rang I was sure I'd hear it from here.

Nothing.

I turned to go back into my room. And then I caught it. A faint, muffled ringtone.

It was coming from across the landing.

From Dad's study.

For exclusive **bonus** materials,
character playlists, **downloads**
and **competitions** go to
www.themedusaproject.co.uk

THE NEW BESTSELLER
BLOOD RANSOM
SOPHIE McKENZIE

BY THE RICHARD & JUDY'S CHILDREN'S BOOKS WINNER

BLOOD TIES
SOPHIE McKENZIE

SOPHIE McKENZIE

The Richard & Judy's Children's Book WINNER

GIRL, MISSING

And running for her life...

Be the first to hear the latest book news and author gossip at
www.sophiemckenziebooks.com

WIN!

Fancy getting your hands on free copies of all of Sophie McKenzie's brilliant books?

We're giving away ten sets of all nine of Sophie's fantastic books, including all the books in the Medusa Project series, plus signed copies of the fabulous new book BLOOD RANSOM.

For your chance to win go to
http://kids.simonandschuster.co.uk
– click on COMPETITION
and answer the question –
good luck!

**This competition will run
from 27th October 2010 until
midnight on 31st November 2010.**

For full T&Cs please refer to www.simonandschuster.co.uk

For more exclusive competitions and news
join Sophie McKenzie on FACEBOOK:
http://www.facebook.com/pages/Sophie-
McKenzie/355619419770?ref=search